I0831614

BEDLAM

Andrew Matarazzo

BEDLAM

TABLE OF CONTENTS

1 3 2 2 14
2 6
10 19
5 3 4
7 2 4
17
6 8 13 3
10 7 10 7 11 10
2 12
1 11
10
19
7 10 4 3 7 14 10
10 7 11
10
14
19 2 3 5 10 5
17
6 8 3 7
10 7 11 10 2 12
1 14

1.

"You've got to be fucking kidding me!"

Hunter's words stabbed into my head, forcing my eyes open. It felt like I'd been out for hours.

The only thing I could vaguely make sense of was that I was in the backseat of a car with a terrible pain coming from the core of my skull. I touched my throbbing forehead, and like I'd dipped it in paint, it came away dripping red.

One glance out of the window pulled me back to the gravity of our situation. Droves of people zigzagged through the congested line of honking cars, all of them carrying bags, some wearing medical masks. Like us, most of them were of high-school age, or younger.

Hunter was driving; Riley sat anxiously in the passenger seat. She looked like she'd gotten into the same paint that I had.

"Let's just get out of the car and walk. We're getting nowhere!" she pleaded.

"I told you three hundred times—at this point it'll take just as long to walk with all those people out there!" Hunter fired back. "I'm not ditching the car!"

My head pulsed with every word they shouted.

"Hunter, we have less than a half tank! This car isn't going to do shit for us!" Riley insisted, standing her ground. "We need to get to that warehouse and find the others!"

Reality found me once again …

What was reported almost two years earlier as a powerful flu sweeping the States had become a full-blown epidemic. The virus had seemingly died out the previous year, and just when we'd returned to what felt like normalcy only months before, a breaking news interruption had announced *"an unprecedented virus that will go down in history."* Almost overnight, our cities were infected with a more evolved strain and it had already wiped out thousands of people, mostly adults...but they weren't *staying* dead. The virus was said to be airborne, or transmitted more directly through a bite from an infected host. Reports said that older and weaker bodies were most vulnerable to the airborne transmission, but a bite was fatal. Those reports were soon confirmed as fact. My parents were both dead now; the remaining friends I was able to reach were all I had left, and were waiting for us in a warehouse they'd managed to hide in amidst the chaos.

Everything felt like it was happening in a haze. Setting a goal to reach familiar faces was the only thing keeping me going. How many times had I watched a film like this? How often had books and cinema painted this horrific picture of the end of the world? This was it, and it was far worse than anything fiction could describe.

"Let's get out of the car," I managed to say.

They both looked back at me, Riley concerned, Hunter resentful.

"Fine, you both want to walk? Get the hell out of the car, then!" Hunter spat. "No one's forcing you to stay with me."

"Bro, we're not trying to leave you, but we're at a standstill!" Riley shouted at him.

He didn't reply. I knew he'd realize soon enough that if we left him, he'd be alone, and that was something I'd always known Hunter to fear.

I opened the car door impulsively, stepping out of what had become our safety cocoon. There was so much noise. My head throbbed even more intensely.

I started to walk. I had no idea where I was going. I just followed everyone else. That's what most people seemed to be doing, anyway.

It wasn't long before Riley called after me. "Tye! Wait, please!"

I looked back. She was running from the car with her dead smartphone in hand. "Don't leave me with him," she said.

"Give him five minutes. We'll walk slow and he'll follow us," I said.

"I honestly don't care what happens to him."

"Don't say that. He's an asshole, but wouldn't you rather stick with *anyone* we know at this point?"

Barely a minute passed before Hunter came jogging over to join us. "Don't talk to me," he snapped.

I turned to Riley instead. "Ava's car wasn't far ahead. We should still be able to find her if she hasn't left it."

"Did you try calling her back, or is your phone dead too?"

"I didn't try yet. I will now."

My phone was the only one still working. Ava had managed to call me for a brief second to let me know she'd made it to a warehouse next to the iconic water tower downtown before the connection dropped out.

I pulled out my phone. The front screen was cracked from when that *thing* had slammed me against the car door. I was so lucky my two friends had been there. The image of that walking corpse I once called Dad would forever be etched into my mind—that subconscious terror you prayed you would never have to feel... or never thought you *could* feel.

I brought up my recent calls and found Ava's name.

"Hey! Please, man! I have a kid with me! Can I just make one quick call? I need to find my fiancé!"

A woman had broken away from the large group she was traveling with, her expression desperate. All power had gone out, and that meant no phone charging.

"I really can't. I'm so sorry," I said, as apologetically as I could.

"Please! I beg you," she tried again.

I considered it for a moment, but then-

"Hey, he has a phone!" a guy shouted, running over to us. "Is it working?"

The woman answered for me. "Yes, and I really need to use it, but he won't let me. I'm with my kid and he's hurt badly. I need to call my fiancé. I haven't seen him anywhere!"

I stuffed the phone back into my pocket. Two younger girls joined those following us. We quickened our pace.

"Can we use it when you're done? Please, it won't take long!" they called after us.

"Let them use the phone, then I need to make a two-second call to see where my sister is," the guy insisted.

Hunter got up in the man's face. "None of you are using the goddamn phone! Back off!" he yelled.

"Selfish piece of shit!" he spat back, and punched Hunter in the mouth.

Mayhem broke out. Hunter and the man fell to the floor, their arms flailing. The ladies decided it was their opportunity to come at me. They lunged, sticking their hands in my pockets and digging for the phone. Riley and I forcefully pushed them away and then they were not only fighting with us, but with each other.

The man was now on top of Hunter, fisting his face repeatedly.

"Get off him!" I yelled.

It was all I could do. The women would not get off of me, and one was pulling Riley's hair.

Now that half the street knew I had a working phone, more people joined in the fray. It was me against a barrage. I could feel their weight suffocating me. My head wound reopened.

Just when the crushing weight of multiple people was bringing me to near blackout—*BAM*.

Somewhere in the distance, a gunshot rang out. Everyone scattered, screaming. I was lifted by the back of my shirt as Riley and Hunter helped me up. His nose was bleeding more heavily than my head, and Riley had a gash across her face.

I ducked behind a car. They both knelt beside me, out of breath. I retrieved my phone and tapped on Ava's name. My stomach dropped. "*Damnit*, no service!"

Riley looked defeated. "No! *Still*?"

"Told you that was gonna happen. Towers are obviously down," Hunter scoffed.

"Can you stop being so negative?" I shot back.

I put the phone back into my pocket. Sirens whined from far off. We continued onward. It would take at least an hour before we would reach the others.

The warzone we were in now bore a stark contrast to how normally our day had started out. The night before, Hunter and Riley had come over to finish up a biology project. Like most high schoolers, we'd left it to the last minute. They both slept over, and we woke up early to enjoy a sugar-filled breakfast before tackling our homework. Instead, we found my mother's body on the kitchen floor. It looked like it had emaciated overnight. My ears rang in shock, blocking most of Riley's screams. As I came back to my senses, I could hear Hunter dialing 911 in panic.

The TV was on, a soundtrack to the monstrous scene. Images and live footage of various locations around the state slapped me across the face—fires, protests, gunshots, car crashes, thousands of dead bodies, and what looked like horrific, walking corpses…

"-complete chaos on all fronts. We have gruesome reports of what appear to be reanimated human corpses spreading the virus through bites. Experts are urging citizens to steer clear of the anomalies as they are aggressive. Other countries are closely monitoring the situation, but it seems these phenomena are heavily concentrated in the United States. Cross-border travel has been completely shut down and air traffic has been grounded, domestically and internationally. There is evidence that these symptoms are connected to a more evolved strain of the virus as we know it, as well as the mass animal wipeouts

reported last year. The story is still developing, but it's clear this is an unprecedented virus that will go down in history. The U.S. Army-"

The volume of Riley's screams grew tenfold. I turned to see my mom now standing upright. She was drooling foam and blood, and her eyes had turned black in their sockets.

"*Mom*?" I choked out.

Hunter grabbed Riley and shoved her into the nearest room. Her screams didn't stop.

There was a demonic expression in my mom's eyes that burned into my soul. It wasn't her anymore. Her limbs were oddly contorted, and her body was twitching. She croaked a horrible sound.

"Tye, back away," Hunter warned.

In a blink, the *thing* lunged at me, growling and scratching at me like a rabid animal. I froze in shock as Hunter grabbed a kitchen knife and speared it through the neck. It fell to the floor, lifeless once again.

This couldn't be real. But then, Hunter had always pressured me to try drugs for fun. Maybe he'd thought it a good idea to spike our Gatorades the night before. A bad trip was far more logical than this new reality.

Hunter grabbed me, tearing me away from the nightmarish scene. "Riley!" he shouted, still dragging me with him. He banged on the door. "Let's go!"

She came out crying, shrieking louder at the sight of the bloodied kitchen floor.

Outside was a deeper layer of hell. Our perfectly-manicured, gated community was now a tableau of devastation. Bodies littered the streets, alarms filled the air, and cars piled up as their owners attempted to flee. We were running for Hunter's Honda parked near the mailbox when I saw my dad.

"Dad ... ?" I said in a hoarse, barely audible whisper.

He appeared to be in the same terrifying state as my mom. He was standing on the roof of our house, swaying eerily.

"DAD!"

Riley pushed me out of the way as the *thing* jumped down, roaring primitively. It grabbed me and threw me into the dirt, then shoved Riley into the car door. Hunter quickly grabbed a baseball bat from his backseat and swung it violently. Dad ignored the threat, his teeth so close to Riley's face she must have been able to see right into his torn-up throat. She thrashed, managing to break away and maneuver behind Hunter. Dad turned to me, lifted me with ease, and slammed me hard, head first, into the car window. I felt myself start to lose consciousness.

The last thing I remember was a vague vision of my dad's blood spraying over the car as Hunter's bat made contact with his skull before I blacked out.

We kept on, walking by endless rows of cars, which we came to notice were mostly abandoned. It was chilling to see so many kids our age roaming the streets. They all wore the same expression, a sort of emptiness mixed with terror and confusion. We were fledglings, kicked out of the nest way before we were ready.

People began sprinting past me, panicking.

"They're running from something," Hunter realized grimly.

Our pace quickened. I tried to see over the crowd but the stampede was too dense. What was it? We started to run, clambering between cars and people. Riley tripped over a dead body I'd dodged only seconds before. She regained speed, just in time to spot the cause of all the mayhem.

There were several corpses running toward us. Dead in appearance, but full of life. My chest tightened. These were the first ones I'd seen since my parents, their eyes black like soot and flesh rotted in an almost mummified way. We ran as fast as our legs could manage. One of the rancid men sprinted toward us at unbelievable speed. I tried to spot an escape route, but we were now on an elevated highway, a free fall on either side of the road. People poured over the railings, desperate to get away. It was a long way down. Some of them wouldn't make the fall.

The creature was gaining on us.

Hunter opened the back door of an abandoned Suburban. "Get in!" he roared.

Riley and I jumped in after him with no hesitation. In less than a second, the car shook violently as the bloodthirsty man smashed his fist into the metal and headbutted the window. The car alarm blared in response.

"STOP IT!" Riley shouted at it desperately.

It paid her no attention. It was manic, with only one motive: to kill. Its black pupils were fixated, reminiscent of a shark who had just tasted blood in the water. The window began to crack from the force of its skull.

Riley jumped into the driver's seat; the keys were still in the ignition. She turned them and the engine roared to life. But we were stuck. Cars blocked us on all sides.

"What are you doing?!" I asked, panicked as the sound of the exhaust invited more monsters from nearby.

There were now three smashing into the car, growling like hounds. Riley dug her foot into the gas pedal and jerked the wheel to the left. The Suburban smashed into the vehicle in front of us, then swerved in a circle, crushing some of the creatures beneath the wheels. She then plowed through the others on the sidelines, forcing them off the edge of the highway.

She slammed on the brakes, our bodies wrenching forward painfully. She'd saved us. An unnerving silence fell over the street.

Hunter was in complete shock following her quick stunt. "Damn ..."

"Let's get out of here before more come," I urged.

We jumped out and ran off. As far as we could see, there wasn't anyone ahead or behind us. We had fallen dangerously behind the rest of the crowd.

2.

The sun was our most immediate enemy. Although it'd been a handful of hours, it felt like we'd been walking for days. Dehydration was already taking its toll and the last beads of our internal water supply dripped defiantly from our skin. We'd been tempted to grab some water bottles left in the cup holders of abandoned cars, but refrained when we realized contamination was a very real risk.

There was still no sign of any living person, but at least we didn't see any dead ones either. The city had evacuated en masse. I was already starting to get used to the eerie silence of the world. Or maybe it was the numbness of shock. It had all happened so fast that my brain was still processing this new reality. I still wondered whether I was having the most vivid nightmare of my life—so vivid I could bleed, starve and feel pain.

Hunter picked up a stray golf club and adopted the most irritating pastime ever, smashing the windows of every luxury car we came across. I counted three Cadillacs, a Porsche, and two Mercedes before I tried to argue that the noise would invite unwanted attention. Of course, he fought me on it. I didn't have the energy to fight back. He was blowing off steam. At least it was on the cars and not on us.

There had always been an unspoken tension between Hunter and me since freshman year, and I was convinced it came from his unrequited feelings toward Riley. Despite Riley being attractive and in high demand at our school, she seemed to lock on to me. I was confident and decently attractive, but I never thought I had anything over the other guys who fawned over her.

We met the day I sat next to her in our ninth-grade Lit class. She was a guys' girl. Very few female friends, even fewer acquaintances, but she seemed to have a friendly rapport with every guy at our school. Her tough demeanor was adopted after she lost her sister in a car wreck only four years prior. She didn't get too close to people after that, so she'd mastered the art of the friend zone, but with me it was different. Hunter never liked that.

The three of us actually had a great friendship up until Riley and I made it official, and his envy toward me lingered long after she and I broke up the following summer. He had his own imagined fantasy with her.

"Guys ..." said Riley.

I followed her gaze to find a break in the river of cars ahead of us. Within the traffic jam were two army Humvees. They must have weighed at least a ton, so the sight of one overturned left a hollow feeling in my stomach. *What happened here?*

Riley and I approached with caution. Hunter meanwhile ditched the putter and climbed into the backseat of the upright vehicle. "You're not gonna believe this," he said, in a tone hard to read.

"What?" Riley asked, clearly dreading another setback.

"We got ourselves some protection!" he exclaimed.

"No way! Condoms?" I joked.

Riley rolled her eyes, but a faint smile appeared on her anxious face.

Hunter just stared blankly at me. "Guns, dipshit."

He threw me one. I mulled it over in both hands. Looked like a shotgun. It was the first time I'd held one since an uneventful hunting trip I'd gone on with my dad years back.

Riley grabbed a handgun, while Hunter picked up an intimidating-looking automatic rifle.

"Jackpot, baby!" he said, waving it haphazardly. He then dragged a huge canvas bag from the backseat and slung it over his shoulder. I saw him eye the gun I was holding. He snatched it from my hand and handed me his.

“Hey, what the hell?” I asked, annoyed.

“I like this one better.”

Despite the underlying tension we were usually able to keep up a decent comradery, but since junior year began six months earlier, our friendship had been running on empty. It seemed his unspoken issues were giving way to spoken ones. If Mrs. Reingold hadn’t grouped the three of us together for the Bio project, he would’ve definitely declined coming to my place, especially with Riley there. It was the first time we had all been together, like the old days.

“I like this one better too,” I said, keen to avoid conflict.

I switched the safety lock off and sprayed a couple rounds in the air. My ears rang for a moment and I felt the kickback of the gun against my shoulder. I played it off casually. “Sweet.”

In the brief second I’d held down the trigger, it had fired about four bullets. All that power made me feel safer...but only slightly.

Hunter shook his head disapprovingly. “Hmm. Well, I’m glad you’re over the noise attracting *unwanted attention.* Check this out.” He held up the shotgun. “Cover your ears.”

Riley and I did so a nanosecond before Hunter cocked the gun and pulled the trigger, aiming it at some soccer-mom van nearby. The shot was much louder than those I’d let off, echoing for a few seconds before we heard the clink of the shell on the sidewalk. The van’s window was obliterated.

Hunter wore a smile from ear to ear. “My god ... ” he said in awe.

“My turn?” Riley prompted, raising her pistol.

My gun education had come solely from first-person shooter games, but I was almost sure the gun she held was a Desert Eagle, like those in Counter-Strike.

One shot, and the gun flew right out of her hand. For a brief moment Hunter and I started cracking up, but I quickly swallowed my mirth, my brain reminding me that laughter wasn’t appropriate under the current circumstances.

"Dude, shut up! I didn't know the kick would be that powerful!" she complained good-humoredly. She picked the Eagle back up and cocked it. "Wait, I'm trying again."

We tried to hold it in, but we couldn't contain our snickering. She shot into the air, with confidence this time, holding it firmly.

"Good job, Ry!" Hunter said earnestly.

Just like the shotgun, the sound hung in the air. Riley blew the smoke off the end of the barrel.

"What are you, a freakin' cowboy?" I teased, making her laugh.

"Sure am," she said, faking a southern twang. "So, what's in that bag, Hunter?"

He unzipped the canvas sack and started to unpack it, shuffling through our new inventory. "A canteen, a knife," he said, laying them on the asphalt. "Ammo for our guns, other random ammo..."

Everything he laid out was a major score. Although I was hoping we wouldn't actually need to fire any, we were bound to run out of bullets sooner or later.

"And... a fucking *grenade*!" said Hunter in disbelief.

"No way!" I said, doubting him until he held up a green sphere with the signature pin on top.

Riley stepped back. "Sheesh... I mean, that's like a last-resort type of thing, right?"

"Duh! But it's awesome that we have one," he said, looking at it up close like it was some foreign relic.

"Anything else?" Riley asked, nudging the bag with her foot.

"That's it." Hunter zipped up the bag and leaned over the backseat of the overturned Humvee for one last look. His head resurfaced a few seconds later. "*Blood.* A *lot* of blood...We should go," he said gravely.

We traded nervous looks in mutual agreement, then continued down the highway with our new bounty.

The heavy quiet became the soundtrack to our new life. Only random bangs and distant sirens would break it momentarily. Or when we'd deliriously chat about pointless crap, knowing full well that underneath the shallow banter was the terrible pain of the events that had tossed us into this alternate universe.

My fight or flight instincts wrestled to determine which one would ultimately take the forefront. Every time my thoughts flashed with the image of my parents, I forced it back like a dog on a leash. It was half agonizing, half numbing. I never got my last moments with my true parents. The *things* they had become felt unrecognizable to me. I started wondering where Hunter and Riley's parents might be, when—

"Look! Ava said it was next to the water tower, right?" Riley asked, pointing ahead.

Hunter's eyes glazed over as they landed on the city's landmark water tower. "Water..." he said, mostly to himself.

"That's it," I said, relieved.

The tower stood less than a half mile down the road, but with our soles blistered and heads pounding from the sun, reaching it was no small feat.

Not far from the tower was a warehouse facility, just as Ava had quickly described before the line dropped.

Hunter lifted his weapon. "We don't know who else could've found refuge in there, so let's just keep our eyes peeled and our guns ready."

Riley and I followed his lead, walking on with vigilance. We shuffled between cars for only a few minutes before Hunter suddenly cocked his gun.

I panicked. "What?"

"I see people."

I followed his aim. About a football field away, I could make out two people, one a girl and the other a guy. He was on the ground, seemingly in pain. She was kneeling beside him.

"Help, come quick!" she called to us.

These were the first people we had come across in hours.

"Should we go?" I asked.

We didn't fully know how easy the new virus spread, but what I did know was that neither of them looked anything like the creatures we had seen.

"I think it's alright. He looks hurt," Riley whispered.

Hunter was still in defense mode. We walked closer.

The girl grew more frantic, seeing how slow we were approaching. "Please!" she shouted.

I started to walk a little quicker when I felt Hunter grab my shoulder.

"Keep your guard up," he said to me. "He could be bit."

A few moments later, we drew close enough to see there was no blood.

"Please help, my cousin's hurt!" the girl begged.

The guy next to her was turned on his stomach, groaning in pain. I noticed a military dog tag hanging out the neck of his dirty white tank.

When I met the girl's eyes, I was caught off guard by how beautiful she was. Her hair was long and dark, her fatigued eyes a deep green. I then noticed a series of harsh bruises on her neck—followed by the barrel of her pistol, now pointing directly at my forehead.

In the same instant, the boy sprang up with a pistol in each hand, one directed at Hunter, the other at Riley.

"What the fuck, man?!" Hunter spat.

The girl had turned fierce. "What's in the bag? And don't move, or I swear to god I will pull this trigger."

So, this was a trap. My face burned with embarrassment. No one answered.

"What the fuck is in the bag?!" the guy pressed, more intensely.

I had to diffuse this. "We got some basic things, a knife and some other crap. Nothing you need," I said calmly.

The guy laughed. "We need anything we can get at this point, buddy. Drop it, slowly."

Anyone in a survival situation would realize what we had in our bag was beyond valuable. Once they saw, they'd *want*. I couldn't let this turn into a shootout. I wasn't ready to go.

"Why don't you just put down your weapons?" I suggested evenly. "I think we're all trying to do the same thing here—stay alive. See that warehouse? A few of our friends are in there. You guys can join us."

"*Fuck* no they can't!" Hunter said aggressively.

"Hunter!" I shot back through tight lips.

"No! Who the hell made you captain? They're trying to rob us! We're not letting them join us... Well, the girl can, but that's it."

Her cousin's knuckles went white around the grip of his gun. "Who's the one with the gun to your head, buddy?"

"You're a pussy. Shoot, then," Hunter urged.

"*Hunter*!" This time it was Riley trying to rein him in.

The girl lowered her pistol. "Hah! I like this kid."

For a split second my heart skipped, but I realized she was referring to Hunter.

"So, we goin' with them?" her partner asked, as if it were her call.

"Why not?" She turned to us. "I'm Elle."

This was a quick change in circumstances. I never thought the offer would actually stick.

She held out her free hand in a truce. Hunter shook it hesitantly. Riley and I did the same, all our weapons now at our sides.

"This is Caleb," she said.

Caleb straightened, towering over me. Even without the dog tag, he had the typical cornfed army brat look—buzzed head, wife-beater tank, and the build to match. He had the same green eyes as Elle, but whereas hers had an intriguing confidence behind them, his held something vaguely dark. "Where'd you guys get those guns?" he asked, eyeing them.

"Abandoned Humvee," said Hunter, still with a hint of distaste in his voice. "Came across one on the way here."

"My pop's in the military. That's where I got these two Glock 18s. Elle's is from his closet. It's an XD9."

I had no idea what he was talking about, but for the sake of staying on good terms with them, I tried to sound friendly. "You know your stuff, then."

He visibly lit up. "Hell yeah. You have an MP5SD3, he has a SPAS-12 shotgun, and she has a Desert Eagle."

I'd been right about one of them, but the rest was foreign to me.

"Weapons are my thing. So, let's go to this warehouse," he said, casually slipping his dual pistols into the waistband of his jeans.

"Any family there?" Elle asked us.

No one answered. I figured these two probably had similar stories to ours.

Hunter broke the tense silence, his hand resting on Riley's shoulder. "She and I don't know about ours, but his are gone...I think mine's gotta be too."

Elle's eyes glossed over. "Caleb's and mine are long gone. They turned into those ... *creatures.*"

"I'm so sorry ... I'm Riley, by the way. This is Hunter. That's Tye."

"I thought we were never going to see people again," Elle said glumly. "A mob of them came running through here a while ago, but no one after them until you."

"Well, we shouldn't wait around for anything else to happen. Let's get to the others," I urged.

Our new pack trudged ahead.

3.

"Sorry about before," Elle announced as we walked.

"Don't sweat it. We're all just trying to get by," Riley replied.

"So how'd you guys end up here?" I asked. "You're the first people we've had a chance to talk to."

I was happy Elle was the one to answer. Her features darkened.

"Everything seemed normal yesterday. Caleb picked me up from my place, we went to a family barbecue together. When we walked in, everyone was glued to the TV watching the news... That's when my aunt went fucking crazy. She started screaming. We thought it was a panic attack at first, but then she... she grabbed hold of my parents, and started biting them... Blood, *everywhere*. Just when the others pulled her away, my parents started going wild too. It happened so quickly. Like a domino effect. We got out of there before anyone else turned..."

Caleb's forehead had tensed during her retelling, but he took over when her voice cracked with emotion. "After Elle and I got in the car, scared shitless, I rushed us back home to check on my ma and pop. It was hard to even make it down the street. Everyone was suddenly leaving town. When we got to mine, it seemed like no one was there so we grabbed the guns and rushed back downstairs. That's when I found them... They'd turned... I had no choice but to kill my parents. They went apeshit, man. I'm telling you. My pop almost choked Elle out. When 911 didn't pick up, I knew we had to get going. Next thing I know, the world's upside down. It was like a light switch."

The two of them suddenly felt familiar to me, the mugging attempt a distant memory. I knew exactly how they felt.

"I'm sorry," I said. "These two were at my place when it happened to my parents. We barely made it out."

Caleb nodded somberly. "Yeah, man, this whole thing's beyond fucked up."

"So, who's at the warehouse?" Elle asked, making a welcome change to the direction of the conversation.

Hunter went to speak, but I quickly jumped in.

"My good friend Ava and this kid, Dustin. They're friends from school. I've known Dustin for a minute, but Ava's like my sister. Known her forever."

"She's a sweet girl. You'll like her," Riley added. "Not sure what their story is, but she managed to call Tye and tell him where she was before the line cut out. Nothing seemed like a better option than trying to find people we know. Best we can do for now."

"You guys are damn lucky. Elle and I couldn't reach anyone," Caleb said.

"Where you from, Caleb?" Hunter asked him, friendlier now.

"Downtown, much more on the south side. Can't say it's a nice place to live. Elle lives near me too."

"Did you go to Ponchester Middle?"

"Yeah, Elle and I both did. You?"

"No wonder you guys look familiar. I think you were in my English class first quarter," Hunter said.

"Mrs. Zibrachi?" Elle asked.

"Yes!"

Of course Hunter would be bonding with them right out of the gate. *Great.*

Caleb's mood had brightened. "Bro, she was such a *bitch*! I think I remember you. You were in my lunch period too, right? A-block?"

"Yeah, I was. Not sure why we never linked, but I think I remember you guys now."

I felt myself wanting to be included. "So, what do you guys like to do for fun? I mean, like ... you know, before this all happened?"

Elle chuckled at my clumsy words. No one answered.

"I spy a warehouse," she said, shifting gears again.

"Oh *man* ... Look at Ava's ride," said Riley. She pointed out the dark red Mazda parked in the grass field near the warehouse.

It was covered in deep dents, its windows blown right out. Ava's orange dreamcatcher charm still dangled from the rearview mirror. Since we'd seen what those monsters could do to a car, it was clear that the Mazda had fallen victim to a similar fate. I hoped Ava and Dustin were in better shape.

We passed the water tower and crossed the stretch of grass until we reached the rear side of a rundown, two-story warehouse facility. We followed the tall perimeter gate around to the front where a sturdy metal entryway greeted us. Beyond the solid panel, we could see the warehouse windows were boarded up with wood and sheet metal. Caleb was analyzing the fence, trying to find a way in, but there was no climbing this beast of a barricade.

"Count of three, we all shout *Ava*!" I said.

"What if she's not inside anymore? They could've got her," Hunter said grimly.

"Shut the fuck up, Hunter," I shot back.

I could see him flinch in anger. He hated when anyone talked to him like that, but when I did it, it truly tested his temper issues.

I jumped as a gun went off. Elle had shot a round into the air.

"What was that for ... ?!" I yelled, the end of my question softening as I made eye contact with her.

Riley answered for her. "To get Ava's attention."

Elle and Riley traded smirks. Seemed like the new kids were hitting it off with everyone but me.

My eyes darted to an opening that appeared in the sliding door of the warehouse ahead. Two heads peeked around the corner. A beat later, Ava and Dustin came running out onto the driveway, waving excitedly. Both of them grabbed the large chain on the side of the entrance gate to lift it.

We poured into the driveway as the heavy entryway closed behind us. Ava jumped into my arms with a huge smile on her face, tears welling up as she scanned the wounds on my face. She only broke away when she noticed the gun I was holding, her eyes growing wider with each one she spotted in our hands. As emotional as this reunion was, tears were a common occurrence for her. She was a sensitive soul.

Ava and I had grown up together in suburbia. In middle school, we had gravitated toward very different circles of people but always maintained our friendship. It was tough being that age and having to explain our odd dynamic to other people. They refused to believe we didn't have feelings for each other, but she truly was like my sister. As we got older, changed friend groups, started new schools, and had significant others, we always upheld our bond.

"You're okay!" she said to me, squeezing my hand in hers. "I was seriously starting to think something happened to you." She let go of me, turning to Riley. "Hey!" She hugged her as if they were best friends.

They liked each other, but it was more the excitement of seeing someone familiar, from the 'old world.' They'd never really gotten to know each other beyond having a mutual friend in me.

I gave Dustin a bear hug. "Hey, dude, how ya been?" I asked breathlessly as he squeezed the air from my lungs.

I immediately realized how misplaced the question was.

"I mean, good as I can be, Tye. Glad to see you, though."

"Yeah… Sorry it's not under better circumstances."

Dustin was an athlete, in every sense of the word. His build was proof of his dedication to our school's wrestling team, and his sun-bleached hair was a result of all the surfing he did in his free time. His energy always made him fun to be around, but he was known to be a bit headstrong, which probably stemmed from growing up with both parents being cops. I was glad he was here.

I started the introductions. "Ava, Dustin: this is Hunter, Caleb, and Elle. We just met Elle and Caleb on the way here."

They all shook hands.

"Hey, nice to meet you guys," Dustin greeted them. "So, where'd you get all these guns? You look like a little army."

"We kinda are, huh? We found an abandoned army car. Elle and Caleb got theirs from their place before they fled," I explained.

"Well, I feel much better knowing we have some protection around here. The gate seems solid, but it's been tough to rest easy since we got here."

"Are you guys the only ones here?" Riley asked.

"Yes, luckily," said Ava. "We saw a couple groups passing through, but no one gave us any trouble. Let's get inside."

Our group filed into the warehouse. The bottom floor was a cavernous, mostly empty space with only a couple power tools scattered around. Sawdust and scrap metal covered the floor. Stray wires decorated the industrial ceiling, along with rusted pipes and air ducts. A set of metal stairs led to an upper level. Because the windows were boarded up, the main light source came from a glowing fire lit within a tin barrel at the center of the room. Two tarps were laid around it to form a makeshift rest area.

"We've had all day to explore. There's lots to use around here. We'll show you around so you get an idea of things," Dustin offered.

"That'd be good," I said.

I took in the space around me. It only now hit me that I most likely would never see my home again.

Just when I felt the emotion flushing into my face, Dustin broke my train of thought.

"We've been calling this open space the main room. It was a lot more cluttered when we got here, but we threw most of the stuff out back. I think we can agree we should prepare as if we're staying here long term ... or at least until some sort of help comes through here."

There was a slight ripple through the group, and I was sure the others had come to the same realization I had. This was home now.

Dustin continued. "To your left is a garage. Nothing really in there, besides a broken down lawnmower. Out back is a huge junk pile we haven't finished going through."

Ava started up the stairs, and we hurried after her.

"There are six work rooms, one bathroom—completely out of order and the faucet water is black, so don't bother. Over there are some closets with brooms and old junk. We found a few towels, cleaning products, and scrap wood, but mostly it's been cleared out. I don't think this place has been functioning for a few years."

Dustin caught up with us and pushed open a door to reveal a walk-in pantry.

"*This* is by far the jackpot, and why we decided to stay here," he said joyously.

My heart leapt as the dim firelight from the hall illuminated the small room.

Piled on a series of shelves was a dusty assortment of canned foods. It seemed to be some sort of emergency ration storage. None of it looked mouthwatering by any means, but it was enough to lift everyone's mood. In that moment, my stomach growled, the first hint of an appetite in nearly twenty-four hours.

"I counted earlier, and there are a hundred seventy-six cans altogether," Ava said. "Divided by seven of us, that leaves us with about twenty-five cans each. I know you just got here, but I feel like we should have a group meeting and kinda talk things out. Set some ground rules now that there's more of us."

"Okay, good idea. It would be good to get everyone on the same page, and you can fill us in," I said.

"Well, this is pretty much all there is to see," Dustin told us. "I mean, there's a shitload of stuff around the warehouse outside the gate, but I don't know how safe it is to go out there. We haven't seen any of those *demons* around here yet... Would rather keep it that way."

"We didn't see any for the last half of our trek," Riley assured him.

"What about you two?" Hunter asked Elle and Caleb. "You guys run into any in the area before we bumped into you?"

"Not near here, no. But we did see some further downtown. Caleb and I found a rooftop to get a bird's-eye view of where we were. We watched a group of them for a bit. Weirdly, they seem to drop dead again after a while," Elle revealed, a hint of disgust in her voice.

"When they turn, I'm pretty sure their burst of rage is temporary. We saw some scavenging, but then they just dropped to the floor," Caleb added.

There were still so many questions about what these creatures were. Any observations or knowledge about what we were dealing with was fully welcome. I hoped their apparent temporary mobility meant we didn't have to worry about them invading in large droves.

I felt a sense of ease to have finally arrived at the warehouse. Because there was no telling how long we'd be spending here, I felt the urge to organize our group. "So, let's go downstairs? Get stuff sorted out?" I suggested.

"Yeah, sounds good," Dustin agreed.

I caught a quick eye roll from Hunter as I took the initiative.

In what was now established as the 'main room,' we sat on the nylon tarps by the fire barrel. After what felt like an endless day, night had finally fallen. A small ticking sound accompanied the crackling fire, coming from a battery-powered clock hanging on the wall that read 8:25p.m. Thinking of all that had happened today made my stomach clench. I took a deep breath and slowly let it out, trying to subdue the stress.

"I know this is gonna sound cheesy, but we don't all know each other well. Maybe we can take turns introducing ourselves a little better?" Ava proposed. "And everyone can suggest any rules or thoughts now that we're here."

There were some muffled laughs around the circle. We couldn't deny this was going to feel like a first-day-at-school exercise, but we had nowhere to be but here.

"Elle? You first?" I prompted. I was excited to know a little more about her.

She cracked me a beautiful smile. "Hmm. Um, I'm Elle. Caleb's my cousin. Love him to death. We grew up together and my family comes before anything. If you're cool with him, you're cool with me. If you're not, you're not...Just throwing that out there so no one fucks with him. But overall, I just want to keep things chill. I don't really think we *need* rules right now, more like just figuring it out as we go and seeing what works and doesn't, you know?"

She ended her speech with a shrug, and the tension that had formed in my forehead after hearing that hint of a temper in her intro started to relax.

"Okay... Caleb?" Ava prompted over-pleasantly, possibly starting to regret suggesting this roundtable.

"My pop's in the army. It's what I've wanted to do my whole life, so I've done a bit of training and prep for that. I noticed we've got some serious firepower under this roof, so anything you want to know about weapons, just ask me. I know a lot of survival shit, so that'll come in handy too. Only rules I want to make clear are: don't touch my guns, and don't touch Elle...thanks."

I swore his eyes landed on me for a split second when he said the last part. These two were not making this intro thing fun. Microscopic looks of disapproval bounced from Dustin to Ava and back to me across the circle.

"My name's Hunter." He couldn't have looked more bored. "I suggest we get ready...to *fuck! Some! Monsters! Up!*" he shouted dramatically.

Caleb found this hilarious. "Fuck yeah, bro!" he agreed through laughter.

We waited for Hunter to continue sharing a bit about himself, but in typical douchebag behavior, he ended it there.

This was going *great.*

"Yo. Riley," she started, her tone more thoughtful, like she was trying to get things back on track. "I return the energy I receive, so if you respect me, I'll respect you. That's my personal rule. I kinda get annoyed easily, so just give me space if I'm being a bitch. Tye will tell you. We dated."

She delivered the last part with the clear intention of embarrassing me, as evidenced by the devilish smirk she shot me.

My relationship with Riley was defined by two summers. It began one summer and ended the next. When sophomore year began, we walked the halls holding hands and the entire school buzzed with talk. We were quickly branded 'Ry and Tye.' Riley had always been the unattainable cool girl in school. She seemed to be part of every group and no group all at once. Not exactly one of the popular girls, but by no means was she unnoticeable. All girls admired her nonchalant disposition that somehow made every guy want her. Maybe it was the fact that I was always off in my own world that made me oblivious to who she was and how people thought of her, but Riley immediately caught on to my initial indifference of her, and she loved it. We vibed and got close quickly. We dated passionately, sometimes complicatedly, and when things eventually ended, we broke it off amicably. I never knew if her impartial reaction to the breakup was just another emotional burial of hers, or if she truly agreed that we made better friends than we did a couple.

"I'm Dustin. I liked to work out and surf. My parents were both cops," he started.

The past tense of his words tugged at my heart. I saw a couple of the others look away in sympathy.

"I liked to skate, too," he went on. "Wrestling was a passion of mine. Um, I've known Tye and Ava for a little over a year. They were in my class, that's how we met. About the house rules, I think we should just live here for a few days and see how things work out, but we should definitely have more of these group meetings here and there so we can keep a good vibe going. We need to communicate what's working and what's not if we're going to make this place livable ... We don't know when help's coming."

When he finished there were nods of agreement all around.

"I'm Ava. Been friends with Tye since fifth grade. He's like my brother," she said, smiling at me. "I just want everyone to know I'm really easy to talk to, so if you need a friend, I'm here. I'm really easygoing, a pro people pleaser, smart, beautiful, funny, perfect—no, I'm kidding."

We all laughed.

She went on more seriously. "I think tomorrow when we wake up, we should team up and search for useful things lying around. Maybe fix some stuff up now that we have more hands. And if Caleb's up for it, I think it'd be a good idea for him to give us a crash course on how to use the weapons, maybe?"

"Yeah, that'd be good," Caleb said confidently.

"I know a few things about shooting a gun too, so I'll help," Dustin offered.

Caleb was blunt. "It's cool, man. I got it."

"Are you sure? I go to the shooting range with my dad all the time. I could teach them, too."

"Trust me, I know more about guns than anyone. Just let me do it," Caleb said, a note of finality in his voice.

The energy in the room gained weight. Dustin shrugged it off, clearly the bigger man.

I cut in to dilute the tension. "So, yeah, I'm Tye... Uh, I like art, music..." I shifted gears. "Can we just look around the room at each other for a sec? I want everyone to realize that, for now, we're all we have. I don't want to just survive, I want to thrive. I'm trying really hard to convince myself I'm fine, and I know you guys must be doing the same, but we're not. And we're allowed to feel that. This is real, but we need to keep our shit together and stick this out as a group. This is our home for now, so let's treat it like that. Sound good?"

There was a small beat, but everyone's expression lightened in understanding—except Hunter's.

My stomach dropped. "Hunter, is there something wrong?"

He gave me a look like I used to give my mom when she'd get on my case. He stood up to leave.

"Where are you going?" I asked flatly.

"Upstairs to pick a room."

Ava called after him. "Can you wait?"

"No, it's cool. Tye's the leader, so he can make all the decisions. I'll be upstairs," he said passive aggressively, then left.

The rest of us sat there awkwardly in the wake of his abrupt exit.

"Let him cool off. He has a really short fuse," I explained to the others.

For the next few hours, we recounted our individual journeys on how each of us had arrived at the warehouse.

Ava and Dustin lived in the same neighborhood and found themselves running out to the street to see what all the noise was about. Several of their neighbors wore contorted expressions and were ravaging the people closest to them. They both ran inside to look for their parents, but neither could find them.

Ava locked herself in her bedroom for nearly an hour, trying to call for help while listening to the screams and gunshots outside. She only opened the door when Dustin said it was him. He'd come for her.

They bolted for Ava's car and sped out of their gated community, passing several military vehicles heading the opposite way. After hours on the chaotic road and a run-in with more of the infected, the warehouse was the nearest reasonable refuge after Ava's car gave in from the damage.

As corny as the intro exercise seemed at first, by the end of our sharing we felt bonded. We had been talking for so long we had no energy to choose rooms upstairs, so we tried to double up the tarps for more cushioning, but to no avail. Only when Dustin found a large roll of bubble wrap were we able to enjoy an ounce of comfort.

With our weapons close by and exhaustion finally overtaking the adrenaline of the day, we drifted off to sleep. The last thing I saw was the hanging clock, reading 12:20a.m.

4.

I'd been asleep for what felt like only a few minutes when the roaring of helicopter blades woke me up. It took me a full beat to process the thought. *A helicopter!* I jolted upright and sprinted for the exit. Dustin was up and beside me in a blink. We both slid the metal door aside and ran into the front driveway.

Above us, like a metal god, was a U.S. Army chopper. It flew by at speed, passing overhead within seconds.

"DOWN HERE!!!" I screamed through a dry throat.

Dustin and I tried everything to wave it down. This was our way out. All the mental preparation and talk of living in this warehouse long term seemed so silly now. We were out of here sooner than I could've ever hoped for.

"HEY! OVER HERE!" Dustin shouted at the top of his lungs.

It kept flying, putting distance between us with every moment that passed. We let our arms drop to our sides, realizing there was no chance they'd see us from this far. Just when I turned away in defeat, I heard the roaring blades get louder. The chopper made a wide turn and came flying back in our direction.

I rejoiced. "Dude! It's gonna land! It saw us!"

The helicopter turned its nose toward us.

"Over here! Help us!" Dustin called out.

There was a loud *click*, then-

BAM, BAM, BAM, BAM, BAM, BAM, BAM, BAM, BAM.

Gravel and glass exploded around us. They were shooting at us!

Dustin and I dived through the doorway, dropping to the ground with our hands over our heads. The others, who had gathered around the entryway only a second before, beelined for cover. The artillery rounds left giant holes in the aluminum walls, creating thin beams of light that crisscrossed through the dust and debris.

As quick as it came, it went. The roaring propellers grew faint until silence fell again. No one moved until we were sure it was over.

My heart pounded so hard, it felt like it was trying to break free from my body. I could feel Dustin's panicked breathing on the ground next to me. We were all clearly shaken by the betrayal of our only beacon of hope.

"What the *fuck* was that?" Elle demanded.

"They must've thought we were infected," Dustin said.

"Or worse," Hunter added as he cautiously came down the stairs. "They could be making sure there's no survivors to spread it."

We all let that hang in the air for a moment.

Ava broke the silence, her voice shaky. "Let's not jump to conclusions. Maybe they realized and went to get help. That's why they stopped shooting. If we let our morale down, we're going to have a hard time staying alive. We need to keep ourselves busy...How about we all take some time to cool off, then start working around the warehouse? Get some stuff done."

"Solid idea," I said, my voice still trembling. "Let's make this place the best it can be. Seems like we'll need to plan for a long stay."

Riley was quick to agree. "Okay, so, what do we do first?"

"I don't know about you, but I'm thirsty as hell. We really need to figure out our main source of water, or that's going to be our first downfall," I said.

I had watched enough survival shows to form a small mental handbook in my head. I remembered thinking I'd fare well if I was ever put in a situation like the ones the contestants were thrown into. Sure, this was nothing like TV, but the fact remained.

"Ava, I think you should be in charge of food rations and dividing it up. Make sure we have a set number per day, and an idea of how long it'll last," I said.

Ava gave me a nod. I looked to Hunter, who already wore an irritated expression. I bypassed him and directed my question to Caleb and Dustin instead.

"Will you two take Hunter and try to find anything you can to fortify this place? Board up any holes—including these new ones—and look for weak spots that could be problematic if any of those things show up here. We need to be sure nothing can get in...Sound good?"

Dustin put a friendly arm around Caleb and Hunter. They didn't reciprocate. "We got this," he said. "There's a bunch of tools laying around, but you might want to check the junkyard out back while we do that. See if there's anything else we can use."

"Will do. Riley, how about you and Elle go to the water tower and see what you can do? Take your guns."

The two girls picked up their pistols, snatched up the canteen from the backpack and headed off to the tower, albeit with some hesitation.

"As a matter of fact, we should all keep our guns on us. Even when we're inside the warehouse," I said. "Just because we haven't seen any of those things around here yet, doesn't mean we shouldn't be ready for them at all times."

I picked up my automatic and headed out back as everyone else got to work. My head still hurt under the dried blood in my hair, but now that we were taking our situation by the reins I felt charged up and motivated.

As I explored more of the area, I got a much better feel of the landscape. The expansive barbed-wire fence that bordered the perimeter of the warehouse gave me a slight sense of freedom in walking around the grounds.

In the driveway out front, I didn't find anything with potential lying around. There were just scrap metals, rubber tires, and some rusted, abandoned machinery. I made for the junk pile at the back of the property.

Beyond the back fence, I could see the water tower across the vast, grassy field. Riley and Elle were just passing Ava's wrecked car, which marked the halfway point.

I got back to rummaging through the promising-looking trash mound and right away spotted some useful items: a bunch of Styrofoam blocks, more bubble wrap, buckets, old cans, and a few empty water and Coke bottles. As I dug deeper, I found a bunch of PVC pipes, some broken pieces of metal and a long rubber tube—none of which had any obvious use, but it all seemed potentially valuable.

Near the gate was a conveniently placed flatbed on wheels, which I used to wheel the weight of my new collection inside.

The other three guys were nailing metal plates to some weak points in the walls. I could see they were working diligently.

I walked upstairs to see how Ava was managing and found her in the cramped storage room, cans all over the place. "How's it going?" I asked.

She jumped at the sound of my voice. We started laughing.

"I hate you! Scared me," Ava said.

"Sorry!"

"I got it all sorted out. We have one hundred seventy-six cans. Like I said before, that's about twenty-five cans for each of us, and I'm thinking we could give them out so everyone's in charge of their own rations."

"That could work, but what if someone doesn't ration correctly and runs out? We're going to have to help them... or not, which will cause problems."

"We're being fair and giving everyone the same amount. I don't feel comfortable dictating who gets what, or when. Once hunger sets in, I don't want to be the target of their resentment. Hopefully help will come long before we get to that point."

"Yeah. We just have to make it clear that when it comes to food, we're all responsible for our own."

"So, what do I do? Should I bring them downstairs and split them up?"

"No, I think keep them here for now. We'll pick rooms later, I'll help you pass them-"

BAM!

Ava and I jumped at the sound of a gunshot. *What now?*

We ran down the stairs to an empty main room. I heard another gunshot out back. We sprinted outside.

Three figures ran at full pelt across the field toward us: Riley and Elle, and one of the infected only a few feet behind them. My stomach felt hollow at the sight. The gory man was bleeding from every orifice, flailing his scabbed arms at the girls in an attempt to grab them. He clearly wanted nothing more than to take a giant chunk out of each of them.

Caleb aimed his gun through the back gate. Two shots went off. Riley screamed as the bullet made contact with the man's shoulder. Blood sprayed, but the man didn't flinch.

I ran to open the latches on the gate. Elle pointed her gun behind her and shot a few times. She only hit him once, but again, it barely slowed him down.

Hunter ran inside and came out moments later with his shotgun in hand. The girls were close now. I readied myself to hold the gate open then slam it quickly behind them.

Hunter aimed, then fired. The round shot through the fence links, zoomed past Elle, and blasted the man's head off. The body fell heavily to the grass.

The girls didn't falter. They barreled inside, completely out of breath. I latched the gate behind them. Riley was coughing and gagging while Elle was flushed, drenched in sweat. Caleb ran to his cousin's side.

"Are you okay?" he asked Elle worriedly.

"Yeah, I'm fine. Just give me a sec," she said, panting.

"What happened out there?" he pressed.

"Just give me a sec, Caleb!"

He backed off.

None of us expected to see one so close to the warehouse. We couldn't catch a break today, and it just confirmed my fears that leaving this place would not be easy. I looked over at the dead body in the grass, then quickly turned away from the gory sight. We moved inside.

Elle and Riley lay flat on the tarps, still trying to calm themselves down, their heads resting on the makeshift pillows I'd crafted from Styrofoam squares encased in bubble wrap.

Dustin started a fire in the metal barrel, which also had a new addition; Caleb had taken a rectangular sheet of metal and punched some holes into it to make an impromptu cooktop. Earlier, he had prepared to boil the water we'd anticipated, but thanks to their run-in, the girls' mission had failed.

Ava began distributing the cans, twenty-five each. "Keep these in a safe place, because this is all you'll have. If you run out, you're putting a huge burden on someone else's survival, so be really smart about it."

The way Elle looked at Ava as she spoke gave me a vibe that she wasn't too fond of her.

Hunter, on the other hand, seemed a lot more receptive to any rules coming from her rather than me.

It took us a while to open our single cans of food; we each had to use a jagged piece of metal and a hammer to puncture the top and peel it away.

After we'd virtually inhaled the contents, there was not a single person in the room who didn't want to open another. Most of us were smart, but Caleb and Hunter both downed one can and went straight for a second. I rolled my eyes at their stupidity.

They made a toast with the cans raised high.

"To living the good life," Hunter proposed sarcastically.

They clanked their cans together.

I changed the subject to deflect the attention they wanted so badly. "Did you guys look through the stuff I found?"

Dustin was holding one of the buckets. "Yeah, I had an idea. If we figured out a way to redirect the gutters so when it rains it'll pour into a few buckets, we could get some water. I found some mesh screening on the windows upstairs that we can rip off and put over the buckets. It'll strain out any crap that we don't want. The rest we can boil and drink."

It seemed like Dustin had his own internal survival handbook as well.

"You're a legend, Dust. I'll help you guys finish boarding the place up, then we'll get on that...Caleb, you wanna give us some weapon lessons later?"

"Hell yeah. We can't waste too much ammo, but I'll give you guys some tips and shit about the guns and how to hold them," he said confidently.

"Sweet," I replied.

For the next few hours, we utilized every last piece of wood and metal we could find. We continued to barricade the doors, reinforce the windows, patch up some more bullet holes, and fix some torn areas of the fence. We even found a hatch that led up to the rooftop. The four of us guys climbed up to take a break.

The view was far-reaching, but there wasn't much to see. I scanned for any more of those things around our border but thankfully saw none. I looked out at the beyond. This was the first time I truly got to take in the level of desolation.

As far as I could see, the whole city looked abandoned. Not a soul roamed the streets and cars had been ditched on roads by the hundreds. Our once manicured city had begun to dismantle over the last few days. I could see some distant store windows shattered, their interiors most likely wiped clean of supplies.

We all stared in silence. How could we have ever known that our normal lives would completely change overnight? Was this the end of life as we knew it?

The rest of the evening was dedicated to checking more things off the to-do list. The buckets were set up to collect rainwater, bathroom holes were dug outside, and we'd picked our rooms.

I was with Dustin and Ava. Hunter was with Caleb, and Elle was with Riley. There was enough room for all of us to have our own space, but after some minor disagreement, we concluded that we shouldn't separate. In the same vein, I suggested we take shifts doing night watch, and to my great surprise, Elle volunteered to take the first shift with me. I smiled internally.

It was already dark out, and Caleb had crashed. The weapons schooling would have to wait until morning. Everyone dispersed to their rooms while Elle and I made our way up to the rooftop. It was a little chilly outside. With guns in hand, we sat on top of the dead radiators.

The lack of city noise fed the awkwardness of being alone with Elle for the first time. I tried to make conversation.

"God, it's cold out."

She was braiding her long hair and looking distracted. "Not really... You're cold?"

"Yeah, you're not?"

"No." She didn't even smile.

The more time I spent with her, the more I realized she was extremely dry by default.

"That was crazy what happened to you and Riley today," I said.

"Yeah."

"I wouldn't have sent you guys out there if I thought it was a risk. I would've told Caleb to go with you, you know?"

"Why, 'cause we're girls? Riley's a lot tougher than you think, and I can handle myself."

"Oh, no, I didn't mean-"

"I'm glad you told us to go together," she said, finishing the braid. "I like her."

“You do?”

“Yeah, why? You don’t?” she prodded.

“No, no, I like her. We dated-”

“She said. When we did the intros.”

“Right. She tells everyone. I don’t know why,” I said lightheartedly.

“She still likes you, peabrain. I can tell.”

“Yeah… Everyone tells me that. But I always thought she agreed we make better friends.”

“Because it’s easier than feeling rejected. You should clear that up with her. Anyway, we talked about other shit too. She’s down to earth, which I like. Not dramatic like most girls. And we both hate other girls, so there’s that.”

“Yeah, she’s always been like that. What about Ava? You like her?” I asked, appreciating the flowing conversation.

“Not really, to be honest. A little too bossy for my taste.”

Even though I had already gathered that, I couldn’t help but get slightly defensive. “She’s not bossy. She’s… motherly.”

“AKA, bossy. I don’t *not* like her, but she’s just kind of annoying.”

“Right… Well, I love her,” I countered.

“Yeah? Well, you should date, then,” Elle retorted.

“Why does everyone say that? Can’t a boy be good friends with a girl without them *liking* each other?”

“Wow, chill. I’m kidding.”

“I know, but for real, *everyone* says that. Our parents always...”

She made a face. *Parents, touchy subject.* I changed it. “So, what do you think about Hunter?” I asked, semi-hoping we shared similar tastes but knowing deep down we didn’t.

“Hunter? He’s really cool. You guys don’t like each other, huh?” she asked bluntly.

“We do...I think. We just butt heads sometimes. But I mean, we’ve known each other for a while.”

"Hmm. Yeah, I like him. Caleb loves the kid. He said he feels like he's known him for years."

"Really? I can see they get along, but I didn't know he felt like *that*."

"Yeah, I'm surprised too. Caleb doesn't get close with a lot of people. You like Caleb?"

"Me?"

Elle blinked.

"Right, duh…Um, yeah, he's cool," I said. "I don't really know him, obviously-"

"He doesn't vibe with you."

That seemed harsh. "He doesn't?"

"Well, he didn't say that, but I can tell," she said.

"How?" I asked, feeling my face get red.

"The way he looks at you, the automatic friendship with Hunter, his tone when he talks to me and mentions your name."

"What does he say about me?"

"Look, I'm not trying to hurt your feelings, I'm just telling you straight up what he thinks," she said, clearly noticing my discomfort.

"Yeah, I know. It doesn't bother me."

It actually kind of did.

"He just doesn't like when people tell him what to do," she explained.

"Hey, I'm just trying to-"

"I know you got the whole 'leader' thing going on, I get what you're trying to do. Just don't expect everyone to be okay with it," she said pointedly.

"Okay…"

"I'm not."

Elle got up and walked away to climb down the hatch.

I called after her. "Hey, our shift isn't over..."

No response.

I didn't know what the hell her problem was. I'd never tried to impose myself on the others as the leader. I just happened to be the only person taking the initiative to get things in order.

As I sat there alone, her words kept repeating in my head. I brushed them off, excusing them for probably being due to her time of the month.

I sat there for another full hour, hearing occasional far-off sounds. Finally, I switched with Caleb and Hunter. I couldn't help but send them both dirty looks as I passed them at the hatch. Caleb just scoffed.

I went to my room and laid my gun down next to my craft bed. Dustin and Ava were sleeping, the former snoring. *Great.*

I lay down on some of the bubble wrap we'd brought up, and tried my hardest to breathe out my bad mood. Another day down. Eventually, I blacked out.

5.

I was yanked out of my sleep by the sound of a gunshot. *Are these abrupt wakeup calls going to be a daily thing?*

I bolted down the stairs as fast as I could, only to find Caleb and Hunter starting the weapons lesson early. Of course; completely inconsiderate. I was livid.

"You guys can't go shooting off like that!" I told them. "I thought someone was being attacked again."

Caleb gave me a smartass look. "I'm sorry, *Mom*. I was just teaching Hunter a few things about his shotgun. Is that okay with you?" he asked condescendingly.

They both laughed. I didn't think it was funny at all.

"Okay...Well, you should wait 'til everyone's down here," I said.

"Why don't you go wake them up, then?" Hunter suggested, in a tone reminiscent of an overbearing boss addressing his employee.

"Too late," Riley said sharply.

She had come down the stairs with an exhausted look on her face.

"Everyone else is awake upstairs, too, except Ava. Seems she can sleep through anything," she added, shaking her head.

I'd just noticed the makeshift targets. Two spraypainted pieces of wood were propped up against one of the warehouse doors.

Caleb reloaded his gun. "Well, get everyone down here so we can start, officially."

Riley and I skipped some steps on our way up to get the others.

"Good morning," I said to her wryly, halfway up the stairs. "How was night watch last night?"

"It took me so long to wake up for it... Dustin and I had a really deep conversation about, well, everything. Mostly our parents... and I told him about my sister."

Knowing her the way I did meant I knew the significance of sharing that information with someone. She kept that part of herself closed to others, so she must have felt really comfortable with Dustin for him to bring that out of her. Losing her parents had to have been just as hard as losing her sister, but she was handling it better than most, at least externally. She already knew how to cope with loss.

We stopped in the hallway. "How'd that go?" I asked.

"There were tears... He's a really sweet guy," she whispered.

"He is, he is. You okay?"

"Yeah, it was a nice conversation," she assured me.

We turned the corner to find Elle curled up, apparently trying to stay asleep through all the talking and commotion from downstairs.

Riley put a hand on her back. "Let's go, girly. It's rise and shine time," she said.

"Uuuugh. Go away, Riley!"

I watched from the doorway, laughing at her grogginess.

"Uh, rude," Riley said playfully. "Come on, we're all heading downstairs to learn about guns. Should be more interesting than any of the classes we had in school."

Elle took several beats to pull herself out of bed, her hair still braided. My jovial mood evaporated as the tense exchange I'd had with her the night before flashed into my mind.

"I hate you guys," she joked.

I couldn't tell if I had imagined her eyes lingering on me as she said that.

The two girls grabbed their weapons before heading down the stairs together, neither of them waiting up for me. My insecurity urged me not to tag along.

"I'll go wake up Ava..." I said, more to myself.

I made my way to her room where she was sound asleep. I smiled to myself. "Ava! We're all downstairs. Caleb's giving us a lesson."

She didn't even flinch. I walked over to her and shook her gently. "Ava." She didn't move. I shook her harder. "Avaaaaa."

Now I was convinced she was faking. I laughed. "Ava!"

She opened her eyes slowly. "What?" she asked innocently.

"What do you mean, 'what?' Everyone's downstairs. Caleb's giving us a weapon lesson," I said, still laughing.

"Hmm? Okay," she said softly, her eyes starting to close again.

"Oh, no, you don't," I said, tickling her.

She immediately burst into laughter. "STOP!" she begged, laughing uncontrollably.

I persisted. "Then wake up, sleepy butt!"

"Okay, okay, okay! I'm up, I'm up!" she said, sitting upright.

Another gunshot went off downstairs.

"You ready to go?" I asked.

She stood up and pushed her messy hair away from her face. "Yeah," she yawned.

In the main room, the targets already sported a few major holes. An improvised table was set up, two trash cans with a piece of sheet metal laid over them. All the guns in our possession were laid out on display, along with some of the ammo we'd found in the Humvees.

Caleb stood in front of us. We all sat around him like students in a lecture hall. Suddenly I felt like I had been drafted.

"When Elle and Riley were being chased, you guys used a lot of ammo on those missed shots. A moving target's much harder than these stand-still practice targets. After you get the basics down, moving targets and high-pressure scenarios are going to be the biggest challenges," Caleb said.

He picked up each weapon and addressed them accordingly.

"This shotgun is a SPAS-12. It's about four pounds and shoots twelve gauge, three-inch shells. It shoots four rounds at a time, so ammo goes fast.

You got to cock it each time you shoot. It's very dependent on ammo, so this gun shouldn't be used unless we have a real encounter. We don't have many shells in the bag. You saw what Hunter did to that thing with it yesterday. Head came clean off. If you're using this, be really careful with the kick."

He really did know a lot about weapons, and I could tell he had a passion for them. Despite my distaste for him, it was pretty impressive.

"This, here, is the XD9," he continued. "Elle uses this one. It holds sixteen rounds in the magazine-"

"What the hell is a magazine?" Riley interrupted.

"Yeah, I'm already lost," Ava added.

Caleb smiled. "Sorry—this." He pulled out the small cartridge from the handle of the gun and held it up. "It's where you put in the bullets. It has a nine-by-nineteen millimeter Parabellum," he said.

I barely understood, but I listened. He put the gun on the table and picked up his two pistols.

"These babies are mine. Used to be my pop's. There's two. Who doesn't have a gun?"

Dustin and Ava raised their hands.

"Dustin, you can have one of these," he said, handing him one with a hint of resistance.

Ava looked disappointed, but Dustin's face lit up.

"Sweet. Thanks, man," he said, looking over the handgun.

"These are Glock 18s. They're pretty lightweight. They also have a nine-by-nineteen millimeter cartridge. This baby has thirty-three rounds in its magazine. I brought some more ammo too. It's an awesome gun and shoots really quick- Am I going too fast?" Caleb asked suddenly.

Elle answered. "No, we're good, bud. Do your thing."

This was the first time I'd seen a spark of life in Caleb. He didn't seem so empty now that he evidently cared about something. Still, I couldn't forget my conversation about him with Elle.

"Whose is this?" he asked, holding up my automatic.

"Mine," I replied.

A little flutter happened in my core. It was strange, but I felt emotionally attached to the weapon. Not only was it a comfort, but it was the only thing that I felt belonged to me. That had seen what I'd seen.

"This beauty right here's a little under four pounds. It's an MP5SD3, barely has any kick and is a really quick shooter. Again, nine-by-nineteen millimeter cartridge. It has a box magazine and holds about thirty rounds. This guy originated in Germany, if you were curious."

I loved my baby and was glad to know a little more about it.

"Moving on ... Last gun," he said. "My favorite of them all. The Desert Eagle."

"Fuck yeah, bro! That's mine," Riley blurted out, making all of us laugh.

"You should be happy," Caleb continued. "It shoots up to two hundred meters. It's gas-operated though, so again, we can't use it unless we need to. You *really* need to be careful with the kick on this thing. Hard to aim but if you hit, it's deadly. It holds seven rounds and the cartridge has point fifty action express."

Again, I had no idea what he was saying.

"We don't know how long we're going to be out here, so we need to be smart with these. I can teach you individually how to hold them when we're killing time, but in general, make sure to hold them as firmly as possible when shooting 'cause the kick on these things is crazy. When you do have to take a shot, just make sure to aim the best you can. Every bullet counts. Any questions?"

I raised my hand. "Which one of these has the most firepower?"

"Well, the shotgun's a beast, but they're all pretty powerful weapons. It depends where you shoot them and how you use them. A Desert Eagle to the head can be just as effective as the shotgun," he answered. "Anyone else?"

Ava spoke up. "Um, yeah. Do I get a weapon?"

I walked over to the canvas backpack and took out the combat knife. "There's this, for now," I offered, knowing it was significantly less effective.

She took it disappointedly.

"It's all we have at the moment. Better than nothing," I added, trying to sound positive.

"I guess this-"

Ava's words broke off. An engine could be heard in the distance, and it sounded like it was approaching the warehouse.

We readied our guns. The engine hum grew closer until it was eventually out front. It was definitely a car. A big one at that.

Ava looked nervous. "Should we go outside?"

Caleb started for the exit, gun raised. He pulled the giant metal door halfway open.

A black Ford Expedition was parked outside the front gate. The sun's glare off the windows made it difficult to see who was inside.

Was the weapon lesson already going to be put into practice? I hoped not.

Hunter and Dustin joined Caleb, creeping toward the car in defense mode. I joined them once they had the vehicle surrounded. I guess I wasn't the bravest of the four.

"Get out of the car!" Dustin yelled.

Nothing happened.

"Shoot at it," Hunter said aggressively.

"No, don't!" I countered.

Something about it felt nonthreatening, but when the SUV door swung open, we all jumped and our guns clicked.

Two boys stepped down. They both had big guns in their hands, but neither were raised.

"We come in peace," one of them called to us.

In an apparent act of trust, they laid their two weapons on the hood of the car. I wasn't sure what to do. They looked healthy, but were they friendly?

"Should we open the gate?" I wondered aloud.

"They look alright," said Caleb. "Let's open it, but keep your weapons up."

Hunter ran for the chain and pulled the gate open. The two kids got back inside the SUV and pulled into the courtyard. We kept our weapons trained on them. Looking more comfortable, the girls came outside too.

The engine shut off, and three boys jumped out of the car this time. I hadn't spotted the one in the backseat. He too had a gun.

"Hey, guys, no worries," the driver kid said.

The third kid slowly put his weapon down next to the others. No one did from our end.

"Who are you guys?" Hunter asked them forcefully.

The driver spoke up first. "I'm Gage."

Gage looked like he was the one in control of the trio. He was tall, dark hair, blue eyes. He was also freckled, and his smile was suspiciously charming. Right away I felt there was something off about him. I couldn't pinpoint whether it was coming from my unease about new arrivals, or if my gut was waving a red flag.

"This is Otto."

He pointed to the short kid who had been sitting in the passenger seat. He had messy, curly hair and dirt smudged on his face, and reminded me of the type I used to see coming out of the Robotics Club at my high school.

"And this is Xander."

These kids looked like they had just jumped out of a *Lost Boys* remake. Xander had long straight hair, a bandana around his head, a white V-neck, ripped jeans, and pointy leather shoes that looked old and stylishly faded.

"What do you guys want?" Hunter asked bluntly.

They looked at each other. Gage spoke again. "Well, we didn't realize people were already going to be here, but we're looking for a place to stay-"

"You can't stay here," Caleb shot back curtly. "There are plenty of abandoned buildings you guys can choose from."

They were visibly taken aback.

I wasn't sure if turning them away would be the best course of action. Of course the food rations would have to be rearranged, but these kids had more weapons, an Expedition and more eyes for the night watch. Plus, I'd already caught Ava's eyes sparkling as she stared at Gage.

"I think we should let them stay. Or at least, talk about it and vote," I said.

Hunter's eyes speared me. "What's there to talk about, Tye?" he asked through gritted teeth.

"Just hear me out," I said, beckoning my group back inside. "Don't go anywhere, you three."

I shut the metal door behind us.

"What the fuck are you doing, Tye?!" Hunter yelled at me.

"Just listen! They have a working car, weapons, and I'm sure they have even more to offer if we give them a chance. This isn't a club. We need to think what's best for us to survive. Right now, we can't walk out in the city because we'll get mauled, but with an SUV, we can go places!"

Now, everyone was listening. Ava backed me up.

"I think Tye has a point. Why don't we ask them what they're going to bring to the table if we let them stay, see what they have to say, and then decide? They don't seem threatening," she proposed.

It was probably, in part, due to her seed of interest in Gage, but I still appreciated it. I could see Caleb and Dustin thinking about it.

"Okay, but if they don't have anything worthwhile, they're out," Caleb said. "The SUV's great, but more people doesn't really mean better chances."

I looked to the rest for agreement. Elle approved, then Riley, then Dustin.

"Hunter?" Caleb asked.

His look was harsh. "Whatever," he said.

We opened the metal door. The trio were leaning on the car, waiting for our answer, their weapons still untouched.

Dustin delivered the verdict. "Okay, so, we decided that if you guys can sell us on why we should let you stay, we'll consider. We're limited on supplies, so this has to be worth it."

"We got plenty of reasons," Otto said. "First off, you won't need to worry about food. We got the Expedition and we're planning a raid on the nearby supermarket. It looks like it's been looted already, but there's a shitload of stuff left. We can pack all we can fit in the trunk."

More food? This was the best thing they could have started with.

Xander spoke next. "Second, you won't find a better mechanic than Otto. He builds things for fun. He's always making us look dumb with his enormous brain."

Now, it was Gage. It was like they had this all planned out. "I've got guns, and I'm good company," he said, charmingly.

Hunter and Caleb laughed. Then, there was a long pause.

"Want us to keep going?" Gage asked with a smile.

"No, you're good," Hunter said.

"So? What's our decision?" I prompted.

"I like them," said Riley.

"Me too," Ava added, a little too quickly.

I turned to the others. "Elle, Dustin?"

They nodded in approval.

"Hunter... Caleb?"

"Sure, but only if this kid can make us a shower," Hunter said, wiping a little dried blood from his nose.

Otto smiled. "Your wish is my command."

"Come on in," I said.

The three teens could not have looked happier. They picked up their stuff and eagerly joined us in the main room.

After we'd finished surface introductions, Dustin started a fire and we sat around it with the new arrivals.

"So, what's your guys' story?" he asked them.

"Where do we start? I mean, we really thought we were screwed, dude," Xander said. "So, the three of us went on a camping trip we'd been planning. We didn't bring much 'cause it was only overnight. Our day already started off bad when we arrived at the campground and found tons of dead animals laying around. Park ranger told us it'd been happening for months. We'd seen articles about it but never saw it in person. We chalked it up to pesticides, but the next morning we woke up to a bunch of groaning in the woods. Thought maybe it was more animals since we were so deep in the forest, like *way* in, but when we got out of our tent we were surrounded by fucking monsters, man. Obviously, we didn't know what was happening. We just ran for our lives. It took us hours to get out of the forest-"

"We had to leave everything behind," Otto cut in.

"And when we made it out of the woods, we lifted this SUV and tried to get back to our houses. Things just got worse from there. The roads were so jammed we couldn't make it back to any of our places... We still don't know what happened to any of our fam. Not for sure."

"We were able to get this far by off-roading," continued Gage. "Got around all the military roadblocks over this way. We even jacked an extra tank of gas, and took some stuff off a squad of dead soldiers we found."

"Dead soldiers?" I asked. "I thought they'd be getting things under control... "

Otto nodded. "It's gotten worse in the past couple days. There's barely anyone around that's not dead. We were surprised as hell when we saw you guys come outside. We've seen a few people, but they weren't friendly at all. Everyone's still trying to evacuate, but no one knows where to go."

"Did the government just give up on us?" Elle asked, her tone resentful. "They *have* to have a plan."

"The only thing I heard were reports saying it could be biochemical terrorism, but they never elaborated. Information's been scarce. I don't think they're even sure exactly what happened."

Biochemical terrorism. That repeated in my head several times. Had they been experimenting on shit they shouldn't have? Was another country trying to take us out? I had seen protests and news items of theories that suspicious aircraft in U.S. airspace could be linked to the various virus strains breaking out around the country. Funny how terrible news can become background noise when it's delivered so often.

"Fuck the government," Xander said.

Caleb immediately tensed.

"They don't give a shit about us," Xander went on. "They sent in some reinforcements to act like they were doing shit, but now that this place is a lost cause they're not sending their guys in just to die."

There was a long silence. I doubted any of us wanted to accept that no one was coming to help us.

I fought against the thought. "Well, they can't just be sitting there doing nothing. They have to know there's still survivors and people who couldn't make it out. Nothing like this has ever happened in the history of the world. They're probably just trying to figure out a rescue plan. Find a new vaccine to give to their soldiers before sending them in again."

"The only fact that seems true is us younger ones being the main ones to survive the sickness," said Otto, gesturing to the group. "Might play to our advantage. They'll feel pressured by other countries and world leaders to act. You know how things get when kids are involved..."

"Why do you think they even care about survivors out here at all? We had a helicopter fly by and shoot right at us," Elle countered.

"That's because they must've thought we were those *things,*" I rationalized, weakly.

"Exactly!" she said. "They probably think everyone's infected. Especially if they don't know exactly how it's spreading. They're not going to come help us. Caleb, your dad's in the army. What would they do for something like this?"

Caleb's eyes were still locked on Xander. He finally turned and spoke to Elle. "Honestly, I know they'll do whatever they can for their country and they'll try and find a way to help. They could very well be testing a cure before sending more men out here. There'd be no point if they're just sending bodies for the virus to get a hold of and make the problem bigger."

"You know what I think?" Hunter interjected. "I think we should forget sitting around, get our stuff, and get the fuck out of here. I bet we'll find help somewhere out there. If we're cooped up in this shithole, no one'll find us. No one's going to look in a random warehouse on the outskirts of town."

Anger boiled inside me. I didn't want everyone to start getting ideas. We needed to stay together and stay put. We had what we needed to survive for a few weeks. There was no point in leaving right now. Help *could* come, after all. "Hunter, you know that we'll die out there. Much sooner than we would if we stayed and waited for a better option. We can create a signal on the roof so people know we're inside."

"No, Tye, that's what a pussy would do. We have an SUV! I say we get in there and drive as far as it'll take us. There's ten of us, and it's an eight-seater, we can make it work."

"Stop trying to impress your boyfriend Caleb," I shot back, the words coming out before I even put the thought together.

Hunter and Caleb both stood up and came at me. Dustin stepped between us and pushed Hunter to the floor. Caleb punched Dustin in the face.

"Stop it!" Riley yelled.

Her hand caught Caleb's jaw. Elle got up and pulled Riley by the hair. I grabbed her and yanked her off.

Hunter and Dustin were laying into each other on the floor. Elle broke free and went for Riley again. Then, everything went black for a second as Caleb's fist made contact with my stomach. I choked. Through ringing ears I could hear the muffled voices of the three new boys yelling at us to break it up.

Gage pulled Hunter to the other side of the warehouse, trying to defuse his temper as his lip bled. We were all panting. Dustin stood beside me with his guard still up and a cut on his face.

"You okay, dude?" he asked me.

"Yeah, thanks ..." I said, coughing.

I was stunned at how quickly things had gotten out of hand. We were much too early into our survival journey to have everything crumble.

Ava was next to Riley, helping her untangle her hair from her earring. Xander held Elle back by the shoulder. She looked furious. I could hear Caleb cursing upstairs now.

"This is not okay, guys, we need to cool down," Ava pleaded. "We can't do this stuff. We're not going to get through this if we don't pull it together!"

"Shut *up*! Damn, you're annoying as fuck!" Elle yelled across the room.

Ava ignored her but her face paled. She spoke softly to me. "We need to fix this."

I knew she was right, but I was so enraged, I could care less to take any of it back. I couldn't stomach how much I hated Hunter and Caleb in that moment.

The tension had reached its maximum capacity. It took an entire, very drawn-out two hours for everyone to come back to earth. No one but the three new kids had interacted since the blowout. They were whispering amongst themselves around the fire, taking stock of the few things they'd brought inside.

I saw Ava join them and attempt conversation with Gage, and to my mild surprise he actually seemed to be flirting with her. I walked over to their huddle, keeping my manner friendly.

"I'm really sorry about that, guys. I didn't mean for it to go that far," I admitted.

"It's chill," Xander assured me. "Looks like you guys have some issues to work out, though."

“Yeah, I’m hoping this can blow over peacefully,” I said.

“I know something that might lift some spirits,” Otto said. “I was talking with my friends here, and I’m pretty confident that I could upgrade our SUV. Add some things to heighten our chances of getting away from here alive.”

“How would you do that?” I asked, intrigued.

Dustin joined us, a bruise painted on his swollen cheek.

Otto gave us a smile reminiscent of a mad scientist. “Well, I’d need a few things, but nothing drastic. I’ve already seen some stuff around here I could use. I would reinforce it. Try and make it a little lighter so that our weight doesn’t slow it down and burn more gas, and I can see if I can get some weapons on there. I saw in that sack over there that you guys have some ammo for Humvee guns. Where’d you get it?”

“We found it in a Humvee,” I said with a laugh.

“Well, perfect. I want to see if I can mount a gun on top of the Expedition. And, I already figured out how I’m gonna make that shower Hunter wanted.”

My stomach jumped at the mention of his name. I looked over and saw him sleeping against the wall on the other side of the room. Elle had her head in his lap.

“Really? How’s that?” Dustin asked Otto, thrilled.

“You’ll see,” he said.

These kids had arrived at the perfect time. They brought good energy, innovation, and a boost in morale. Ava took a seat on the floor next to Gage, joining the circle with me, Xander, and Otto. We spent a little time getting to know each other. Telling our stories to the new kids made them feel less new.

Otto eventually left our conversation and began his hunt for materials he planned to use for his new projects. I kept seeing him come in and out, each time with something new in his hand. It reminded me of a little bird gathering pieces of straw to build a sturdy nest.

I spotted mechanical parts he'd taken off some equipment out front including chains, some metal, a bunch of nails and screws he'd gathered, and other trinkets I couldn't place. At one point, I saw him take an enormous fiberglass barrel he'd found somewhere and move it outside to the back.

The energy in the warehouse began to settle. Elle and Hunter moved upstairs to get away from everyone. Riley and Xander were having an intensely deep conversation about who-knows-what. Dustin was helping Otto bring things inside.

After Ava spent some time upstairs showing Gage the rooms and rooftop, she came back down without him.

"Where'd he go?" I asked, raising my eyebrows.

"He wanted to take a nap," she said.

I smiled at her. "Why didn't you stay with him?"

She blushed and shoved my shoulder. "*Tye*. Because..."

"Don't even act like you don't have your eye on him," I teased.

"I wasn't gonna say I didn't... I just don't want to seem desperate. We just met. I just think he's cute. Nothing else."

"Whatever you say. Just don't get too attached," I said, feeling protective.

"Oh, shut up, Tye."

"What? I think it's adorable...*but,* I wouldn't trust him."

"Okay, we are not having this conversation. I've known him for a few hours, of course I'm not going to trust him," she assured me.

"Okay, okay. I'm just saying. Out of all three of them, he's the one I have my eye on."

"You're just being overprotective." She rolled her eyes and headed back upstairs.

6.

The tension from the fight was even more prominent the next morning. I could feel the separation seeping into the fabric of our group. As we sat around the main room, eating our canned goods, a stifling silence weighed heavy on the air.

Elle and Hunter were sitting next to each other, which wasn't a surprise at all. I'd heard her unabashedly moaning all night. Caleb, who hadn't even glanced my way since waking up, was playing tic-tac-toe on the floor with Gage. They'd used a rusted nail to scratch it into the concrete. Otto was out back with Dustin and Xander, banging something together. Ava was still asleep upstairs, per usual. Riley finished eating in a hurry, then stood up and walked out back to join the boys. I tossed my empty can onto the corner pile and followed suit.

I found her with a repulsed look on her face, staring out into the grass field. I followed her gaze and made what was probably an identical expression when I spotted the vultures feeding on the headless body at our back gate. Maggots and flies had made it their Holiday Inn.

I guided her away by the shoulder and we walked together around the perimeter fence of the property. "What's up?" I asked her, sensing she needed to vent.

"I want to stick Elle in the face," she said.

"You're still mad too?"

"Hell yeah, I'm mad. She turned on me in a second. Like, bro, I know I barely know the girl, but I didn't think she'd go at me like that. We've been cool. She's fake as hell."

"Trust me, she's not exactly an easy-going person, but she was just sticking up for her cousin," I said, playing devil's advocate.

"Yeah, I got the point, but still. I can't look at her without wanting to break her perfect nose," she said, kicking a tin can like it was Elle herself.

I laughed. "Just try and stay calm. I'm hoping it'll settle down. We've been cooped up-"

"She screwed Hunter too, you know that?" she asked.

"Yeah ... I heard..."

"When I went upstairs last night, I saw them spooning, then I wake up an hour later to his heavy breathing and her gross moans."

It was a little funny to see Riley mad. I let her get it off her chest.

"And I'm sorry, but she's trashy...God, I could really use a cigarette right now," she said with a deep exhale.

"I thought you quit?"

"Yeah, I did, but I want one so bad."

I shook my head with a smile. "You're gross ... So, look, I hate to bring it up again, but I was thinking. Do you think we should stay put or go for Hunter's plan? What do you think will actually be better for us?"

"I really don't know, Tye. I want to stay here because I never want to see one of those *things* again, but there might be somewhere out there that gives us a better chance for getting help. Honestly, either way, I'm sticking with you," she declared. "Whatever you do, I'm down."

"Thanks, but that's the thing. I don't actually know what to do. I'll see what Otto does with the SUV and we'll go from there."

We walked a little longer under the gray clouds until we reached the other side of the warehouse. Otto, Xander, and Dustin were standing under a strange contraption that was not there an hour before.

"Is this the shower?!" I asked, amazed.

A wooden frame was holding up a large fiberglass barrel that had been cut in half to form a giant bucket. A black hose was attached to the inside of the warehouse gutter and snaked down inside the barrel.

"It is," Otto said proudly. "I'll show you how it works, but the rain has to fill this thing up first. I heard it thundering last night, so I worked all night and day to get it done."

"You're fuckin' awesome," Riley said. She walked around the hefty rig, checking it out in awe.

Dustin walked over to me. "How you feelin'?"

"I'm good. Stomach's a bit sore," I said with a laugh. "Actually, can I talk to you for a second?"

"Sure, what's up?" he asked, following me a few feet away from the others.

"I just really want to thank you for sticking up for me yesterday. I was gonna get my ass kicked if it wasn't for you."

"Don't sweat it, dude. I seriously have your back," he said, his hand on my shoulder.

"Yeah, and I know that now, and that's why I just want you to know that I really appreciate it. You're a good friend. Not many people would've went at Caleb and Hunter like that."

"Oh, come on, they're all talk. We can take them both," he said.

"*You* can take them both!" I laughed. "But in all seriousness, I don't want something like yesterday to happen again. I know you got my back, and I have yours, but I want to avoid fights if we can."

I could tell by his expression that he wouldn't mind another one.

"Please, Dustin," I urged. "I know you'd love another go, but we're living together and there needs to be some order, you know?"

"Yeah, I got it. Don't worry about me. I'm not gonna start anything... but if they come at me, or you, or anyone else, I'm not just gonna sit there. Is that fair?" he asked seriously.

I smirked. "Yeah. Sounds fair."

He held his fist out, and I bumped it with mine.

We headed back inside the main room. Otto and Xander were carrying some scrap metal out to the SUV in the driveway. Otto had been working non-stop. It was impressive, and I caught myself thinking how terrible it would have been if we had turned them away. Dustin saw Otto struggling to move a large piece of machinery and went over to take it from him.

In a new development from the day before, I found Ava sitting in Gage's lap as he ran his fingers through her hair. They were whispering and chuckling. I tried to send an authoritative stare at Gage, but he didn't take his eyes off Ava long enough to notice.

I shook my head and turned away, my gaze accidentally landing on Hunter and Caleb, who were at the far end of the main room talking about weapons. Thankfully, Caleb was engrossed in Otto's gun he'd picked up. I could hear him ranting.

"U.S. soldiers usually carry one. Holds about sixty rounds and can shoot up to forty-five rounds per minute. It's a semiautomatic," he boasted.

"Sick," Hunter said flatly. "What's it called?"

"M16A2 assault rifle." Caleb picked up Gage's identical weapon. "My god, these kids are lucky as hell. Two?!"

Hunter looked bored. I thought about going over to talk to them, maybe sort things out, but I wasn't sure that was a good idea when they were both currently armed.

Caleb held Xander's gun now. "And this right here's a fuckin' weapon *god*. Soldiers usually don't carry these. This is the FN SCAR-H. Gas operated, rotating bolt. It's got an eight hundred meter per second muzzle velocity, twenty round box. Mega powerful and big kick-"

Without warning, his eyes met mine and he stopped mid-flow. Hunter noticed and looked over to see me staring.

"What?" he asked me, annoyed.

It was now or never. I walked over to them.

"I...I just wanted to apologize for yesterday." They didn't say anything, so I went on. "It was really dumb...and I think we should just forget it happened. At least for now, so we can come up with a plan."

Caleb put the gun down. "Listen, man, I don't start shit for no reason. If you give me respect, I'll give you respect," he said.

"Fair," I agreed.

"I don't speak for Hunter, but unless you provoke me again, I'm not gonna start shit with you."

"Yeah, that's all I want. A little respect," I said, trying to sound friendly. "This isn't a pride thing. I just want everyone to get along for as long as we can. A couple days into this is a little too soon."

Hunter was staring blankly at me.

"Hunter? Anything to say?" I asked.

"Same thing Caleb said," he said, disinterestedly.

It seemed the problem was at least temporarily solved. "Cool...Thank you."

I walked away as they jumped back into their conversation as if nothing had happened.

My head hurt a little. It was probably the lack of water taking its toll, but I needed a nap. The windows were all boarded upstairs, so it was suitably dark, unlike the main room. I walked past Gage and Ava who were now playing a flirty game of slaps. I smiled at her, then went up the steps.

Riley was singing in her room. I walked in.

"Hey, I'm gonna take a nap," I said.

"So, basically you're telling me to shut up?" she asked.

"Yeah, basically."

We laughed.

I walked down the hall to my room, lay down on the bubble wrap, and forced myself to sleep.

It wasn't long before the constant pattering sound dragged me slowly out of a deep sleep. When I opened my eyes, I could hear laughing and shouting out back. I got up, stretched out the aches I had absorbed from the hard floor and dehydration, and ran down the stairs.

The back door was open, and everyone was playing under a summer downpour. I rushed outside, the rain hitting my skin and sending a euphoric sensation through my body. It was so refreshing.

Xander was in his underwear, standing underneath the homemade shower, shaking out his long hair like a wet dog. Otto pulled a lever that slid out a piece of sheet metal from under the tank. The holes in the bottom now streamed water from the basin.

Xander scrubbed himself down. I took my shirt off, ran at him and pushed him aside, laughing. The cool water washed away the dirt and dried blood.

We splashed each other and took turns rinsing off the grime we'd collected over the last few days. The aura of happiness that surrounded the group made me optimistic that all the built-up stress would pass.

Eventually, all of us ended up in our underwear, and for the first time in ages we were having fun.

Dustin shoved me out from under the tank and took his turn. "Otto, this is fucking great!" he told him, scrubbing happily.

"You really are a genius," I added.

Caleb grabbed me from behind and gave me a friendly noogie. *What's this? An act of peace?*

I laughed and pushed him off. "Dude! Your bulge is touching me!" I yelled through the laughter.

He started cracking up. "My B. It's hard to keep it under control when it's so big," he boasted.

"How original," Riley teased, rolling her eyes sarcastically.

The rain was working miracles. We were all getting along again.

A good hour filled with laughter and reconciliation had passed, and the rain was finally relenting to a drizzle. I didn't see Elle and Riley interact much, but Caleb and Hunter were being cool. It had only taken ten minutes for Xander to lose his trunks, securing the title of the wild one amongst us.

It was strange to reflect on what the world had become, and realizing we were still able to have fun at a time like this. The mental gymnastics of human survival were impressive.

As the rain simmered down, Otto eventually plugged the tank, which was now filled to the top with gallons of rainwater. Some decent shower time and potential drinking water lay in our futures.

We hung our clothes on the fence to dry and went inside in our underwear. After many a "Dude, come on," Xander finally put his back on.

It was easier to start fires now. From his messenger bag, Otto produced matches from the camping trip. We sat on the floor around the flames, occasionally throwing some old newspaper or scrap wood into the barrel.

"How's the SUV coming along?" Elle asked Otto.

"Great so far. I want to make it a super SUV. Gonna try and attach Xander's gun to the top and make the trigger controllable from the inside. I'll try and make a bigger cartridge for it too, so it'll hold more ammo," he explained enthusiastically.

"Otto, where'd you learn how to do all this?" Ava asked, clearly impressed.

Otto smiled sweetly. "My dad owned a big car shop in town...Grew up around it my entire life. He was so good at making things from random parts. My house looked like the inside of some giant robot. Tons of scrap parts and contraptions. He was an odd one...I mean he literally named me Otto, like *auto*," he said.

We all burst out laughing at the revelation.

"That's the best thing I've ever heard," said Riley.

"What did you work on today?" Gage asked him.

"Luckily, some of the power tools still have battery charge, so I was able to add another layer of metal to some of the exterior. Those creatures have wicked strength, so I don't want us to be vulnerable if we get stuck in a group of them. I also attached a really wide piece of metal on the grill so we can push things out of the way. We saw lots of debris out there...Plus, the infected seem to drop dead after an hour or so. Might have some pileups," he said.

"Have you ... seen it happen?" I asked hesitantly.

"Yeah. I didn't know what I was witnessing at first, but from what I've gathered, I believe this plague kills its host, then something kicks in and causes the body to go on a rampage, but once that something runs out of juice, the body just falls limp again-"

"Doesn't that mean that, eventually, all the infected are just going to drop dead? We can wait this out?" I jumped in, feeling like I was onto something.

"No ... because as long as there are hosts, the virus'll keep spreading. And the wild card is that when the infected feed on the dead bodies, the bodies reanimate again. I've seen it. It'll be a never-ending cycle."

"Fuck, dude ... " Dustin said quietly.

Otto's tone lightened. "I'm going to work on a help signal tomorrow. Too tired to think right now, but I'll come up with something."

"Otto, don't wear yourself out. You just got here, relax," Gage insisted.

"I'm fine. Trust me, I love this stuff. It's giving me a purpose," he reassured us.

The gutter rig Dustin came up with worked as planned. It gathered the rainwater and directed it into the bucket we had placed at the end of it. The filter he'd crafted from a piece of mesh caught all the icky fragments that came from inside the dry shaft.

Gage filled some empty cans with water and boiled them over our improvised cooktop. After letting it cool down for a while, he passed the cans around. I drank mine in a blink. I was too dehydrated to let the strange taste bother me.

"Since we're all here, I think we should talk out some of those rules. We've been here enough time," Ava said.

I heard Elle mutter something under her breath.

"I think that's a wonderful idea, Ava. We'll come up with them together," I said, directing my remark at Elle. Her appeal level had gone from a hundred to zero in the last few days, and I was immune to it now.

"I got a rule," Dustin said. "Night watch. We can start with that. The other night I did way more than my shift because *someone* didn't wake up." He smiled and stared good-humoredly at Ava.

Her cheeks flushed. "Sorry!"

"How about this: two at a time, we pick our partners, and rotate every hour?" I suggested.

Everyone seemed satisfied with that plan.

"I call Ava!" I added quickly.

I saw her quickly glance at Gage and felt a hint of rejection.

Everyone else shouted their choices. It ended up being me with Ava, Gage with Elle—Ava was really annoyed by this—Riley with Xander, Caleb with Hunter, and Dustin with Otto.

"Rule number two," Caleb said. "Always have your weapon on you."

"Yes, that's gotta be a rule," Gage agreed.

"Well, you guys left your weapons lying around earlier. Has to become a habit," Caleb warned the trio.

"It will," Gage said with a lighthearted salute.

"And I think we should make it a point to always be with a partner if we're outside for *anything,* even just out back... and let everyone know so we can keep track of each other," Otto said.

At first, I'd thought this rule thing was going to bring back the tension, but it was actually working out great. So far they seemed pretty logical and no one was challenging them.

"I redid the food rations. We have about seventeen cans each, but hopefully we'll be doing that market raid in the SUV, so it shouldn't be too bad," Ava said.

"Until more food arrives, let's treat it like it's truly seventeen cans each. Use wisely," I cautioned.

Otto jumped back in. "Oh, and the shower. I think we can limit it to forty seconds each, once a week. And that's the best we can do with a full tank."

No one was happy about the limited hygiene, but we knew it was necessary. At least we *had* a shower.

There was a beat in the conversation.

"Anything else?" I asked, addressing the whole group.

"No stupid arguments," Riley suggested, not making eye contact with anyone specifically.

Dustin smiled. "Good one."

"Definitely," I said. "And I'm gonna end this with something super cheesy, but I'm serious. Everyone needs to look out for each other, always."

No one contested this, so the rules were set. We scratched them into one of the walls with a stone, like cavemen.

DON'T LEAVE THE PERIMETER WITHOUT A PARTNER OR BEFORE TELLING SOMEONE.

EVERYONE LOOK OUT FOR EACH OTHER, ALWAYS.

ALWAYS HAVE A WEAPON WITH YOU.

KEEP YOUR NIGHT WATCH SHIFT, ROTATE EVERY HOUR.

17 CANS OF FOOD PER PERSON.

FORTY SECOND SHOWER, ONCE PER WEEK.

AVOID STUPID ARGUMENTS.

7.

I half-stirred a few times during the night to the sound of voices downstairs, but they were too faint to drag me out of my sleep entirely. I should've known something was up.

A lot earlier than any of us wanted to be up, Dustin came to wake us with urgent news.

We all congregated in the main room, fuming.

"I can't believe this shit!" he shouted, thumping the wall with his fist.

During the night, Gage, Hunter, Caleb, and Elle had taken the SUV and were gone. My heart was pounding, but still I tried to calm the situation.

"Dustin, we have to keep our heads straight. Relax," I said, covering my own anxiety.

"I'm not gonna relax 'cause I know *you're* not relaxed! They screwed us over!" he shouted.

Otto was visibly upset. "I can't believe Gage left with them...He barely knows them."

"What if they just went on the food raid without us?" Xander asked hopefully.

"They took our guns, the canteen, the food, and the grenade. They're not planning on coming back," said Dustin, fired up. "It doesn't make sense to leave without telling us if they weren't up to something shady."

Otto kicked the fire barrel over. Ash poured onto the floor. "I can't believe he just left like that!" he snapped. "That's insane. He's been our friend for years!"

Ava hadn't said a word. She looked stunned.

"I hate Elle. I hate Caleb and I *really* hate Hunter! And fuck Gage, too!" Riley yelled.

Her angry words echoed around the main room.

So there we were, our group down to six. Betrayed by our own kin. Even though they were in the same situation as us, they were able to detach themselves from all empathy and leave us to die.

The only items they'd left behind were Ava's knife, mine and Xander's guns and a handful of canned foods. I was near a breakdown. What next? Everything was completely screwed now. We were low on food, low on weapons and low on morale. I'd had a feeling a dead end would eventually come, but I'd never considered a curveball like this.

We walked out to the driveway. I still had a tiny glimmer of hope that they'd maybe come back and it was all a misunderstanding, but as soon as I saw the entrance gate, I knew I was dead wrong.

The giant metal entrance was torn apart. They'd driven right through it, deciding to add insult to injury by leaving us completely vulnerable.

"This is unbelievable," I said under my breath.

Otto tried to comfort me, but I knew he was equally affected.

"I'll get this gate back up," he said. "I'll need some help, but it won't be too hard since it snapped on the hinges."

I was spaced out, just staring at the broken chain link. I couldn't fathom the level of evil it would take to execute something like this. None of them had given me good vibes from the start, but I'd never expected this. Not after things had ended so well yesterday.

We lifted the metal gate and hammered out the dents. We then reinforced it with some sheet metal and reattached it to the pull-chain. It wasn't as sturdy-looking as before, but it was fixed for now.

Sweating, we went inside to boil some water. Half of the bucket was depleted from the overnight pillage.

There were still no words from Ava, who was sitting in the corner eating a can of fruit half-heartedly. Riley was on the opposite side, her arms around her knees. Xander was taking the bed mats out of the traitors' rooms and moving them into ours for extra cushioning, a small way to reclaim some of the comfort they'd taken from us.

I joined Xander upstairs to lend a hand. He was laying more bubble wrap over my bed. I patted his back. "Thanks, dude."

"No prob. What's up?" he asked, giving me his attention.

"Nothing. I'm just still trying to understand what happened," I said.

"Yeah. It's messed up."

"Gage was paired with Elle for the night shift. Caleb and Hunter's shift was right after. I'm thinking they planned the whole thing out carefully. That's why no one heard or saw them. But I don't get how the hell they broke that gate down without waking any of us up."

"I thought I heard something, but when you think there's people on the roof looking out for you, you don't think much of it," said Xander.

"You and Riley were before Elle and Gage, right?" I asked, trying to piece it all together.

"Yeah."

"When you woke them up for their shift, they weren't acting suspicious or anything?"

"Well, Gage was already awake ... " Xander said.

"Why?"

"He was hanging with ... I don't know."

"Hanging with who?" I prompted.

"Nothing. Riley told me not to tell anyone," Xander said, busying himself with a stray piece of bubble wrap.

I could see he was regretting the words he'd let slip. "Okay, well, you already brought it up. Tell me, Xander," I pushed.

" ... I don't know. She asked if I could handle the night watch alone. Said she needed to take a breather, so I let her...but after the whole shift went by,

I went to get water, and...they were in the main room. Hooking up. She told me not to say a word, not to start any pointless arguments."

This was getting out of control. Gage hooked up with Riley in the shadows while he was all over Ava in plain sight, and underneath it all he was planning a betrayal with the others. Now I knew why Riley was acting so weird today. Thinking of Ava learning this information gave me major anxiety... I didn't know if I wanted her to find out.

"Gage is a snake, man. How could you be friends with someone like that?" I demanded.

"I'm really disappointed in him right now, but you don't know him like I do. I can see why he went with them. He's impulsive and he doesn't ask questions. They pressured him, I know it."

"Pressured my ass. That's a huge thing to go through with if you're a good person," I said, coming off more aggressive than I meant to.

"Hey, don't get mad at me. I'm just telling you what I know about him," said Xander.

"Sorry... but you saw him with Ava. He was clearly being manipulative. What do I tell her?"

"*Don't* tell her! I told you, Riley said not to tell anyone," he pleaded.

"You don't think she deserves to know? Maybe it'll help her get over him leaving. She'll realize he's a dirtbag and move on. I'd tell her in a heartbeat if I didn't think it'd cause a rift between her and Riley," I thought out loud.

"I don't know. Lie and say you saw them going to the main room or something. Just don't say you heard it from me," said Xander. "You know the girls way better than I do. Do what you think you need to do. I just don't want to get involved."

I made to leave the room, but he called after me. "Tye?"

"Yeah?"

"I... I think you're doing a hella good job being the leader," he said softly.

I forced a smile. "Ha, thanks. I'm trying my best."

Back in the main room, Ava and Riley were still where I'd last seen them. I looked from one to the other, deciding who to approach first. I locked onto Riley. I wanted to see what she thought about this mess and if she'd own up to her part in it.

"Can I talk to you for a second?"

"No, I don't feel like talking right now," she said flatly.

"Okay... When are you going to feel like talking?"

"Go away, Tye. I'm not in the mood."

"Gimme a break, Riley. I want to talk to you about last night," I said.

She gave me a deer-in-the-headlights look, knowing full well what I was referring to. "What *about* last night?"

"Hmm, the fact you ask me like that tells me you know what I'm talking about," I said sharply.

She looked over at Ava, who was making her way upstairs. "I'm not talking about this here," she said.

"Then let's go outside."

"No."

"*Riley.*"

"*Tye.*"

There was a pause. I spoke softer now. "I saw you go downstairs with Gage last-"

"Bullshit, Xander told you," she concluded immediately.

"...I just want to know what you're gonna do about Ava. She's really upset about him leaving like he did," I said.

"Are you serious? She's known him for, like, two days. They're not together," she fired back.

"Doesn't matter. She's hurt and she needs to know he isn't who she thinks he is. If you were her friend and not being a mess-"

"How do you think *I* feel, Tye? He was a flirt. He flirted with Ava, he was checking out Elle when we were in our underwear, and he kept coming to my room every time I was in there alone. I was just having fun, but he fucked me over too. Anyway, does any of this really matter? The world is fucking over! This conversation's dumb."

"It *shouldn't* matter, but it does. It does because we're all in this together. We need to be there for each other. I'm not saying anything else. All I want you to do is tell Ava, so she'll move on from this," I said.

"Oh my god, I can't with you ... "

"If you don't tell her, I will," I said.

She stared at me, frustration clear between her furrowed brows. "Do whatever you want," she said, defiantly.

"Then, I'm telling her." I started to walk away.

"Fine, bro, but you're an idiot. You're just going to start stupid drama for no reason. He's gone. Who gives a shit?"

I wasn't sure if I truly should tell Ava. As my long-time friend, she deserved to know, but Riley was right about the unnecessary drama part.

I walked upstairs, partially to scare Riley into thinking I was about to do it. At that same moment, Ava came down the steps from the rooftop.

"Hey," I said, feebly.

She took a second to answer. "Hi." Her energy seemed depleted.

"You okay?" I asked.

"Yeah. I just don't know why I feel this devastated over a days-old crush. But I felt like we really connected, like I knew him. I know I'm being ridiculous, but-"

"No, I totally get it. You weren't expecting this. None of us were. But I did tell you-"

"Not to trust him, I know. I didn't. It's just the fact that it happened so abruptly. I'll get over him," she said.

I thought she was trying to convince herself more than me. "You sure? I know you weren't in love with him or anything, but...I know you."

She gave me her signature expression, a look I'd seen many times over the years. It always bookended my conversations with her involving guys that she gravitated toward. Guys who usually waved multiple red flags.

"Yeah, he's an asshole. I'll be fine ... I always am," she said sadly.

From the past, I knew that was not the case, but I was willing to see if she'd pull through before I brought up Riley's mistake. If I brought up Riley at all.

I jumped at the sound of the rooftop hatch bursting open. Otto, Xander, and Dustin stormed down the steps, Xander with gun in hand.

"What's going on?" I asked, on guard.

Each of them wore different shades of panic.

"The Expedition just pulled up!" Dustin fumed. "They came back. They fuckin' came back."

We bolted downstairs.

Riley handed me my gun as we sprinted for the sliding metal door. Dustin pulled it open. He snatched Xander's gun from his grasp, pointing it straight at the SUV parked outside the gate.

"Open it, Tye," Dustin ordered.

"Dustin, do not shoot," I said nervously. "Let's hear them out."

"Open it!" he repeated sternly.

I ran for the chain and pulled it with all my strength.

The entrance opened and the vehicle slowly rolled in. It was covered in heavy dents and the back bumper was missing.

Looking livid, Dustin pointed the gun into the driver-side window. The engine shut off and both Hunter, behind the wheel, and Gage, in the passenger seat, held their hands up in surrender.

"Get out of the car!" Dustin yelled at them.

The traitors had the nerve to come back. We were all seeing red.

Hunter's door was the first to open. Gage followed suit. Neither of them was armed. Hunter's head was bleeding and Gage had bloody scrapes on his arms.

"Caleb, Elle, get out here, *now!*" Dustin demanded.

I had my gun up for intimidation purposes, but I could see something wasn't right. Hunter and Gage both looked pale with fear.

"Caleb, Elle, get out of the car!" Dustin repeated, squinting at the tinted windows.

Hunter jerked his head, prompting Dustin to raise his gun an inch higher and place his finger on the trigger.

"I will light you up-"

"They're not with us, man!" Hunter shouted. "They're not fucking with us! Goddammit!"

His words rang in the air.

A primal wave of emotions seemed to wash over Hunter and Gage. They both broke down crying.

"...Where are they?" Otto asked, hesitantly.

Gage responded in a shaky voice. "They're... dead. Those things got them... Got them bad."

There was an intense pause.

Less than twenty-four hours earlier, each of the cousins had been one of us, and now they were gone forever. We had an infinite supply of hate for the four of them, but it was set aside as the two boys shook with grief and we processed the news.

Mercy was short-lived. Riley went off.

"This is bullshit! You guys can't take our stuff, turn your backs on us and then act like you can just come back here and everything'll be fine! It's *your* fault they're dead-"

"Riley, not now!" I yelled.

"No, they're not staying here. Kick them out and leave them with nothing, like they did to us," she spat.

Dustin had opened the trunk and was rummaging inside. "The guns are here, but our food supply's gone," he said, seething.

"We went to the market complex, but we couldn't get any," Gage said. "We had carts filled with everything, but we were attacked before we could get in the car."

"So, you *did* go on the food raid?" Ava asked, seemingly hopeful that their betrayal was all a misunderstanding.

Hunter answered. "... We did. We were planning on coming back once we-"

Dustin grabbed Hunter by the throat and slammed him against the hood of the car. "Liar! You took everything from us! You know damn well you were going to make a run for it. You came back 'cause you had nowhere else to go," he said, squeezing Hunter's neck.

I could see the guilt in Hunter's face. That, plus he was turning red from lack of air.

"Dustin ..." I warned.

Hunter was blue now.

"Dustin!" I said, tapping him on the shoulder.

He shoved Hunter to the ground.

"So, what do we do now?" he asked, directing the question to the rest of us. "Do we play saints and let them stay?"

What *should* we do now? It was against my morals to toss them out to die, but I could see it in my friends' faces that some of them were hoping we would do just that.

"We should vote," Otto suggested. "All in favor of taking our stuff back and kicking them out, raise your hand."

There was a tense moment. Then, Riley and Dustin raised their hands high.

Dustin shot a look at the rest of us with our arms down. "Oh, come on, you gotta be kidding me," he said in disbelief.

"All for giving them another chance?" Otto continued, like he was treading carefully.

He and Xander put a hand up. Ava followed them a beat later.

"Tye, you need to vote," said Otto. "Let them stay or kick them out?"

I held my breath for a long minute. Flashbacks of my early friendship with Hunter blanketed my seething anger. I looked out into the city beyond, knowing full well how brutal of a fate it would be for anyone to be sent back out there.

“I’m going to say...they get *one* last chance. They’ll be under constant watch, and if they fuck up even the tiniest rule, they’re out ... with nothing. Is that clear?” I asked the returnees.

Hunter and Gage nodded, desperately.

“No, answer me. Is that clear?” I repeated firmly.

“Yes,” they said together, not making eye contact with any of us.

We moved into the main room and established some changes. Dustin was now in charge of the car key. Hunter and Gage were not allowed to hold any weapons unless absolutely necessary.

I was Hunter’s new night watch partner, so I could keep an eye on him, and Dustin was with Gage for the same reason. Ava was now paired with Otto, and Riley was still with Xander.

We sat around the fire like usual, but with an entirely new dynamic.

“So, you couldn’t get more food, but what happened to the cans you stole from us?” Ava asked bluntly.

Gage was embarrassed. He didn’t look at her. “We had them in the trunk. We left so fast it was hanging open and they...fell out when we were attacked,” he said.

Ava scoffed.

“You at least owe us an explanation of what happened,” I demanded.

Gage cleared his throat nervously. “We were at the supermarket-”

“No, you’re going to start from when you guys decided to betray us,” Dustin cut in.

Hunter had so much hate in his eyes. I could tell he was on the brink of exploding, having to swallow his usual contrarian attitude.

“I-I was doing the night watch with Elle,” Gage began again.

My eyes inadvertently landed on Riley for a fraction of a second.

“And Elle told me that...Caleb and Hunter were planning an escape during their shift. When Elle woke them up, she told them I knew about the plan ... and they said I had two choices. They could kill me, or I could go with them-”

"You fuckin' liar!" Hunter shouted at him. "You said you wanted to come!"

"Hunter, don't do this to me, man. You and Caleb held a gun to my head and asked me if I was with you or ready to die!" Gage said adamantly.

I couldn't tell whose version was true. It probably landed somewhere in the middle. Hunter palmed his forehead and pressed his lips together.

The conversation had stalled. "Keep going," I ordered.

"I didn't want to die, so I went with them. I knew what we were doing was completely fucked up. I'll admit, part of me was hoping we'd find help, but it was hard to think of ditching you guys," he said.

I looked to Ava and saw that she was totally caught up in what he was saying. Part of it seemed genuine, but I didn't know how much I could believe. According to what Xander had told me, it made sense for him to have been coaxed into joining them, but I was determined not to fall for any more of his manipulations.

"Elle and Caleb were the ones who pitched the idea to me," Hunter said.

Of course he'd blame it on the dead kids. They couldn't dispute it.

"That true, Gage?" Xander asked him.

"I don't know. Elle just said there was a plan... I don't know who started it," he said.

"It was Elle and Caleb, I promise you," Hunter insisted. "We took some stuff and got the keys from Gage. We drove to where he said the big market was, but it was completely wrecked from looters. Gage stayed in the car while we went in to scope it out. Most of it was ransacked. All the obvious things were gone, like basic survival shit. Water and whatnot. We packed carts with everything we could find. Thought we'd hit the jackpot... That's when we heard Gage shouting and his gun going off."

We all seemed to be fully engrossed in the story. I could hear my heart thumping in my ears.

Gage continued. "I-I saw a bunch of them running my way. I shot as many as I could, but they're hard to take down, and they just kept coming.

Then Caleb, Hunter and Elle came running outside with the carts. They helped me fight back, but then even more came... I think the sound of gunshots drew them in. We tried to get the food in the trunk and make a run for it, but that's when everything..."

His words trailed off as the emotion audibly tightened his throat.

Hunter picked up. "We were totally surrounded. One grabbed me and threw me hard against the car, another tossed our cart. The food went everywhere. Everything we'd just collected. Elle... She didn't see the one behind her, and it... it started biting her shoulder. Gage and I managed to get in the car, but Caleb wouldn't leave Elle. We kept telling him to get in, we knew she was done for... If she didn't die, she was definitely infected."

Gage took a deep breath and finished the story. "He tried his best. There was so much blood, and he couldn't get up. We... drove off, and realized there was nowhere to go but back here."

My stomach was in knots, and suddenly, I was aware of the tear that had crawled down my face. I could see why they were traumatized, despite their ill intent.

"I don't know what else to say... I'm sorry, for what it's worth," Gage tried.

No one responded for a long moment. I looked around the warehouse.

"We don't have what we need to survive here anymore. At least, not for long, not without food. We gotta solve that quickly," I said.

There was an uncomfortable shift in the room.

"What are we gonna do?" Xander asked, looking to me for the answer, but Otto spoke instead.

"Don't think we have much of a choice. We have to make a food run. Let me finish the SUV, add a few more things, and some of us can try the supermarket again. We know what to expect now, so we won't be caught off guard. We'll come up with a battle plan."

"Can't we look for another grocery store? Or a superstore? Why go back to a place where we *know* there'll be a ton of them?" Ava countered.

"Because we can't waste any more gas than what's already been wasted by them, and we know that's the nearest one. We can't risk venturing too far and coming back empty-handed."

"I think that's our best bet," Dustin said.

"You can't go back there," Hunter argued.

Riley glared at him. "Bro, you have absolutely no say in this."

"Fine, get yourselves killed! You didn't see what we saw. It's crazy out there. It's been a week but it looks like the world's over. Do you think I would've come back here if there was anything worth it out there?" Hunter asked angrily.

"Well, if you didn't steal the damn food, we wouldn't have to make this choice!" Dustin argued back.

Hunter held his tongue.

"How's the signal coming along?" I asked Otto, trying to change the subject so the plan would no longer be up for discussion.

Otto didn't look very confident. "There wasn't much I could do. I took a bunch of old scraps and wrote out the word 'help' on the roof. Pretty basic, but any aircraft should be able to see it. I'm going to try and make a flare with some of the gunpowder from the shotgun shells, in case anything flies by. Then we'll have a better chance of them spotting us."

"Okay. Do your thing, Otto. We trust you," I said.

He smiled at me, the first positive expression I'd seen in hours.

8.

Night watch was rough. It crawled by and Hunter never said a word to me. We stared out at the silent city, occasionally hearing a car alarm somewhere far off.

At one point, I tried to start a conversation, pointing out all the dead vultures who had been feeding on the body out back. Although they were clearly not immune to the virus, it was a relief to see they didn't reanimate the way infected humans did.

The next morning, the first thing I did when I woke up was find Dustin. He was in the main room separating nails from screws for Otto.

"Hey," I said as I took a seat next to him on the floor.

"'Sup?"

"How was Gage last night?" I asked.

"Weird. We didn't talk the first half, but then he started apologizing to me. I gave him the cold shoulder for a while, but then I kinda started feeling bad, if you can believe it," Dustin replied.

"What'd you say?"

"I just told him to relax and do what he can to prove us wrong. Simple as that," he said.

"Yeah, I want to believe him because I think he really does feel sorry, but it's just hard to swallow."

"What about you and Hunter?" he asked me.

"Not a word out of him. I don't think he really gives a shit. He still wants to get out of here," I said.

"He didn't say *anything*?"

"No. I tried to get him to talk to see if he was maybe even a little sorry, but no, nothing," I said. "But he's shown us he has no concept of loyalty, so..."

"Asshole. Well, you make sure he knows I'll wreck him if he tries anything else," Dustin said, with some cockiness.

"You're having wrestling withdrawals, aren't you?" I teased.

We both laughed. Ava came down the stairs.

"Good morning," she said to us as she walked past.

"Hey, where are you headed?" Dustin asked.

"I'm going to help Otto out with the Expedition," she said, with little energy in her voice.

"Tell him I'll be out there in a sec," I told her.

"Will do," she called from outside.

Before we could resume our conversation, Gage came down. He looked over at us as if we were going to say something, but we didn't. Instead, Dustin gave him a sarcastic wave. Gage turned and went after Ava.

"You're such a dick," I said with a laugh.

"What? I'm not going to be all dandy and wish him a jolly day," said Dustin.

I laughed harder. "*Dandy*?!"

Gage and Ava walked back in together. This was unexpected.

"Where you guys going?" I asked, sounding a bit too protective even to my own ears.

"Do you have to know where I'm going every second? He wants to talk," Ava said.

She fixed me with an *It's okay* look.

"Don't take too long," Dustin warned.

Ava's eyes became daggers. "No matter how long he takes, it'll be longer than you've ever been with a girl," she shot back.

"Ouch," he said, laughing.

She smiled, knowing she'd landed the jab, and she and Gage walked out back. There was a short silence, and then Dustin and I appeared to get the same idea.

"Go to the roof?" I pitched with a smirk.

He nodded, and we both shot up the stairs to find a vantage point.

The two of us lay flat on the rooftop floor, peeking over the edge to listen. We could hear them perfectly. We each held a hand over our mouth so we wouldn't laugh. Ava was talking seriously.

"I know, Gage, but what you did was wrong and I can't just forget about it. I think you're sorry, I do, but it's going to take more than that for me to trust you."

"Okay, but I really do like you... I know it's so cliché, but as soon as I *saw* you, I liked you," he pleaded pathetically.

Images of me vomiting directly onto his head threatened to make me blow our cover. He was lying straight to her face. I realized that Dustin didn't even know about the other douchebag move Gage had pulled the night before.

"Okay, Gage... I like you too, but I don't really *know* you. We just met. You should work on proving your trustworthiness to me—to all of us, before we get any closer," Ava said, standing her ground.

"Yeah, I understand. I just don't know what to do. How can I gain you guys' trust?" he asked her.

"It's just going to take time. I don't know."

"Okay, I'll do whatever. I just want to be able to talk to you," he said.

"You can talk to me, but just know that in the back of my head, I'm thinking of what you did. Just give me time and show me. Don't just say you're sorry," she restated.

"Okay."

There was an awkward silence. Ava kicked at a bottle cap on the ground.

"So, yeah," she said awkwardly.

"Hug?" he asked.

Dustin and I held our laughter back. We waited until they went back indoors, then I turned to Dustin, all jokes cast aside.

"Dude, if I tell you something, do you promise not to repeat it?" I asked.

"Yeah, shoot."

"...Gage and Riley hooked up the night he left," I said in a whisper.

"What?" he asked in disbelief.

"Yeah."

"He hooked up with Riley? Did she know he was leaving?"

"No, no, I don't think she had anything to do with the plan. Think she went to bed afterward, and he stayed up. It was during her shift with Xander," I clarified.

"Does Ava know?" he asked.

"No, of course not. I didn't tell her because she was so hurt about him ditching us like that. I didn't want to make things worse, especially when I thought he was gone for good...but unfortunately he came back," I said.

"You gotta tell her, dude. You can't let her get close to him if he's that kind of person," Dustin said, echoing my own thoughts.

"I want to tell her, but I don't know if now's the right time for more drama. She'll bitch at Riley, and Gage'll get caught in the crossfire. All hell's gonna break loose."

"I don't think there is a right time for it, but I know it sure as hell isn't going to be when Ava gets close to him again," he said. "She's gotta know sooner rather than later."

"Yeah ... This sucks. Maybe we shouldn't have let them stay."

"Well, they're here. It'll be better for her to know in the long run," he assured me.

It was a hard pill to swallow. These all seemed like very trivial problems. The city was destroyed, and here we were dealing with the same things that ran rampant in every high school.

"I'll think about how I'm gonna do it. Get it over with," I said.

We both opened the hatch and jumped down.

We found Ava standing alone at the foot of the steps. Her arms were crossed and she wore an irritated smirk. She knew exactly what we'd been up to. Dustin and I swallowed a fit of laughter.

"What?" I asked nonchalantly.

"What were you guys doing upstairs?" she asked suspiciously.

"Kissing," I joked.

Dustin and I started cracking up. Ava's face was priceless.

"I'm sure you were. I hate you guys," she said, a smile breaking through her scowl.

"Brotherly love, Ava, brotherly love," Dustin teased.

The three of us followed the sound of drilling and joined Otto out front. Xander and Gage were assisting him with a large, pointed piece of metal that he was attaching to the bottom of the car.

"I found more nails and screws," Dustin told him. He handed Xander the cup of hardware.

Otto was lying on the flatbed underneath the car. He slid out, hammer in hand. "Thanks, Dustin."

"No problem."

The jagged metal was protruding from the underside of the car like a wing. "What's the spike for?" I asked.

Otto stood up, wiping the sweat from his brow with his forearm. "I'm gonna put three of these on each side of the car. If we're surrounded, god forbid, we can spin the car out and these things will cut those suckers' legs off," he said proudly.

"Dude, I love you," I said.

"No rush, but how long do you think this is gonna take to be finished?" Xander asked.

"Probably a week. The thing that's gonna take the longest is getting your gun on top. I don't know if it's even possible yet, but I'm gonna try some ideas. Xander's gun is definitely the heaviest artillery we have."

"Well, keep working while you're feeling up to it, but don't kill yourself over it," I said. "Take a break whenever you need and don't hesitate to ask us for anything you need help with."

Otto gave a thumbs-up. "Will do, but like I said, I love doing this stuff. Don't worry about me too much."

Later that day, we divided three meager cans of food between the eight of us. Gage offered his portion to Ava, who wouldn't accept. I knew he must've been starving, we all were, so his effort was noted.

Even more disappointing than the lack of food was the harsh reality that our water supply was already running low. It hadn't rained again so we were forced to take some of the water from the shower tank to boil for drinking.

After what one could barely call dinner, Riley and Xander killed some time by grabbing brooms from the upstairs closet to sweep the main room floor. Riley would distract herself with anything if it meant avoiding Gage and Ava. Hunter also seemed distant, like he'd taken a vow of silence, having not spoken a word to us all day.

Night came fast. Thankfully, the clock on the wall was still ticking. It helped the days go by faster, being able to keep track of time. It read 9:07p.m.

Throughout the day, we had all taken part in reconstructing the SUV, so as soon as I made it to my room and laid my head down, my exhaustion caught up with me.

Riley and Xander had taken the first night shift. I could faintly make out my name at one point in their conversation, but was too tired to care about the context.

Since we'd decided it was best to take rooms with our designated night watch partners from now on, Hunter was sleeping beside me. His presence was hard to relax around, especially when I had to relinquish his gun to him during our shift. It was the only time he was allowed to be armed. Even with mine in hand, it was unnerving that I couldn't read him anymore. It wasn't too long ago that we'd been working on a class project together. A start to what, I thought, could've been a rekindling of our friendship. Now, I was scared for my life being around him at all. I knew Hunter had some demons, but the betrayal he'd pulled on us made me feel there was a whole side to him I'd never known was there. The anxiety of it all kept me in limbo between sleep and high alert.

I felt Xander shake me before long.

"Wake up, sleepy, it's your turn."

"I'm up ..."

I grabbed my gun and nudged Hunter with my foot. He shot up, startled.

"Let's go, it's our shift," I said, trying to keep my tone light.

He took his gun from my hand, obviously annoyed that his least favorite part of the day had arrived, and followed me up to the roof.

Xander called after me. "Goodnight, Tye."

"Night, X."

I saw him smile softly at the nickname.

I perched on one of the radiators while Hunter sat with his feet hanging off the edge of the rooftop. I could tell this was going to be another awkward shift. I just wanted to know where his head was at. It was making me uneasy.

"You gonna talk tonight?" I dared to ask.

He didn't even turn to look at me.

"I don't get why you're not talking."

Still no response. We sat in silence for another ten minutes until I tried again, friendlier this time. "This isn't necessary, Hunter, you can-"

"Does anything I say fucking matter? You make all the decisions. You're the one that's got everything under control, Tye," he said to me with venom.

Finally, words, but I didn't like where they were going.

"I don't know why you've tried to make me out to be some controlling leader who wants power over everyone," I said. "We've all made decisions together. Your say *did* matter, but you went ahead and-"

"I fuckin' get it already! I screwed up! I acted on impulse. I didn't think it through. Do you know how shitty I feel about what happened to Elle and Caleb? They were the only two that gave a shit about me here!"

Now, his walls were coming down. I could see the hurt behind his eyes. I softened my tone.

"Look, I know it's been a while since you've believed it, but the friendship you, me and Riley had, it's still there. Things got off track when she and I were together, but you never once told me directly why you shut us out. If you had feelings for her, how was I supposed to know if you never told her? Never told me? You made us feel like we backstabbed you," I explained.

"She *did*. She knew my feelings for her long before you guys even spoke. I tried to open up to her so many times, but she played her part so well. The girl that no one could get close to. She 'didn't want a relationship because she didn't want to get hurt.' She 'has a hard time letting someone in because of her sister.' And for a long time, I believed it. And I was okay with being her friend if it meant I could *feel* close to her. And then you came out of left field. I couldn't believe she fell for *you*! You didn't give a shit about her-"

"Don't tell me how-"

"Why are we even talking about this?! The damage between us three is so far beyond repair, and the world's done for, so who gives a shit?"

"That's your biggest problem. You keep thinking we'll never get out of this, and it's sealing your fate. What about the rest of our families out there? And did you ever stop to think that your parents could still be alive? I saw mine die...but you and Riley, what if yours got out okay-"

"They're fucking dead, Tye! They're dead! Everyone is fuckin' dead!"

He was impenetrable. In that moment, I felt that Hunter was truly a lost cause. I shook my head.

"Okay, Hunter. I've tried to be helpful. You want to go dark? Be my guest."

"I'm acting like I should be acting. You and the others act like this is just some screwed-up dream that's gonna go away and we're gonna be fine. Everything's going to be fixed up. School's just gonna pick up where it left off! Everything is *over*, Tye. Get it through your fucking head-"

"You are literally the biggest piece of shit I've ever-"

He got up and came at me. I pointed my gun at him, but he didn't stop. His gun wasn't up but his fist was. It froze an inch from my face.

The fog from his heavy breath clouded between us. Every thread of tension that had festered over the years had built up to this very confrontation, and yet, I knew he wasn't going to hit me. Our past friendship still glowed dim like an ember amongst ashes.

I lowered my gun. There was a beat. I slowly walked around him and sat on the floor in the corner. He sat on the radiator with his back to me. Nothing else was said.

Our shift was finally over. I woke Ava and Otto for their turn, making light conversation to delay seeing Hunter again in our room.

When I finally made it to our quarters, he was in the midst of dragging his mat into a separate room. I released a breath I didn't even realize I was holding.

As I prepped my minimal sleeping area, I replayed the earlier events, contemplating what I could've done differently. It took me a long time to fall asleep again, but I'd accepted that we were at an impasse.

9.

A productive week went by. The Expedition project became the glue that kept our group together. Even through malnourishment and dehydration, we worked diligently, knowing that if we could finish the SUV, we had hope.

Now, the vehicle brandished razor-sharp metal pieces protruding from all sides, metal wiring supporting the windows, and a pallet on the grill to act as a battering ram. Otto had also added a layer of thick metal plating for reinforcement.

The star feature was Xander's FN SCAR gun mounted on the sunroof. Otto had managed to override the gun's factory settings by adding a longer barrel and a slew of stray parts to enable it to shoot five-inch rounds. A revolving piece of wood made it easy to turn the gun from the inside, and a piece of twine tied to the trigger hung down to the middle seat. When the twine was pulled, the gun fired. The only downside was the mere ten bullets remaining.

I didn't bother making sense of the mechanical details, but what I knew for sure was that Otto was a prodigy. Our days of scavenging for scraps to contribute to the super SUV had proven to be a success.

By the time it was finally complete, the conditions we had dug ourselves into had become even more pronounced. The food supply was entirely gone. With no rain in over a week, we hadn't showered in days. We resorted to completely repurposing the contents of the shower tank into drinking water.

The water tower taunted us from a distance. Since Elle and Riley's attack, no one wanted to risk a trek over there.

Ava and Gage functioned on their own timeline. In the last several days, their coy smiles had become laughs and their laughs had become kisses, until they were basically inseparable. I did my best not to be overbearing, but I knew it was mostly her loneliness making her crave company.

The scandal with Riley was buried so deeply now, I only ever thought of it when I would catch her avoiding Ava on purpose. Luckily, Ava hardly seemed to notice, so there really was no point in dragging it back up. I only worried about the day Ava did find out.

Xander also started to worry me. At several moments throughout the week I had to ask him if he was okay. Most of the time, he wrote it off to exhaustion, but I noticed that he'd grown quiet around me. Each time I checked in with him, he brushed me off. I was too drained to pry further so I took his word for it.

Dustin seemed to be keeping the most level head, until he found out about the night Hunter had freaked out on me. It took a great deal of restraint for Dustin not to confront him, but I was able to convince him an altercation would only ignite Hunter further. The compromise was agreeing to switch night watch partners, so my roommate was now Gage, and Dustin paired with Hunter to keep him in line.

My first lookout with Gage landed on the night before the planned market raid. A weighted anticipation buzzed in the air. The entire week of labor had led to the following day's showdown, and like two soldiers waiting for a battle at dawn, we paced around the rooftop with weapons in hand. Gage gnawed at the corner of his fingernail.

"You nervous about tomorrow?" I asked him. His last trip there had turned into a nightmare, after all.

"Very. I don't really want to think about it," he said.

"The Expedition came out amazing though. I think we're gonna be okay."

"We just have to be really careful and plan everything out this time," he said, anxiously.

I saw him go at his nail again and decided to change the subject. "So, you and Ava a thing now?"

He planted himself on a radiator, not making eye contact. "There's really no point in a label, you know?"

"Hmm… Ever gonna tell her about Riley?" I asked bluntly.

He shifted where he sat.

The jibe was solely a result of my extreme boredom. I really had moved on from the issue. I smiled to myself, waiting for him to answer.

"I… uh…" he stuttered.

I laughed, alleviating some of the tension that had built up. "You didn't think I knew?"

"Guess not… It was really nothing with Riley. We just made out, I swear. I kind of forgot about that."

"You forgot? Asshole," I said, punching him lightly on the shoulder.

"I *tried* to forget. I really like her, Tye, I do," he said sincerely.

"Ava or Riley?"

"Ava!" he said.

I laughed again. "Alright, just checking. Do you plan on ever saying anything?"

"What's the point?" he asked.

Guess we were on the same page there. "Well, I'm not gonna tell her, but you guys seem to be getting closer by the hour, so it might be a good idea to at least let her know it happened before she finds out another way."

He wouldn't make eye contact with me.

"You really care about her, huh?" I asked gently.

He finally turned to me. "A lot."

"I think at first it was hard to let you get close to her. She's like my sister...and I didn't trust you."

"'Didn't?' So, you trust me now?" he asked with a smirk.

"Still have my eye on you," I said impishly, "but no doubt she's happy when she's with you."

We both turned to see Xander coming up to the rooftop.

"Hey. Our shift isn't over yet, is it?" I asked him, feeling like it had gone by quickly.

"No, in a few minutes it will be," he said, "but Riley told me to ask you if you'll take her shift. She has a huge headache."

"Me?" I asked.

"Yeah. She wants to sleep it off. She said she'll take yours tomorrow."

"Ugh. Fine, probably won't get much sleep tonight anyhow," I said begrudgingly.

"You can go crash, Gage. I'm up, so I'll just stay up here," said Xander.

"Sweet," said Gage. "Thanks, man. Goodnight, guys."

"Night," we said together.

It was ironic that I would end up with Xander of all people. The recent distance between us had come very suddenly and with no real reason. At least, none that I was aware of. I'd always thought Xander had an easy energy to be around, so it was slightly concerning that he was recoiling into himself. The loss of his past life might have been finally catching up with him.

I tried to sound warm, testing if this new behavior was directed at me or about him. "Everything good?"

"Tired, man. It's hard to wake up like this every night. Turning me into an insomniac."

"I know, I know...Reminds me of how my mom used to be." I felt an unexpected smile stretch across my face. "She would stay up all night painting these birds. She loved painting birds. I'd sometimes wake up in the middle of the night to get a snack, and there she'd be at the easel, covered in paint, wide awake. I'd try to sneak past her because she'd always want to tell me about the artsy meaning behind each painting. It was adorable, but I was always dying inside, just wanting to get back to sleep. Next day she'd be sleeping in 'til noon. I'd give her shit for it every day, but she'd always say 'I paint better at night!' Total insomniac, all in the name of art."

His expression lightened a bit as I cracked up. "Sounds like you guys were really close. That must've been nice ... Can't relate."

My laughter died. "You weren't close with your mom?"

"Neither of my parents. Basically disowned me in middle school."

I was happy that our words were flowing openly. I started to feel like my perception of our situation had, in fact, been wrong. Maybe he was just tired after all. "Why's that? Were you a troublemaker?"

"Nope. Just gay."

I tried very hard to make sure there was no awkward pause, but I was caught off guard. "That's—That's terrible...I'm sorry."

"Yeah. It wasn't easy. I do wish we could've been in a good place before all *this* happened."

"Well, if they're gone...I really believe that stuff doesn't matter when you pass on. Not to get heady, but I feel like souls just have a higher understanding of things when they leave here."

His dewy eyes bore into mine. He smiled. "That means a lot. I like that."

"Of course," I said.

After a beat, I looked down at my gun, the anticipation of tomorrow creeping back in. It was a while before I looked back up again, but when I did, Xander was still fixated on me with the same expression I'd caught him wearing throughout the week when he grew quiet around me.

"What?" I asked uncomfortably.

He shook his head with a pained smile and walked over to the roof's edge, gazing out at the blacked-out cityscape.

The rest of the shift was a strained effort to make conversation. It came as a godsend when Hunter and Dustin lifted the hatch, cutting off the drawn-out tension.

"Lucky you, you guys are done. Go catch some Zs," Dustin said.

I grabbed my gun a little too eagerly, then took my time fumbling with it so Xander could walk ahead of me. After a moment, I hurried down the steps into the hallway below.

As I headed to my room, I contemplated how I was going to wind down with the thoughts of tomorrow and Xander's new energy around me flashing through my head.

My stream of consciousness was interrupted as he stepped in front of me. "What's up?" I asked, trying to mask my confusion.

"I'm sorry I've been weird lately." Sadness swelled behind his eyes. "I really think it's just me being lonely, and everything piling on top of me...but I feel like I care about you, more than a friend. I pushed it down because I don't want to be the cliché gay guy who falls for his straight friend, but tomorrow...some of us may not make it and I don't want to go my whole life hiding who I care about."

My heart pounded, feeling absolutely terrible for Xander, but not knowing how to handle such a delicate moment.

He continued through his tears. "Now that I got that off my chest, I won't keep being weird around you, but I hope now that you know, you don't change around me."

I pushed my discomfort aside and smiled. "Xander, I appreciate you telling me. It won't change anything...Promise."

Dustin came down the steps from the roof. "Everything okay?"

"Yeah, we're good," I said.

I saw him clock Xander's wet face, but he didn't push the subject. "Okay, well, get some rest. Tomorrow's the big day, boys," he said.

I gave a half-laugh. "Yeah, goodnight."

Dustin returned to his shift. I stood in the hallway for a second, making sure Xander had gotten everything out. He smiled and gave me a hug. Then, we parted ways.

Day broke, and a frenzied mood enveloped our camp. We were finally going to put the battle car to use. This would be the first time we would have real food in weeks and the thought had us preparing to leave in a hurry.

We all stood in a circle in the main room, rehashing the plans. Hunter and Gage were visibly anxious, but for the most part there was a good energy flowing.

Otto looked intense, as if delivering a war speech. "This is going to be an in-and-out mission. I'll be driving, and I'll keep the car on in case we need to haul ass. That means the longer we take, the more gas we're using, so once we get there, we get right to it. Hunter, I want you to man the turret gun. As soon as I park, you girls get out, pop the trunk, and wait there providing cover while the rest of you go in. Grab carts, get whatever you can fit in them, then head back to the car. Just in and out, don't overthink it. You'll hand the carts off to the girls, who'll load up while you surround the car and give us cover fire in case anything comes at us. Once we're loaded up, we hop in and take off. Done."

"Genius, Otto! Magnifique!" Xander exclaimed, clapping.

He seemed to be in good spirits. I was happy to see our exchange from last night had made things better.

"Any questions?" Otto asked.

Riley spoke up. "Just one. What happens in the worst case scenario?"

"Like if we're attacked?"

"Yeah, 'cause what you described sounded like the best case."

"Well, if we do come in contact with the infected, drop whatever you're doing and do whatever it takes to get back in the car. We worked our butts off to make this SUV a tank. As long as we're inside, we're good," he said.

"Everyone ready?" I asked confidently.

On that note, we geared up. Xander now wielded Hunter's shotgun, and with Otto driving, Ava was armed with his automatic. Our canteen was filled, and after pouring in the last of the fuel reserves the trio had stored away, so was the SUV.

Otto pulled on the chains outside, lifting the giant door to the street beyond. Dustin helped him wedge a thick metal rod between the links to jam them in place so the gate would stay open.

With a collective deep breath, we hopped into the Expedition and strapped in. The engine roared to life.

"Judgment day, y'all," Otto proclaimed in a country accent, then swerved onto the street.

My stomach fluttered with jolts of excitement that churned into fear and back again. It felt weird being outside the warehouse boundaries. It had been so long since I'd seen more than the street out front and the field out back.

Dustin was in the passenger seat. Behind him in the middle row, Xander and I sandwiched Hunter. Riley, Ava and Gage sat in the backseat. I figured the sweat forming on his brow was half from mission anxiety and half from being between the two girls.

We drove in silence, our eyes glued to the disconcerting view outside. Hunter had warned that the world had become something far worse than we could imagine in such a short time. He was right. Decay had blanketed the city: trash everywhere, car windows shattered, countless bikes deserted in the grass, storefronts smashed, bodies littered every mile, and house doors left eerily ajar, their owners never coming back.

Dustin tried to turn the radio on.

"It's broken," Otto said.

"My heart's racing, dude," Dustin said. "The nothingness is getting to me."

"It's not too far, just don't look outside. Stay focused," Otto encouraged him.

We drove another ten minutes. Several times, we hit blockades of abandoned cars and either had to off-road or reroute, but eventually, we saw the large green sign that read *TEETERS*.

Otto slowed down and pulled into the vacant lot. "Here we are," he said quietly.

Everyone's eyes widened, trying to spot any sign of movement, but the lot seemed stagnant.

"Make sure your gun safety locks are off," Dustin reminded us.

"And remember the game plan," Otto added.

There was a symphony of clicks as we cocked our guns. The SUV came to a crawling stop directly in front of the disheveled grocery store. It had definitely seen many unwelcome visitors. The shattered glass panes and littered parking lot served as proof.

After a cautious beat, Otto turned to us.

"Looks like you guys are clear."

Dustin pushed open the car door, instantly bringing up his gun. Xander, Gage and I followed him on high alert. The girls jumped out of the back, leaving the trunk open and taking up arms as instructed. The turret gun Hunter was manning locked and loaded with a clank.

As we slowly made our way to the storefront like a rookie SWAT team, I spotted blood on the sidewalk. I knew all too well that it must have been from Elle and Caleb's struggle. I swallowed thickly, realizing their bodies were nowhere to be seen.

We crossed the threshold of a smashed automatic door. It was dark inside. The once organized establishment, with its many sectionalized rows, was reduced to chaos. I grabbed two carts to my right.

"Here." I rolled one over to Dustin.

Gage and Xander snagged two more from the corner. Gage was already drenched in sweat.

"Let's make this quick," he said, wiping his forehead.

We dispersed into different aisles.

I started on aisle five, throwing box after box of cereal into my cart. The bountiful start made me optimistic about exploring the rest of the store, but as I made my rounds through the clutter, I quickly realized there was very little left. As expected, there was no more bottled water or even a single can of food on the shelves, but what was more disheartening was the lack of niche items like batteries and lighters, all completely gone.

I added a few non-perishables to my cart as I ran through a mental checklist, but nearly everything I'd had in mind was missing. Once the city went to the dumps, people had taken every opportunity to secure what they needed to survive. Where were all those people now? If they were surviving out there somewhere, why hadn't we seen anyone? I tried to push the thoughts away, but my mind continued to race. *What if I never went to the warehouse and just kept on? Would I have found help that the others managed to reach?*

After a couple laps, it became apparent how slim the pickings were. I did manage to grab a handful of juice boxes, peanut butter, and some crackers. I could hear the others rummaging through things and throwing them into their carts with urgency.

"Everyone alright?" I called out.

"We're good," Dustin answered.

"I think I got everything I could find," Gage added.

"Why don't you go pay, then? I'll be right there," I said, waiting for a laugh, but none came.

Gage's tone was flat. "You're hilarious, Tye."

"I don't see much else over here, either," Xander said from another aisle.

I quickly strode down aisle seven toward the back wall where all the cold goods would have been. With no power, most of the freezers' contents had been left behind to spoil. My eyes watered as the stench of rotten meat and poultry wafted from the open doors.

I scanned for anything I could salvage, and my gaze landed on a single remaining glass bottle of cranberry juice.

I eagerly reached for the crimson prize ... and instantly pulled my hand back. My heart stuttered. I was sure I'd seen something moving behind the shelf in the freezer room beyond. I held my breath as I made out the silhouette of a gaunt-looking body, pacing the stockroom. I stepped back, aiming my gun between the shelves-

"We're ready to go, dude."

I jumped at the sound of Dustin's voice. The thing behind the shelf turned abruptly, its onyx eyes gazing between the racks.

"Run!" I shouted, loud enough for the others to hear.

The shelf came crashing down as the infected man charged at the two of us. My gun went off but the bullet didn't make contact. I made to sprint away but felt a hand grab the back of my shirt and turned to see the monster towering over me, its apron splattered with blood and vomit.

"Dustin!" I called out.

Two bullets zoomed past my head. With a violent grunt, the thing's grip loosened. I ran around the corner and down an aisle behind Dustin. I heard Xander and Gage's guns go off.

CRASH. In its frenzy, the infected man had knocked over a massive shelf. It set off a domino effect throughout the store as one shelf crashed into another, then another. Items rained from all directions, the creature barreling through the mess to get to Xander who was firing his shotgun repeatedly. I could see the bullets making contact, but the thing didn't slow.

"Get to the car!" Dustin yelled.

The beast turned its attention to Dustin. I fired multiple times. One of the monster's eyes exploded, but like an angry bull, it kept charging forward. It managed to grab me again, this time by the ankle. Dustin stopped firing and grasped my hand as it pulled me away.

I screamed so loud my throat burned. "Dustin, don't let him get me! *Please*!"

Dustin fired a round into the creature's skull. Blood sprayed onto my shirt, and I fell on top of Dustin as the man finally collapsed.

I was wheezing, completely out of breath. My friend helped me get to my feet, our need for escape still vital.

"Holy shit!" I choked out.

Dustin pushed me toward the exit. "Let's get out of here!"

We grabbed our full carts and ran for the car.

"Come on!" I called to Xander and Gage, who both looked to be in shock.

Outside, Ava and Riley were still by the trunk, guns ready.

"Are you guys okay?! What was all that?" Riley asked.

Dustin pushed the carts at them. "We're okay but we gotta go! Get this stuff inside, now!"

As the girls stuffed the trunk with everything we'd foraged, the rest of us encircled the car with guns reloaded. My body was shaking so badly, I could hardly aim at anything.

"Forget the stuff! Get in the car!" Gage commanded.

I turned to him, confused—we'd thrown off our attacker. "What, why?"

Xander and Dustin were looking up at something. There, on the rooftop of the store, stood a crowd of the infected. My knees nearly buckled.

BANG! The turret gun went off as Hunter fired a five-inch bullet into one of the bodies. It doubled over and toppled off the roof, smashing into the concrete lot below, now sporting a giant hole in its midsection.

The four of us opened fire as the masses began jumping down toward us, crazed and animalistic. Ava slammed the trunk shut, leaving many items still in the carts. Riley joined our shootout with her Desert Eagle.

BANG! Another of Hunter's rounds blasted through an infected woman grabbing at Gage. Otto shunted the Expedition forward, slamming into a group of them with the metal front panel and smearing their blood over the asphalt like paint.

It was impossible to gain enough leeway to make an attempt at getting inside the car. If one of us let up our firepower, the horde would be on us in seconds. We seemed to be making progress, but eventually the tides turned.

Both mine and Gage's guns ran out of ammo. Gage quickly hopped in the car, but at the very moment that my gunfire ceased, one overweight man managed to grab me from behind. I kicked and flailed, but its power was overwhelming. I used every ounce of strength I had to push the thing's face away from me as it tried to take a bite from my shoulder. Dustin shot at it, but amid his distraction, two more were upon him.

Xander was also cornered, until Hunter blasted the head off the one blocking his path. Riley's gun clicked, declaring it was also out of ammo. She jumped into the backseat, head first. Our friends watched Dustin and I struggle, their only option being to save themselves...

Suddenly, Otto held down the horn. The infected turned their black eyes to the car, giving us a split second to break free of their hold. As the horn blared, four monsters pounced on the car, smashing their heads and fists into the metal. Otto put his foot down and swerved the SUV in a circle, the protruding metal spikes slicing through the monsters' legs, doing exactly what they were designed to do. Their bodies dropped helplessly to the ground.

Dustin and I raced for the car and jumped in, slamming the door behind us and locking it. *BANG!* Hunter fired one last round before we spun out and made it back onto the road.

"Headshot!" he boasted.

We gasped for air, our clothes bloody and our bodies bruised.

The excursion had been brutal, and I couldn't believe we'd made it out alive, but our mission was a success. Otto stepped on the gas and we sped full-throttle down the road. I could sense the adrenaline collectively pulsing through us.

"Hell *yeah*!" Dustin burst out.

I could hear the smile in his voice. I turned to Gage, Ava, and Riley in the backseat. "You guys okay?" I asked, panting.

Ava nodded, tears in her eyes. "Are *you*? I thought you were done for."

“Me too. But I’m okay. Dustin? You good?” I asked.

“Yeah, I’m fine. Damn, those things are crazy!”

Otto made a sharp turn. “Do we have anything we can eat on the way? My stomach’s legit eating itself,” he said, sounding desperate.

Ava reached over the backseat into the trunk and started moving things around.

“We have a bag of chips, a box of brownies-”

“No way, we got brownies?!” I exclaimed.

Ava laughed. “Heaven has arrived. Everybody want one? We deserve this,” she said, tearing the box open.

The car filled with noises of agreement. Ava handed each of us a soft, square brownie. I ripped the plastic wrapping from it and, with restraint, took a tiny bite. My mouth watered. At that moment, I was the happiest person in the world. This gooey, preservative-filled brownie was the best thing that had ever touched my taste buds.

“Best brownie ever,” Riley said, echoing my thoughts.

“Twelve out of ten!” Xander agreed.

The laughs and the much-needed calories made my near-death experience seem like it had been a dream.

10.

It was only after many minutes on the road that the harsh realities began to creep in again. With every abandoned complex and driverless vehicle we passed, the mood in the car deflated.

"I've been thinking about this for a bit, so chime in if you have any ideas, but...I think we need a nickname for those *things*," Riley announced.

Her prompt was welcomed by us. Anything to pass the time. It was true that we'd never really, properly addressed them. They were so grotesque and foreign, even with all the zombie films and stories I'd been exposed to, nothing could prepare me for seeing one in person. *Zombie* didn't quite feel right. That name felt like a parody compared to what we were dealing with.

"Fuckheads?" Xander suggested in a half-serious tone.

"Bloodheads?" Dustin added, a little more seriously, but with a laugh.

I pictured the demonic being in the grocery store and my smile fell. A chill ran down my spine. "I can't bring myself to give them a funny name. When one's standing in front of me, I lose myself in this overwhelming fear," I said honestly. "Don't think I'll ever get used to it. They need a name that fits."

"Wow, buzzkill," Riley joked.

"No, I think he's right," Otto said. "Something that reminds us not to take them lightly. A serious name so we don't forget it."

The others suddenly seemed to be taking the conversation seriously. I could see that they too were having flashbacks to their own encounters with the infected.

"I have one," Ava piped up, looking thoughtful. "Morts. *Mort* is the Latin root of death."

We all exchanged glances, a few of us mouthing the word silently.

"Honestly, it's fitting," I declared. "They look like Morts."

"Let's hope we've had enough Mort encounters for one day," Dustin agreed with a wink. "Hmm, it works."

"We shall now refer to all infected, as Morts," Otto said in a dramatic English accent as he turned the corner. "It shall be known-"

There was a loud squeal of tires as he abruptly stomped on the brakes. We all lunged forward in our seats, my seatbelt digging into my neck.

Through the front windscreen, I saw a small bus parked in the middle of the street. Intimidating graffiti decorated its exterior. Surrounding it was a crowd of people. At first glance I thought they were infected, but looking closer, I could see their mannerisms seemed normal, though they were definitely taking a defensive stance.

These were other survivors. The first ones we had encountered beyond the warehouse.

No one in the group looked past their late twenties. Like us, they must have banded together to make it through this nightmare.

I'd known in my gut that we couldn't have been the only ones out here, and I was right. I was flooded with excitement.

"Are they infected?" Dustin asked. His tone showed he wasn't nearly as happy to see them as I was.

"Doesn't look like it," Otto said, "but are we sticking around or should I bolt past them?"

"We don't have enough ammo if things get ugly," Hunter said flatly. "We should get out of here while they're off the bus. We have the advantage."

"But who knows where they're heading? It could be somewhere we need to be. Somewhere where there's help. And they might have info we don't," I added.

Otto had his hand on the ignition key. "So, are we going?"

"Yeah...Let's feel them out. Stay friendly, but reload now and be on defense mode," Dustin decided.

Otto shut off the engine as the strangers stared at us.

We stepped out of the Expedition with our guns by our sides and our expressions friendly. A few members of their group cautiously held weapons up.

A guy stepped forward, covered in soot and grime. He didn't seem aggressive, but hesitant. "Thought you might be soldiers when we heard your car. Haven't seen any pass through here after the initial wave," he said.

Otto looked to me to speak, but I looked to Dustin.

"We're survivors too. We were taking a drive around to see what we could find. Just passing through," Dustin said.

I scanned the group standing anxiously behind the man. They were equally disheveled, but younger than him. I saw his judging eyes pass over us.

"...You find any help out there?" he inquired.

His party moved slightly closer, maybe anticipating an answer to their prayers. I had hoped they'd have the same for us.

"We saw a chopper early on but it never landed for us," I said. "Do you have any clue what's going on? Any news?"

"Not much since the blackout, but Mel here knows more than any of us," the guy said, placing his hand on the shoulder of a woman beside him.

She stepped forward, her expression serious. "Happy to share what I know... for a trade," she said. She seemed almost embarrassed to make eye contact.

Dustin and I shared a look.

"What do you have in mind?" he asked her.

"Ammo? Food? Meds?" Mel suggested, a little more confidently this time.

No one said or did anything for a full beat. Finally, I walked over to our car, opened the back door, and took out a small, plastic-wrapped brownie. I turned and threw the brownie to her. When she caught it, she turned it over in her hands like she was staring at the most beautiful treasure she could ever own.

She dragged her hazel eyes away from the precious snack and met ours once again.

"I was on an EIS research team studying that flu a few years back," she began. "It was nothing we hadn't dealt with before, so it was business as usual, until those mass animal die-offs raised the alarm again..."

"I remember the first one," Ava cut in. "That's when those weird plane photos started resurfacing. People saying the smoke trails behind them were chemicals purposely causing these sicknesses ... "

"Correct," Mel said. "There were Government investigations, but nothing seemed to come of them. We kept digging on our end, but the more we studied the virus the more unnatural it seemed. It may have once been found in nature, but the strains were changing."

"But wait, I thought the whole plane thing was just a conspiracy theory. Everyone heard about them but it didn't really seem like it was ever confirmed," Riley said.

"We may never know," Mel explained. "I'm still in the dark for a lot of it...but what I can say is that the newest strain was manmade, and it's definitely all connected to what's happening now."

My insides had gotten colder the more she relayed. I had been aware of new strains spreading, but the news and internet were filled with so much chaos every day that it became background noise. It was the curse of our generation, being so engrossed in our own minuscule lives that the rest of the world could sometimes feel distant and immaterial. Still, there had definitely been no news about the newest form the virus had taken until it was too late.

"So, if this was a government conspiracy or biochemical warfare...does that mean help isn't coming? This was *meant* to happen?" I asked through a tight throat.

Mel took a bite from the brownie, savoring it before she spoke again. "There must be a reason our country got the worst of it. However it started, I don't think it was meant to go this far. A deadly flu's one thing, but this...this is hell."

The man took over. "This city's probably heavily bordered off by now. We're in one giant quarantine zone. All we can do now is do what we got to do to survive until this virus runs its course or they finally send a team in with a cure. Whatever happens, I'm not going down without a fight. It's a dog-eat-dog world." The last part carried a glint of malice.

My friends and I exchanged worried glances.

Another guy spoke from the doorway of the bus, apparently with more pressing matters on his mind. "You guys got any more food?"

It took an overly long moment for one of us to answer.

Hunter finally did. "No. Sorry."

The tension was mounting suddenly, the quiet interrupted by the sound of one of the SUV trunk opening. We turned to find two women climbing inside.

"Back off!" Hunter shouted at them.

He and Dustin ran over to the car and yanked the two women away. Their pack raised their guns almost instantly. Within a second, ours were up too.

"We don't want any trouble...We're going to go now," Dustin said sternly.

"They have food! Loads!" one of the women yelled.

I could see the greed overtake their eyes. The situation was suddenly at boiling point.

"Let's get in the car," I told my group.

We quickly turned to leave. A gunshot sounded.

We scrambled inside the SUV and were seated in seconds. I heard a few rounds ricochet off the back window as we peeled away. An instant later, the bus's engine roared to life. They were following us.

"Shit!" said Otto. He pressed his foot to the pedal, trying to put as much distance as possible between the bus and our car.

"Oh, no ... " said Hunter, his voice strained.

"What?" I demanded.

He pointed at Xander, pale and bleeding heavily from his shoulder.

"Fuck, dude, that bullet hit me!" Xander said, distressed.

I tensed as I watched the blood run down his shirt. This was really, really bad.

"Wrap this around it," Dustin said, stripping off his t-shirt and throwing it to Hunter, who helped Xander tie it around his arm.

All our bodies pressed against each other as Otto made a hard right. Xander groaned in pain. The bus was now gaining on us, bullets hitting the back of the SUV. I heard a crack from the window.

Hunter turned the turret gun toward the bus and pulled the twine. *BANG.* The bus's front window shattered. It swerved slightly, but picked up speed again.

"Don't go back to the warehouse! They can't know where it is," I told Otto.

Xander was groaning.

Otto swerved to the left. "Hunter, you got to get their tire!" he begged.

"I know, I'm trying!"

BANG. One of their headlights blew out.

Whatever they were shooting back at us had major firepower. The bullets busted our rear windscreen, and left deep holes in the trunk's door.

"Shoot the driver!" Riley screamed.

She and Ava ducked behind the seat as Gage fired at the man driving. He missed several times, but eventually scuffed the guy's arm. The bus swerved dangerously, but another man quickly took the wheel.

"Dammit! I don't want to use all the rounds," Gage said, sounding panicked.

"There's more at the warehouse, shoot that fucker!" Dustin yelled.

I shoved my gun under the seat.

"Xander, give me the shotgun," I said as we made another hazardous turn.

BANG. I aimed for the tire, but missed by inches. Another shower of bullets from the bus made our trunk fly open, one of the latches blown off.

"NO!" Ava and Riley screamed, as a ton of food rolled out onto the street.

The fact that they didn't stop to grab what we'd lost proved they wanted much more than our food.

"Get the trunk closed!" Dustin shouted in panic.

Riley jumped into the trunk and pulled the door closed, managing to salvage some items, but most was lost. She quickly ducked behind the seat as more bullets rebounded.

Hunter finally managed to shoot the driver, his bullet making grotesque contact with the guy's head. The bus slowed and swayed, but a woman quickly shoved the body aside and grabbed the wheel. The bus was feet away from us now, our car slowed down from the new damage.

"Otto, faster!" Ava shouted.

"I'm going top speed!"

I rolled over my seat into the back. Gage moved aside, reloading his gun with his head down. I rested the barrel on top of the seat and shot at the bus's tire. There was a loud pop and a hiss of air. Sparks flew as the tire blew off, and the bus skidded across the asphalt with an ear-splitting screech before slamming into a divider in the road.

"Yes! I hit it! I hit it!" I shouted in disbelief.

We watched the smoking bus as we put distance.

Otto slowed down slightly. "Did we lose them? I don't want to waste any more gas," he said, trying to see through the cracked rearview mirror.

"Yeah! Dude, did you see that?" I asked.

I was overcome with relief, but the joy was short-lived. Not only was the food supply drastically reduced, but the fabric of Xander's seat was drenched in red. He was grunting in pain. My heart clenched at the sight of his shoulder.

Dustin tried to offer some comfort. "We're almost home, bud. Hang in there."

"It hurts so bad!" Xander bit out through gritted teeth.

We drove for another ten minutes, doing our best to calm him.

11.

It was dark out by the time we made it back to the warehouse. We rolled in past the open gate and quickly sealed it behind us.

With urgency, Dustin carried Xander into the main room. He'd been saying he felt cold for the last half of our drive. Otto immediately ran ahead to start a fire while the girls unloaded the remaining bounty from the car.

"Tye, can you go upstairs and bring down a mat?" Dustin called to me.

I ran up the steps two at a time, exhausted, but the adrenaline from our chase kept me moving. I dragged Xander's homemade bed down the steps and laid it near the fire's glow. Dustin carefully placed Xander on it, his blood smeared across Dustin's bare chest.

"There's peroxide here!" Riley called to us, having rummaged through our new items.

She tossed a brown bottle of liquid to me. I caught it and quickly checked the label. Amazingly, it was indeed peroxide.

Dustin grabbed it from my hand. "Xander, listen to me. I won't lie to you, this is going to hurt, but we need to make sure the wound stays clean. Good news is, it looks like the bullet made it out the other end."

Xander's face was white as paper, contorted with pain. He gave a curt nod as Dustin unwrapped his dripping shirt from Xander's shoulder and tilted the peroxide over the open wound. A few drops trickled out, then a stream. It bubbled on the skin.

Xander tensed in pain, breathing in sharply. "*Shit!*" he exclaimed.

"Relax. You're good," Dustin said.

Otto brought over a towel. Dustin tied the cloth around the puncture. It looked like it was bleeding a little less now, but Xander was sweating and still void of color. We knew the damage was serious. Especially in these unideal conditions.

Once Xander finally found a position he could bear to lie in, all we could do was monitor him. Staying nearby, we sifted through everything that hadn't been lost during the chase. It was scarce, but we had more than I expected.

"A box of Frosted Flakes, Cocoa Puffs and Apple Jacks. Crackers, a four-pack of juice boxes, peanut butter, jar of olives, Lays, box of granola bars, Pop Tarts and a bag of ramen noodles," Ava reported, like she was trying to sound positive.

"That's not going to last us very long," Gage said.

"This food needs to be rationed to the extreme," I warned.

"We need to try our hardest to live on the bare minimum as long as we can, and once we get low, we'll come up with a new plan," Dustin suggested. "That's the best we can do for now."

Xander was clearly in no condition to take his night watch shift with Riley. The night before, he had alluded to his fear that he may not come back from our mission. His vulnerability with me weighed heavy on my heart, now I knew that tomorrow was not guaranteed for him. I found myself wishing more for him. A fuller life than he got to live.

Riley and I sat on the rooftop with our newly-loaded guns, our bodies melting with relief. It was the first moment we'd had all day to sit still and rest. I was running on empty, and I still had another shift with Gage later on. At that point I was on autopilot.

"That brownie messed me up. I was actually getting used to being hungry, but now all I want is more," Riley complained.

"I know. I feel like it's worse now we know we have food but can't go at it."

Riley put her gun down and sat next to me on the edge of the roof. "Today was insane," she said. "I truly can't believe we made it back here."

"And those people ..."

"They were scumbags. At least that nurse gave us some insight. I don't understand how things got this bad," she said.

I picked up a small twig near the radiator and started fidgeting with it between my fingers. "I feel terrible for Xander."

"Me too. He's such a good soul...He doesn't deserve this. I'm really worried."

"You know, last night he told me he wanted to get something off his chest because he wasn't sure we'd make it back...He told me he had feelings for me. And about his parents not accepting he was gay. Did you know?"

She gave a pained smile. "Yes. About both. We talked a lot during night watch. I understood his feelings completely. Having feelings for you *and* not being accepted by parents," she said softly.

I shot her a look. "You have a great relationship with your parents, though."

"My sister didn't ..."

My stomach jumped. It was rare for Riley to talk about her sister voluntarily.

"Well, with my dad, at least," she continued. "Did you know she was gay?"

I gaped at her for a moment but quickly blinked to cover my surprise. "No, I didn't...So your dad wasn't accepting of her?"

"He was cold about it. When she told him, he dodged the topic as much as he could and avoided it at all costs from that point forward. I think that's why she always tried to excel in everything, to overcompensate for the disappointment. That was my dad's biggest regret when the accident happened. They never closed that chapter. And I found myself trying to follow in her footsteps, be good at everything, be liked by everyone." Her eyes glistened with emotion. "I think that's why I liked you so much when we met. You were just so indifferent with me, and it somehow made me feel like I could drop the act. Made me feel like you saw me so differently than I was used to being seen."

I put my arm around her and pulled her close. "Well, look, even though we split, you know I'll always love you and have your back, right?" I asked, gingerly.

She smiled. "Yes." Her voice brightened. "Did you know I totally thought you were dating Ava when I first met you?"

"You and the whole world," I said.

Her tone shifted again, darker this time. "But now that she's dating Gage, I can see you're not her type at all…"

"Wait, I really want to understand why you're so upset about it," I insisted. "I mean this with love, but it seems so strange to me that you're so upset over a make-out session when you two barely knew each other. It's not adding up. It was clear he was planning on leaving and not coming back...The whole thing was reckless, but it was a quick, meaningless moment-"

"We had *sex,* Tye."

A long beat passed as I stared at her, then looked away. "I thought...I thought it was just…"

"No...and I'm trying not to make it a big deal, but I can't help it. I feel used and it's hard to be under the same roof as him, especially seeing how he came back from his little escape plan, then completely tossed me aside and fed Ava a ton of bullshit."

"Well, now I understand. And I'm pissed he underplayed the whole thing when I confronted him," I said.

"It's not about the drama, I don't want that. It's stupid. But it's really hard being around them…"

I felt my face get hot and my heart speed up. I wanted to swing at Gage so bad at that moment. All the resentment that had been slowly ebbing away after his betrayal was creeping back in. He just wasn't an honest person. Even his feelings for Ava, that I'd been coming to accept, suddenly seemed warped again.

Right on cue, Gage climbed up the rooftop. Riley pretended to be looking at something on her gun.

"Get some rest," I told her.

She gave my arm a friendly squeeze, then walked right by Gage as if he were a ghost. She keenly ran down the steps and out of sight.

Gage had noticed her attitude. "I don't understand why she's still acting like this."

The plethora of choice words I had for him were on the tip of my tongue, but my brain was simply too exhausted from the day to unleash them.

"You know better than I do," I said flatly.

He sat on a radiator and tied his shoe. "I just checked on X. He said he was still hurting. He's in and out of sleep."

I nodded my head slowly, still fighting the urge to berate him.

"What's wrong?" he asked, suspiciously.

"Nothing, just tired. Aren't you?"

"Yeah, but I couldn't sleep...at all," he said, his face losing color.

"How come?"

" ... Elle and Caleb. They were missing from the parking lot."

I felt my face go white too. It was one of the first things I'd noticed when we pulled up to the store, but I'd forced it from my mind since then. "I saw their blood," I said, evading the point.

"But *they* weren't there. I can't stop thinking about how they've turned. They're out there looking for blood-"

"Cut it out, Gage, I don't want to think about that stuff," I snapped.

"Well, that's why I can't sleep. 'Cause I am."

"Okay, well, I plan on getting some rest after this, so let's drop it," I said.

"Okay, okay."

I could see him struggling to find a new subject.

"You know, Otto came up to me today when I took some trash out back earlier. He had a lot to say to me. Pissed me off," he shared.

"What about?"

"Well, I'm sure I know whose side you'd take...He told me I better not hurt Ava because he thinks she's an amazing girl that I don't deserve."

I *knew* I liked Otto. I smiled, but all the words I was holding back were dangerously close to surfacing. "And what could've possibly made him think that?" I asked, the sarcasm clear.

"I know exactly why. He likes her, too," Gage said, hostility creasing his brow. "Wouldn't be the first time Otto liked someone I'm with."

There was a bitterness in his tone that surprised me more than the notion that Otto was into Ava.

"Sounds like there's a story behind that," I said.

Gage was quiet for a moment as he stared out at the city.

"Growing up together, the only falling-out we ever had was when he told my girlfriend at the time he had feelings for her and shit hit the fan. Took us a long time to come back from that. Otto has a hero complex. His mom left when he was a kid. Now he latches onto the girls in his life and wants to save them."

"Well, Gage," I said, grabbing him by the shirt, "maybe there's a reason he feels they need saving from you."

My anger had gotten the best of me. He stared into my eyes with a look of shock. My distaste for him was in the open now, but he didn't comment.

I released my grip on his shirt, shoving him aside. He backed away and looked back out at the skyline, evidently not knowing what to say.

The rest of the session was spent in tense silence.

We woke up to a morning sun shower. This was only the second time it had rained during our weeks here, but it was just as electrifying as the first.

We jumped under the tank, clothes and all, taking turns and dancing in the rain in between. Dustin was still shirtless, but showed no sign of missing his clothes. I caught both Riley and Ava looking him up and down.

"Quit flexin', meathead," I bantered.

He splashed me with a handful of water, laughing. "Shut up, twig!"

Shower time was short-lived as the gray clouds passed over quickly. We moved inside to distribute small portions of frosted flakes and a can of boiled rainwater, catering to Xander first. Riley took a cool, wet cloth and laid it on his forehead.

The night had seen him get considerably worse. He was having trouble breathing and our morale was plummeting alongside his health, but we couldn't lose hope.

Otto and Gage hadn't left his bedside in hours. Every time I saw them sitting with him my heart ached, remembering the bond they'd had before all of this. The way they tended to him was gentle and a testament to their history.

The rest of us spent part of the day helping repair the damage to the SUV. In the remaining time we reloaded our guns with the last bit of ammo still in the supply sack.

The windows of the Expedition were beyond repair and the gas tank was near empty, but Otto managed to patch up some bullet holes and reinforce the pieces of sheet metal that were damaged. Hunter was doing some heavy lifting for him and it was only after a minute that I noticed Dustin wasn't there helping us, which wasn't like him. I walked into the main room to look for him. He wasn't there either.

I finally went out back and spotted him sitting on an old tire. He was gazing out at the sun setting beyond the grassy field and the distant water tower.

"Dustin?"

He jumped, his hand quickly reaching for his gun. "... God, you can't sneak up on me like that," he said, lowering his guard.

"Sorry, I thought you heard me. You okay out here?" I asked.

"Yeah, just thinking. Good to have some quiet time, you know?"

"Oh, yeah. Totally. You want me to leave you to it?"

"No, buddy, you're good."

"You sure?" I checked.

"Yeah, sit," he said, scooting over to make room on the rubber.

"Thanks… So, when are you getting a new shirt?" I teased.

"You're a little shit," he said, laughing.

"Kidding. What're you thinking about?"

He inhaled deeply, as if gathering the strength to voice it all. "I'm just thinking about life before all this. So many things that seemed so important, all pointless. I'm thinking about life *after* all this. Even if we make it out, the world will never be the same. And there's no way this is just happening here in the States...It's going to spread eventually if it hasn't already."

His words came out like a stream of consciousness, and his thoughts were all too familiar. I had many of the same reflections every night.

"One day at a time," I said, trying to sound comforting. "We're in the dark right now, but we don't know what's being done behind the scenes, beyond all this. There are things going on under lock and key that we're totally unaware of. And cures for any new viruses take time. We have to keep going like things *will* go back to normal, maybe a different normal, but we need to stay tough...even when things look bleak."

"I know. Just hard, man...*God,* I miss my parents." His voice was shaky.

"Me too. So much."

A single tear rolled down his cheek. He wiped it away quickly.

"I know it's cliché and doesn't help much, but everything happens for a reason," I said. "Sometimes, we can't understand what in the world the reason is, but there's one for everything… even this."

He looked at me, his eyes brimming over, then smiled and gave a short laugh.

"What?"

"Am I being a pussy?" he asked.

"No way, dude."

"Do you...?"

"Cry? Hell yeah! Almost every night," I said.

He laughed again. "You know, I've heard Hunter crying before bed," he admitted in a hushed tone. "Not sure if he thinks I'm sleeping or doesn't care, but … it's kinda hard to listen to."

"Well, at least we know he has some feelings," I said.

"The kid's got some walls up."

"Forts, more like it."

There was a short silence before Dustin spoke again. "Let's just make sure we keep holding each other down. Talking it out like this. All we have is each other. Being loyal and looking out for one another. Trust is everything."

At his words, my mind drifted to Ava. *Am I being a bad friend to her, keeping her in the dark about Gage's lies and manipulation?* We had too great a history. We needed to talk. I owed her at least that.

I stood up and walked over to the fence. "I wanna go to that water tower again, one of these days," I said.

"Not scared?"

"Course I am, but there's gallons of fresh water in there, and I can't take this boiled, weird-tasting stuff much longer," I said.

"Ha. I'll go with you, but not now. Sun's almost down."

"No, not right now. But you'll go with me?"

"Yeah, of course," Dustin said.

"Sweet. Well, I'm gonna go talk to Ava," I said.

"To see if she'll come with us?"

"No, not about that. Found out Gage lied to me about what happened with him and Riley. He's playing mind games and I can't let him get away with it. This is all gonna blow up if I keep her in the dark...It's not fair to Riley, either."

"Like I said, trust is everything. I got your back if you need me," Dustin said.

"Thanks, dude. I'll catch you later."

I walked back inside with purpose, intent on finding Ava and finally telling her the truth. However, the moment I spotted Xander, eyes bloodshot and heavy, the wind was taken out of my sails. Gage was beside him, tilting some water into his mouth. My priorities shifted; the timing just didn't seem right.

"How you doing, X?" I asked softly.

He gave me a frail smile, as if my presence brought him comfort. "My shoulder's numb. It feels a lot better, but I don't think that's a good sign. I'm scared."

I knelt down beside him. "Xander, you're strong. We're gonna take care of you," I assured him.

"Can I ask something of you guys?" he asked weakly, addressing Gage and me. "It's important."

"Of course, anything," Gage answered.

Xander's face seemed to pale even more. His voice was shaky. "I need to know I can trust you with this...There's a boy. Only one I ever loved. I said awful things to him to push him away when I was ashamed of myself...It's my biggest regret. If I don't make it—if you guys get out of this—find him and tell him I'm sorry and I never stopped loving him. It's important to me."

Gage looked as dumbstruck as I felt. Xander's tone seemed so final, like he'd been preparing for the end.

Gage rested his hand on his arm. "Quit it. You'll be able to tell him yourself-"

"We will," I cut in quickly.

Xander's smile was so fragile it barely registered on his face. "Thank you. His name's Beckett Taylor. He has a brother named Parker," he said.

I repeated the names in my head several times, conscious of their importance.

Otto walked in with a towel in hand. He threw it to Gage, who swapped it out for the one wrapped around Xander's arm.

“What’s going on?” Otto asked, seeing the gravity in our expressions.

“X just wanted us to pass a message to someone...if we ever run into them,” said Gage, helping him with another gulp of water.

The look on Otto’s face told me he had an idea of who that someone was. He motioned for me to step away with him to a corner of the room.

“He’s not doing good. I’m really getting worried,” Otto said, his voice gravelly.

“Me too. There’s nothing we can do but take care of him. Be there for him,” I said sadly.

“That’s the worst part. Just watching him slip away. I feel like he’s giving up.”

Ava walked in, handing the bottle of peroxide to Gage. Her face was drenched in tears. She could barely look at Xander in the state he was in.

Gage stood up and pulled her close, holding her to his chest. I noticed Otto looking away from their embrace.

Once again, my dilemma niggled at me. I wanted to be a good friend and not keep secrets from Ava, but watching her receive even a tiny measure of comfort amid this madness made it so hard for me to deprive her of that.

Another day wouldn’t hurt.

12.

I'd been listening to the arguing on the rooftop for ten minutes. It was the middle of the night and in my grogginess, I couldn't quite determine if it was a dream or real life. It was only when I heard Gage yelling vehemently that I noticed he wasn't in bed. I quickly got up to see what was going on.

Out in the hallway, I found Hunter already climbing up to the roof two steps at a time. I followed to find Ava going off on Gage while Otto sat on the radiator with his shirt ripped. Something had clearly gone down. None of them even noticed Hunter and me arrive.

"How many other nights did you hold hands? What else were you doing up here?!" Gage shouted at her.

Ava was riled. "You're taking something that was nothing and making it into a big deal! There's nothing between Otto and me! Stop it!" she snapped back.

Hunter stepped in. "What's the problem here? I don't get what's going on."

Gage was livid. "I came to check on Ava, and Otto had his arm around her!"

"He's being totally irrational!" Ava countered. "Otto didn't mean anything by it! He was being nice."

"Bullshit! You probably make out every night up here," Gage spat.

"Watch it, Gage," I warned.

I didn't like the tone he was using with her. I found my own temper rising.

"We're night watch partners, asshole, there's nothing going on!" Ava told him sternly.

"Your intentions are different from his, Ava. Otto always falls for girls I care about, right Otto?"

Ava turned to Otto, a hint of confusion on her face, but she stood her ground. "What's that supposed to mean?"

Otto's face reddened.

"Tell her, Otto. Now's your chance. You only want girls if I want them too, right?" yelled Gage. "Wouldn't be the first time and clearly it won't be the last. You're a piece of shit."

Otto tried to sound unbothered. "You're being stupid right now, Gage. Listen to what's coming out of your mouth. Do you not see the state of things?"

"Don't dodge this!" Gage shot back. "Whatever, fuck this."

He shoved Hunter and me out of his way and stomped back down to his room. There was a strained silence.

"You okay, Ava?" I asked, gently brushing her hair behind her ear.

There were tears in her eyes. "Yeah, I'm fine. He's such an idiot. He threw Otto to the floor," she said.

"Why don't we go downstairs and get some water?" I suggested.

I put my arm around her and led her down the steps. Hunter and Otto followed us to the main room.

Xander was sound asleep next to the fire. I dipped the canteen into the bucket of now cooled water and passed it around. Ava took the first sip, still sniffling.

"I'm so sorry, Ava. I really didn't mean anything by it," Otto said, looking disheartened.

"What are you apologizing for? You did nothing wrong. I think he's just stressed about Xander," she said.

Hunter handed me the canteen. I went to take a sip and it was empty. "Really?"

He smirked. I refilled the canteen and drank, then filled it again to take over to Xander.

"*Shit,* dude," called Hunter, now across the room, his voice like ice.

"What?" I called back, thinking he was pulling another move on me.

He stood over Xander, eyes wide with terror.

"What is it?" Otto asked more seriously.

We all hurried over. We hadn't noticed it in the dim light, but up close I could see Xander was lying in a pool of blood. Ava turned away with her hand over her mouth.

Otto dropped beside his friend. "No, no, no, no. *No!*"

There was no way someone could bleed that much and still be alive. I knew it was over. I put a comforting hand on Otto's shoulder.

"No, he can't be dead," he said, tears streaming from his eyes.

I heard Ava sobbing from across the room. Hunter embraced her. I lifted Otto and gave him a tight hug too. He was shaking.

"Otto ... we expected this. Stay strong, man. He's out of this. He doesn't have to live through this anymore," I said, holding back my own tears.

Otto cried heavily. I didn't know what to do other than pull him away from the sight of the body and embrace him longer. I was devastated for him. That was one of his good friends. Like Ava, Riley, and Dustin were to me.

I was caught off guard by the tears now pouring from my eyes. We were not supposed to see our friends die so soon, and not like this. It was unnatural. I'd told Dustin *everything happens for a reason,* but I couldn't even convince myself of that.

The four of us continued to cry in the main room until we all fell asleep, backs against the wall.

The following morning, it took the others a long while to process what had happened overnight. Dustin couldn't even look at the body. He immediately went back upstairs with tear-filled eyes. No one was sobbing as hard as Gage, though. We watched him kneel beside his friend, convulsing with heartbreak.

Otto led us out front to give his friend a private moment. He was still visibly distraught.

"Gage and Xander knew each other much longer than I did. We really need to give Gage some space, take care of him," he said.

We stood out in the heat as the loss sank in. We paced, kicked rocks, and threw bottle caps over the fence and out onto the street.

I found myself repeating the names Xander had given us before he passed. *Beckett and Parker Taylor.* I said them multiple times until, after forty long minutes, the metal door finally slid open. Gage stood there, wet-faced. Otto embraced him. No one said a word.

Gage looked into Otto's eyes. "Did anyone go into the garage?" he asked.

Otto looked confused as to the question's relevance. "What do you mean?"

"There's footprints in Xander's blood, leading into the garage," Gage said.

We hurried inside. The morning sun had revealed bloody tracks leading from the body toward the garage door. Blood dripped down the door frame.

My stomach gave a jolt. "Get your guns," I said.

"What's wrong?" Riley asked, sounding scared.

I was already storming upstairs to get my weapon, and met Dustin in the hallway. He was sitting with his back against the wall.

"We have a problem," I said.

"What?" he asked, springing into defensive mode.

"There's footprints leading away from Xander's body. Something got into the warehouse. It must've come in when we left the gate open, when we left for the raid."

Dustin ran for his gun and followed me downstairs.

I cocked my automatic. Gage and Hunter both had their guns in hand and Riley looked panicked.

"Can someone please tell me what's going on here?!" she asked.

"Something was feeding on Xander," Dustin said, taking in the crime scene with difficulty.

Her face paled. "Jesus *fuck*!"

I spotted Hunter turning Xander on his side.

"Hunter! What are you doing?!" I yelled at him. I couldn't believe he'd touched the body.

"There's a huge hole in his side ... " Hunter said, his voice almost giving out.

Riley ran out back and threw up. I turned to Dustin, who was now examining the laceration too.

"It's got to be in the garage. We never go in there," I told him.

He approached the garage door apprehensively. Gage was already in front of it, his hand on the doorknob. Clearly if there was a Mort inside, Gage wanted revenge.

"When I open this door, shoot at anything that moves ... infected or not," he said. He turned the knob with a creak.

SLAM!

A Mort pulled the door open before Gage was ready, and was immediately on top of him.

The gory creature sunk its teeth into Gage's wrist. He screamed and flailed, managing to breakaway only seconds before we showered the creature with lead.

The Mort finally dropped dead, covered in bullet holes from our barrage. Its raven-black eyes stared blankly up at the ceiling.

Gage pushed it away, yelling in pain. Dustin kept his gun aimed at the body's head, but I dropped mine and ran over to Gage. Without even a moment to mourn the loss of our friend, we'd already been thrown into another catastrophe.

"Calm down, I'm gonna help you!" I urged him.

Blood was streaming from his wrist, tears falling from his eyes.

"Ava, get me a towel and the peroxide!" I called to her.

She was momentarily frozen, watching him scream.

"Ava!" I repeated.

She broke away and in less than a minute she threw me the bottle along with a rag.

I poured some liquid on it and wrapped his wound. He grunted in pain. "Stay calm," I said.

"No, Tye! I'm *infected*!" he yelled, completely overwhelmed with agony.

That thought hadn't hit me yet. Gage would go on to turn on us, and Xander eventually would reanimate. How long that would take, I had no clue, but the realization was disturbing.

I walked him toward the stairs, but his panic worsened when he saw Xander's body again. I turned him away. "Dustin?" I called.

Dustin unglued his gaze from the dead Mort and looked over to me. I pointed to Xander's body and gestured to move him outside. Dustin shook his head *No,* white in the face.

I turned my attention back to Gage, helping him up to our room where I laid him onto his cot. His breathing was ragged. "I'll be right back," I said, running back downstairs.

Ava passed me on the way up, holding a can of water and looking petrified.

Dustin was frozen where I last saw him. "Dustin, please," I said to him, gesturing at the mess.

"I can't, man, I really can't," he whispered desperately.

"We *need* to. I can't make Riley or Otto do it. X can't stay here ... and neither can the Mort."

Dustin eyed both bodies. He took a deep breath, then put his gun down. "Let's hurry. *Please,*" he said, tensely.

I took Xander gently by the arms, and Dustin lifted his legs.

We took him out back quickly. Riley was out there, looking queasy and shaken.

"Please, open the gate," Dustin begged her.

She ran for the latch, turning away and heading inside quickly.

We placed Xander gently on the grass. Otto joined us outside, his hands visibly shaking. In one he held matches and in the other, some sort of cleaning product from upstairs.

"Otto, you don't need to see this," Dustin said.

"We need to burn the body," Otto declared staunchly.

I froze.

"The Mort was feeding on him. The virus could've passed over. If we don't... he could become one of them."

"If we do it, I don't think I can watch," I said faintly.

"I'll do it," Otto said.

"Otto, you don't have to-"

"No, I want to," he said.

He opened the bottle and held it over Xander, hesitating for a whole minute before pouring its contents over him. Still more tears rolled down his face.

"Do you want to say a prayer or something?" I asked gently.

"No. There's no god to hear me," Otto said.

He lit a match and set the alcohol-drenched body aflame. Dustin and I turned so we didn't have to watch.

We never saw if Otto did the same.

The burning smell was rancid. We stood under the blazing sun for more than ten minutes. I didn't turn around once.

"I'm going in," Otto finally told us, sounding even more broken than I felt.

In the main room, Hunter threw a tarp over the red puddle, then helped Dustin take the Mort outside to torch while I ran upstairs to check on Gage.

"The bleeding isn't slowing down," Ava told me.

The entire bandage was drenched in red.

We both jumped at a bang on the wall downstairs, followed by Otto yelling, "We need to get out of here! When is this going to end?! Give me a sign! This is crazy! I'm going crazy!"

"Don't lose yourself, Otto!" came Dustin's voice. "We're going to get out of this."

The garage door slammed and there was silence. After a beat, I turned back to Gage.

"Is there anything you need?" I asked. "I don't know what else to do."

His voice was weak. "Me neither ... I just need more water."

"You got it," I said.

I grabbed the empty canteen downstairs, and realized our water bucket was barren.

Luckily there was water in the shower barrel out back, but it was more than half-empty. I dipped the canteen inside and scooped out a frugal amount of water.

I spent a few minutes sterilizing the water over the fire. I found myself suddenly nervous that Ava was alone with Gage. Without knowing how long it'd be before he changed, my urgency intensified. I ran back upstairs, handing the canteen to Gage. He raised it to his lips, but I quickly grabbed it back.

"You shouldn't put your mouth on it," I said.

He gave me a mournful look, knowing all too well what I was implying.

I turned away from him, pained, as Ava helped tip the water into his mouth.

13.

Month two arrived stealthily. We'd fallen into autopilot, going about our days relying on our routines to distract us from the famine and dehydration that loomed. Conversations amongst us were short-lived despite my efforts to keep morale up. We simply didn't have the stamina we'd had in the earlier weeks.

Gage was in worse shape than any of us. The bite on his wrist had turned his arm black and blue; he was a ticking timebomb. We debated what exactly to do with him. He was clearly a liability, but still fully coherent. The group decided it was best to continue caring for him—a choice that would've been unanimous had Hunter not opposed it, but he was outnumbered.

Gage now stayed in a corner of the main room where we could keep an eye on him, but maintain our distance. Probably the only reason he hadn't turned yet was our constant care and attention. Like clockwork, Ava changed his bandages and cleaned the wound every day, careful to keep a cloth wrapped around her face at all times to avoid transmission.

The heat outside had skyrocketed in the last week, and came with a new set of challenges. The shower tank out back was empty, and rain clouds seemed to pass us by like they had made a game out of it. At night, falling asleep was twice as hard in a pool of our own sweat, which left us sleep deprived, and during the day, headaches from lack of water had become a permanent ailment.

Dustin and I had been avoiding our trek to the water tower until we were down to our last drop. Seeing our friend's decimated body again or having a run-in with another Mort were the last things we needed, but the moment had come. Our water rations were dangerously low. I began mentally preparing for the inevitable excursion.

Night watch partners were rearranged again. Ava was doubling up, covering Gage's shift with me in addition to hers with Otto. Hunter was with Riley, and Dustin was doing his alone. I proposed joining him, but he claimed to need 'quiet time.' I wanted Dustin to keep his mental fortitude, so I relented. It was comforting to feel his sense of leadership in the places where I faltered.

Otto's form of self-care was working on his inventions. He kept himself busy by probing the warehouse for trinkets. His latest achievement came in the form of three flares he'd made by extracting gunpowder from spare shotgun shells.

One afternoon, Otto was tuning up the SUV in the front driveway when I watched Riley hurry across the main room, holding something behind her back. She met him outside.

"Close your eyes," she said playfully.

He was caught off guard. "What?"

"Close your eyes!" she said again.

This time he smiled. With his eyes closed, he held out his hand. Riley placed something in his palm.

He finally took a peek. "Where'd you find this?!" he asked.

It was a small, dusty radio with bent antennas.

"It was behind an old crate in the garage," Riley said. "You said the car radio was jacked up, maybe this'll work."

The discovery caught everyone's attention.

Otto walked into the main room and over to the hanging clock on the wall. He plucked it from its perch, turned it over, and removed the two AA batteries from inside. We gathered around in anticipation.

"That easy?" Dustin asked, hopeful.

After a few minor twists of the antennas, Otto set the radio on the ground and clicked some buttons. We formed a circle around the device, straining to make out any words within the static.

… … … … … … … … … tschhh … … … … … … … … … … … … … … … …
… …chttt … … … … … … … …
… … … … … … … … … …chhhhssshh … … … … … … … … … … … … … … …
… tshhtt … … … … … …
… …
… …
… … … … … … … … shhh … … … … … … … … … … … … … … … … … … …
… … … … … … … … … … … … … … tchht … … …

For nearly five minutes Otto fidgeted with the dials, but still nothing. He switched it off. "Let's save the battery. We'll keep checking in on this. Great find, Ry."

"It would feel so good to hear just one voice out there," Dustin said.

My stomach rumbled audibly. "I'm gonna hit the food closet. Anyone want anything?"

"Can you get me one of those granola bars?" Otto asked.

"I already had my weekly portion," Riley said glumly.

The pantry upstairs had once been home to an assortment of cans, but now looked bleak. Only a few boxes of stale goods remained.

I reached up to grab a granola bar from the top shelf when I heard a rustle coming from inside the box. I recoiled, knocking it to the floor. A mangy rat quickly scuttled away, disappearing around a corner. My heart pounded.

I turned the box upside down and nothing but crumbs fell out. I cursed under my breath, quickly checking the other two boxes nearby. They were also empty.

Sweating with rage, I moved to the last of the items on the bottom shelf, rummaging through the boxes of cereal to check for holes. Painful pricks shot through my hand.

"Ouch!"

My skin was now covered in red ants, adding insult to injury. I grabbed the box of Pop Tarts and crackers and tried to knock them away. After a few more bites, it looked like I'd managed to shake most of them off.

I stomped back downstairs. "We have a problem," I grumbled.

"What?" Dustin asked, standing up with his gun ready.

"It's the food. A rat got into it and now it's covered in ants."

"Are you kidding?!"

I lifted my hand, displaying the inflamed bites. "I wish I was."

"All ruined? Everything?" Riley asked.

"Mostly. We're gonna have to share this." I held up a single pack of Pop Tarts.

"We're fucked," Hunter stated bluntly, echoing my own sentiments. He picked up a rock and went over to the wall of house rules, scratching one out.

~~17 CANS OF FOOD PER PERSON.~~

"I *wish* we still had seventeen cans of food," he said.

Gage mumbled something.

"What's that?" Ava asked gently.

He coughed, then spoke clearer. "Who is that?" he asked, staring at Hunter.

"What?" she asked again, confused.

"Him. Who *is* that?!"

He was frantic now. Ava looked at me. The confusion in her eyes turned to fear.

"Gage, it's Hunter," I replied, trying to hide my concern.

Gage looked even more lost now.

"Who did you come here with, Gage?" I asked.

He stared blankly at me. "Here?"

"Yeah, who'd you come with?" I repeated.

"I-I came alone. Why are you interrogating me?" he asked defensively.

A single drop of blood trickled from his nose.

Ava's eyes welled up with tears. "Gage, lie down. You need to rest," she said, wiping his nose with the sleeve of her shirt.

He put his head back down and turned over, away from the terrified looks on our faces.

My shift that night was dedicated more to preparing Ava for the worst than watching the streets below.

"I know you care about him, but like I told Otto about Xander … they're going to a better place. Out of this nightmare," I said.

"It's not his death I'm scared of. It's..."

"When he turns?" I finished.

Silence. "Yeah," she eventually said, sniffling. Her eyes were watering again.

"We both know what happens next," I said quietly. "I want you to know I'm here for you. I love you. I think you should say what you need to say to him tomorrow morning, and leave the rest to us. I don't want you to watch him turn."

Ava swallowed audibly, then took my hand in hers and squeezed it tight. Her head dropped between her knees. She knew what was coming, we all did. We weren't naive to the ins and outs of this new world anymore.

For the remaining hour, I listened to Ava cry. There was nothing else I could do or say to make her feel better.

Dustin showed up, marking the end of our shift. He went to console Ava, when-

BAM!

The three of us jumped at the sound of the gunshot. Dustin and I ran downstairs.

Chills ran up my spine at the sight of Hunter standing over Gage's body, the smoking gun in his hand still aimed at Gage's head. Blood spilled across the floor.

Dustin instantly charged at Hunter and nailed him in the face. He dropped to the floor, gun skidding away. Ava ran in as the two tussled. Her knees buckled and she screamed at the gory sight of her lover.

"Get off me!" Hunter spat in Dustin's face.

I saw more blood now, but it was coming from Hunter's nose.

"What did you do?! You fucking *killed* him?" Ava shrieked, frantic.

Riley and Otto came running down the steps, grimacing at the scene. Dustin shoved Hunter off him.

Hunter looked manic. "I had to! He was gonna kill us!" he yelled.

"He didn't have to die yet!" I yelled back. "He was still our friend until he turned! Who do you think you are?!"

The only sound in the room was Ava bawling into Otto's chest. He held her tight, clearly trying to stay strong, but Gage was his close friend too. He looked like his heart had just been unplugged.

"If I didn't kill him, he'd have killed *us*! You saw him starting to turn! We waited way too long," Hunter declared.

"What did we tell you when you came crawling back here after leaving? Huh?" Dustin demanded.

Hunter stared at him, flames in his eyes.

"We told you if you tried anything else, you were out."

The tension in the room was palpable. It was only when I looked around that I noticed Riley's face. She was pale as ivory.

"You want me to leave?" Hunter asked, addressing us all. Dead silence hung in the air. "You want me to leave when I just saved your fucking lives?"

Otto spoke through tears. "Hunter, what you did is beyond insane. You killed my friend! Yes, he was turning, but he hadn't turned yet!"

"I did it for us," Hunter said.

"You did it for *you*! You're a coward and you were scared! You had no right to do this!" Ava yelled, stepping up and slapping him across the face.

Hunter recoiled. When he spoke, his lip quivered. "You all know it needed to be done, but no one wanted to do it! Screw this," he said, kicking his gun across the room, then storming out back.

After a beat, Ava ran upstairs. The door slammed seconds later. Otto followed, but Riley lingered on the steps.

I turned to Dustin. "What do we do, man?" I asked, still in shock.

Dustin was breathing heavily. "I want him gone," he said, finality in his tone.

"If we make him leave he'll die out there, and we'll be doing exactly what we're punishing him for," Riley said hoarsely.

The tension grew over more silence. Riley stared at Gage's body, her expression vacant.

Dustin embraced her, but directed his words at both of us. "If he stays, his gun's gone, his shift's with me, and he's not getting a word from any of us. We're shutting him out."

We nodded in agreement, sensing the absoluteness of his terms.

The overnight shifts carried on, but Hunter didn't show for his. No one knew where he went. He could've left, but none of us cared enough to search for him.

The next morning, the depression that enveloped the warehouse was palpable. We were weak with hunger and gravely in need of water. I crawled out of bed, two full hours past my normal wakeup time, and groggily made it downstairs.

The new stains in the main room were sinister. I was caught off guard to find Hunter with his back against the wall, reading an old newspaper. He didn't look up. I was floored to find that he wasn't already miles away from here after what he'd pulled.

My spirit bottomed out when I saw the lump underneath the bloodied tarp.

Otto met me at the foot of the stairs. I spotted the matches in his hand and immediately knew where his head was at.

We carried Gage into the field and carefully placed him next to Xander's charred remains. I was numb all over. After a similar sendoff to Xander's, Otto walked back with me.

The rest of the day went by in a blur. Otto spent most of his time listening to the radio static. I hadn't seen Riley at all. Ironically, Hunter made a point of giving us the silent treatment. Dustin stepped up and tried to clean the blood from the floor, but for the most part, he was unsuccessful. I avoided that spot like the plague now.

Two minutes into my night shift, Ava was sobbing again. It was an aggressive cry.

"Breathe, Ava, please," I said.

"Can you leave me alone? I don't want to talk," she bit out.

"I'm not trying to start a conversation. It's just killing me to see you like this."

"Maybe I want to cry. Maybe I like feeling something!"

There was a tense pause.

"I'm sorry. You've never had a problem feeling anything," I eventually said, gently. "That's always been one of my favorite things about you."

Her breathing evened out slightly.

"Do you remember in fifth grade when I called you 'Waterworks?'" I asked, smiling. "You'd tear up when you were happy, mad, sad, excited ... "

A small giggle escaped through her sobs. She wiped her eyes.

"It was so funny. I loved it, though. I think that's why I got so attached to you so quickly," I said. "You seemed like you wore your heart on your sleeve, so I felt I could be vulnerable around you, right from the start."

She finally looked up at me, her face drenched, but a smile now appearing. "'Waterworks' was one of the nicer names you teased me with."

I smiled menacingly. "What? You mean 'Jellylegs' was bad?"

She rolled her eyes.

I grabbed her by the arms and lifted her to her feet. "It's okay, you're white. Your dance moves are *supposed* to be terrible," I said.

She was laughing now as I did a silly dance around her.

Just as I spun her around, something on the dark street below caught my eye. It was moving. I stopped and lifted my gun, cocking it.

"*Ava,*" I whispered, the lightened mood completely draining from me.

"What is it?" she asked.

"There's one down there."

She raised the gun she'd inherited from Gage and followed me to the edge of the rooftop, all remaining humor evaporating. The Mort was now walking along the warehouse fence.

I aimed for the head, squinting one eye and trying my best to make the shots count.

BAM. BAM. Two rounds fired into the monster's head. It dropped quickly. An eerie silence filled the air, broken only by the clink of the shells hitting the ground.

"Is it dead?" Ava asked softly.

"I think so …"

Minus Hunter, the entire group showed up on the rooftop in a matter of seconds.

"What's up?" Dustin asked immediately.

"One of them, on the street," I said.

They peeked over the edge.

"Not good, dude," Dustin said. "If they're this close to the warehouse, that means they're looking for food...us."

Riley shuddered. "Dustin, don't say that."

"We haven't seen any around here since that one chased you and Elle. Now, one's hiding in our garage and another's taking a stroll outside," he pronounced. "They smell blood."

14.

Otto's panicked voice pierced through my shallow sleep.

"Dustin! Tye!"

I grabbed the gun next to me and ran into the hallway to find him there, Dustin already by his side.

"What? What is it?" I urged him.

"There's a bunch out there," he said.

"Morts?"

He nodded.

Riley and Ava now stood outside their bedroom doors. "What's going on?" I heard one of them ask.

I didn't stop to talk. I opened the hatch and climbed onto the roof.

Down below us, a large group of bloody undead feasted on the body I'd shot down the night before. I cringed at the sight. "Can they get in here?" I asked, eyeing the perimeter fence.

"That many? If they wanted to stampede through that fence, they could." Dustin swallowed. "Girls, get your guns. And tell Hunter."

Ava and Riley wasted no time, reappearing armed a few moments later.

"Where is he?" Dustin asked.

"In the main room," Riley said. "I told him what's up but he completely ignored me."

Dustin didn't miss a beat. "Everyone, check your magazines," he ordered.

We were dangerously low.

"Even if we hit them dead-on with every round, I don't think this is enough to take them out. And we'll be out for good," I said, my heartbeat picking up speed.

The fence rattled. The infected were now trying to move on to their second course: us. In a joint effort, they ripped a small hole in the wire as others started to climb. Dustin fired a round. One dropped from the fence, but got up seconds later, trying again.

I emptied out my cartridge, managing to kill three, but the others barely faltered. The Morts that had torn through the fence were now pushing themselves through the gap. Dustin aimed and fired at one's head. Blood sprayed, but the bullet only grazed its skull and the Mort resumed its efforts. Dustin emptied out his magazine, this time killing a few.

Our chances of maintaining our stronghold seemed slim. Visions of my friends being mauled in front of me flashed through my mind. Once the Morts made it through the gate they'd be on us in minutes, like a flood of carcasses. The body they had feasted on overnight twitched and got to its feet again.

All at once, the horde turned their attention away from us and toward something down the street. They moaned and wailed in fury.

Riley pointed with a trembling hand. "Hunter!" she yelled desperately.

"No ... " I said, so weakly no one heard me.

He was outside the fence, the grenade in the palm of his left hand.

"Hunter! What are you doing?! Get back in here!" I called after him.

All discord was forgotten in that moment. Suddenly, he was the Hunter I used to know. The friend I once had. Everything seemed to slow.

The infected turned their bloodlust on him, racing after him as he ran down the street, drawing them away from our premises. They swarmed, piling onto him just as he pulled the grenade pin.

I closed my eyes. A breath later, the ground shook under me. I felt a wave of heat press against my face. An almost peaceful silence lingered in the atmosphere.

I was only knocked back to reality by the sharp ringing in my ears. The street was covered in limbs. For many long minutes, we just stared.

And then there were five.

I couldn't remember what had happened between witnessing Hunter's sacrifice and ending up in the main room. Riley was staring at the floor, not blinking, her face wet. Ava was completely zoned out. Otto and Dustin were leaning against the wall with their arms crossed and heads down in defeat. Words were scarce. Not a sound from any of us.

What Hunter had done was ludicrous, but we were alive because of him. Nothing needed to be said. We probably all had different opinions on his atonement, but we kept them to ourselves.

My worry now was the amount of loss that shrouded the warehouse. It was overwhelming. I had been watching Ava's sanity gradually dissipate, and I was scared Riley's was next. Otto's pragmatic ways made it easier for him to cope, and I knew Dustin was very resilient with his emotions, but the girls had been more fragile lately. Riley had already dealt with the loss of her parents and sister. Losing anyone else at this point was nearing torture. How many people in someone's life could vanish before they lost it?

I wasn't sure if it was my leadership mentality keeping me from becoming a mental wreck, but I didn't feel the pain I thought I would after having just lost a friend. Death was such a common occurrence now, my system seemed to have developed the antibodies to fight off the effects of loss like it was a foreign invader in my psyche.

Dustin broke the silence. He kicked over the bucket. "Alright, we need to get some damn water," he said, sounding frustrated. It was clear he was deflecting from the harrowing event we'd just witnessed, but the fact remained.

I was glad to have any form of distraction. A productive one was even better. "Let's just make this quick. To the water tower and back," I said, still dazed. "If we go, it's now or never. More of them are gonna show up eventually."

"We need this bad," Otto chimed in. "Without food we can live for a few weeks... but without water, the human body can only function for a few days. Let's not test it."

I snatched up the canteen and Dustin the bucket. When I went to pick up my automatic, I remembered. "My gun's cashed," I said.

Ava handed me Gage's. "There's a few left," she said.

"Hold the fort down," I whispered to Otto.

Both Dustin and I headed out back.

The sun's rays were brutal. It seemed they were trying to drain every last bead of moisture we had in us. We looked out past the fence and across the sizable field. Beyond the blackened bodies of our two friends, the tower offered us salvation.

I unlocked the gate and pushed it open cautiously. We set out, slowly but with purpose.

Five long minutes went by. I could see Dustin's face was already sporting a mild sunburn.

Panting, I said, "It's a lot further than it looks."

We could just make out Ava's demolished car ahead of us, marking the halfway point to the water tower.

"It's ruthless out here," Dustin said. He eyed me, as if trying to read my thoughts.

"What?" I asked, uncomfortable at the shift.

"You okay? I mean about Hunter. I know you guys used to be close."

I was caught off guard by the sudden wave of emotion that bubbled up in me. I'd thought I was numb to my feelings on the matter, but the mention of our past hit a nerve. "I don't think I've processed it yet," I said somberly. "We had a good friendship in the beginning...We just lost our way. Even before all this."

Dustin put an earnest hand on my shoulder. His kindness brought me back to the first time I met Hunter.

"In middle school, he was the very first person I became friends with outside the few people there I already knew. My first few weeks were scary. Everyone seemed more interested in being cool and tough, I just kept my head down. Then in my art class, this kid who sat next to me every day, messy hair, goofy smile, he kept bugging me. Saying he wasn't even gonna try in that class because I was 'too good.' Complemented my drawings every single day. He started sitting with me at lunch too, bringing other friends with him. Pretty much made my year—and we were tight for the rest of middle school. All because he wasn't worried about being 'lame' by actually being friendly-"

My emotions got the best of me and I had to stop.

Dustin rubbed my back. "Hey, that's a good way to remember him. And maybe that's the side of him that saved us today."

I nodded. I appreciated that perspective on Hunter's ending.

Before we knew it, we'd arrived at the tower. Long metal stairs wrapped around its thick trunk, leading up to the massive round tank.

"You first," Dustin encouraged.

I started up the steps, climbing with intent. The thought of having fresh water was powerfully motivating. We climbed to the very top, and there it was, the hatch that opened into the tank's contents underneath.

Dustin yanked on two metal handles and the door opened with a screech. "Holy. Shit."

Right below us was a deep, crystal-clear lake.

Dustin laughed. And laughed, more and more until he was cracking up. "Unbelievable. Why didn't we come here sooner?!" he exclaimed.

He put the bucket down and threw his shoes off, then leapt into the water. "Get in here," he called up to me, the words echoing.

I tossed my shirt, sneakers, and the canteen aside, then dived in. "It's freezing!" My voice reverberated around the dome. "How deep do you think this is?"

"Deep. This has to be a million gallons," Dustin said, right before he ducked underwater.

I tipped my head back and washed the grime from my hair and face. Dustin surfaced and spat water at my cheek.

"Dude! Come on," I said.

He laughed. I splashed water in his eyes. He grabbed my head and shoved it under.

"You're dead!" he warned playfully.

It was an invigorating swim, but the fun had to be short-lived. Though we wanted to, we couldn't stay there forever. The others needed water just as much as we did. We drank as much as we could from the pool, filled the canteen and bucket, then climbed the ladder back up.

"We gotta bring the others here at some point. Our fam needs some smiles," said Dustin, shaking out his hair.

"Definitely," I said. "I feel *new*."

The walk back from the oasis was much easier, despite having to carry the heavy water bucket. We were energized and the sun felt good as it dried our clothes.

When we reached the warehouse, I expected to see everyone in the same place we'd left them, but to my surprise, they were gathered around the small radio.

No one even looked up when we walked in. When we set the water bucket down, there was nowhere near the happy frenzy I'd been picturing. I dipped my hand in the water and splashed a little at their backs to get their attention.

"Anyone want-"

"*Shhh.* Come here," Riley snapped.

It was only now I realized there were some breaks in the radio's static. Dustin and I sat on the floor next to the others.

… … … ..chhhhsssshh… … … ..Federal Communications Commission… … … shtt… … … … ...evacuation routes… … … … … … … … to administer… … … … … … … … … ..tchhh… … … … … … .a… ..developed with some success … … … … … … .testing… … … … … … … … … … … … … shhhhh… … … … … … .

… … … … … … … … … … … .tchhh… … … … … … … … … … … … .b orders… …

I strained my ears to listen, barely breathing for many minutes, but couldn't make out any other words amongst the static and crackles.

I finally spoke, excitedly, but still hushed enough not to drown out any other words. "It said something was developed with success. That has to be a vaccine!"

"Maybe potential cures? Or at least steps being taken!" Otto said with a smile.

We hugged, pressing our heads together. Though vague, it was the first outside contact we'd had since the beginning of the end. Those words were our first glimmer of hope that there could truly be a light at the end of this brutal tunnel.

Dustin grabbed a few of the empty cans and dipped them into the bucket's clear water. He handed one to Otto and another to Riley, then held up the canteen.

"To better things coming!"

The girls' smiles came with some effort, but they couldn't resist the much-needed hydration. The canteen made its rounds and I watched the water visibly bringing my friends back to life, the color flushing back into their skin.

In the midst of the momentary levity, I realized that there really wasn't anything left for us in the warehouse, only memories of death and struggle and sadness.

I glanced over to the bloodstains where Xander had died. And the ones Gage had left. And those the Mort had shed. And the old newspaper Hunter had been reading the day before. We needed out. A change of location.

"I think we need to leave this warehouse," I said.

My words hung in the air as everyone looked at me.

Dustin spoke sarcastically. "Yeah?"

"No, I mean *today,*" I explained. "We need to go somewhere else. Especially after hearing that radio broadcast. Clearly there's moves being made out there, but we've waited around long enough hoping it'll find us. We need to at least try and make it to the border, see if we can find one of those evacuation routes. I'm done being a sitting duck."

"I'm dying to get out of here, but we're not exactly in good shape to make any voyages. No ammo, very little food, and the biggest issue—the car's pretty much on empty," Otto said, looking heartbroken.

"I had an idea on the way to the water tower," Dustin chimed in. "If there's anything left in Ava's car out back, we can siphon the gas out and fill up the SUV."

It looked like Otto's gears were turning. "With so many Morts in the area, it's a bit of a risk for an unsure reward. That grenade going off must've been heard for miles."

"We didn't spot any, but we won't let our guard down," I said.

"I filled up a few days before the evacuation. There should be enough gas to make the gamble worth it," said Ava, her voice raspy.

I'd nearly forgotten what she sounded like. Hearing her contribute was comforting.

"There's more rubber tubes out back in the junk pile," I recalled. "We can use them to siphon out the gas."

"So, we're doing this?" asked Dustin, a hint of excitement in his voice.

"Let's do it," Otto agreed. "Girls?"

It took Riley a second longer than Ava to break out of her daze, but she nodded in confirmation.

Dustin followed Otto and me out back and spoke in a low voice. "I think one of us should stay here with the girls. They're definitely going through it right now. We only need a pair of us to go get the gas."

"I've siphoned gas tanks plenty of times at my dad's shop. I can do it quick and easy," Otto assured us.

"I'll go with him," I said. "I'll feel better knowing you're here with them if anything goes down."

Otto and I grabbed an empty bucket and a rubber tube near the junk pile. Dustin picked up a few stray zip ties.

"I'm gonna patch that gap in the fence while you guys are gone," he said.

"Good call," I told him as we opened the back gate.

For the second time that day, I braved the open field and the high sun. The adrenaline from the prospect of a new plan was fueling me.

Otto was vigilant, looking in all directions as we walked toward the dark red Mazda. Despite the open area, the amount of Morts we had seen congregating outside our perimeter that morning was reason enough to be on high alert. I was suddenly uneasy that Dustin and I hadn't spent a little more time checking our surroundings. Luckily, nothing seemed out of place in the grassy field. We trudged onward.

It wasn't long before the silence became uncanny.

"How are you feeling, Otto?" I asked. "I feel like I haven't had a second to even check in on you. Been so worried about Ava, but Gage was your friend too...and X. Can't imagine what's going on inside your heart right now."

Otto closed his eyes momentarily at the mention of the losses. "It was sick what Hunter did, but I'm glad Gage isn't in pain and suffering through all this anymore. Same with Xander. I just wish we were all in a better place before they went. I feel like so much was left unsaid...but I can't dwell on that now. I just have to make sure we survive this so it wasn't all for nothing. And I'm worried about Ava."

"Me too. I appreciate you caring about her. Gage made her happy, but you have a different way with her. It's more genuine. Something about Gage always had me second-guessing him."

"I've heard that before," Otto said. "In all the years I've known him, that never went away. Loved him to death, I mean, he knew me better than anyone else in my life, but since the beginning I always saw this coldness behind his eyes. Like he had this secret he'd never share. I was never sure where that came from. That dark side didn't usually come out around me, but I did see it around others. Around his love interests, mostly."

I shot him a look. I knew Otto had felt a way about one of Gage's girlfriends in the past, but I'd never gathered the details. "Ava wasn't the first girl you worried about with him, huh?" I asked curiously.

"He told you about the falling-out we had? When we were younger?" Otto asked, surprised.

"Briefly. Not in detail."

"I know what it looks like, but Gage and I have always been a duo. Since we were always together, any time he brought a girl around, I got close with her, naturally. And who do you think they end up venting to when my best friend fucks up with them?" asked Otto.

"Not an easy position to be in..."

"No, and other than that one girl that divided us, I never crossed that line again. That was young love. It wasn't worth the friendship falling apart. But Ava brought up a lot of those mixed emotions in me. I tried so hard not to get involved, but being on that rooftop every night with Ava, and the connection we have, just really made me feel like we were more of a match than her and Gage could ever be. And I..."

I looked at him when his sentence trailed off. His eyes were wide.

Not far from the Mazda, a Mort limped toward us, uncharacteristically slow. We clutched at our guns, but it didn't seem crazed or threatening. Instead, it fell to the grass.

"I think the virus just ran out of juice," said Otto.

"Don't drop your guard," I said sternly as we got closer.

Creeping nearer, like stalking leopards, we noticed the infected woman was clad in SWAT attire. Her bulky gear and face mask covered most of her decaying body. She was as rigid as concrete.

"Dude," Otto said, gripping my shoulder. "Dude!"

I spotted the source of his sudden shift from fear to excitement. The Mort's stiff hand was clasped around a pistol, and strapped across her back was a hefty-looking automatic weapon.

"Holy shit. Is she *dead,* dead?" I asked.

"I'm almost positive they need to be bitten again to get a second wind. Let's hurry," Otto said, putting his gun on the ground. "Cover me."

I aimed my gun directly at the woman's head as Otto advanced guardedly. He nudged the Mort's hand to test its reaction; luckily, the body did not move. He kicked the pistol from its grasp. I quickly picked it up and tucked it inside the waistband of my jeans.

Otto hustled over to her other side, kneeling down for the automatic. "Damn. I can't unclip the strap. The clasp's underneath her." He looked up at me.

"What?"

"...I need you to help me turn her over," he said, regret in his voice.

I froze for a moment, looking down at the body, then lowered my gun. Both of us lifted her from the side and flipped her over. A pool of blood soaked the grass beneath her.

"That's a fresh bite!" I blurted, spotting the cavity in the back of her neck. "She could reanimate!" I lifted my gun again.

"Wait! Don't waste ammo, the bite could've been from before," Otto pointed out.

He quickly unclipped the strap and grabbed the assault rifle. We both backed up closer to Ava's car.

"Let's do this quick," I said, grabbing the rubber tube and handing it to Otto, keeping my eyes fixed on the Mort.

Otto set his gun down and funneled the tube into the gas tank. I heard him working quickly, but my eyes stayed glued to the Mort. I heard the sound of liquid streaming into the plastic bucket. The smell of gasoline wafted under my nose. I turned for a moment, a smile of relief stretching across my face.

A nanosecond later, I turned back to the Mort... except it was gone.

"Tye!" Otto yelled, diving for his gun in the grass.

The Mort rushed toward us like a rabid predator. It jumped onto the car, stumbling when its feet dropped through the broken front windscreen. It thrashed and grunted, giving me a split second to point and shoot. Two rounds went off before Gage's gun clicked. The Mort went limp once again.

We stood frozen in shock, only coming back to life when the tube suddenly made a gurgling sound. The gas tank had run dry, its contents now within our bucket. We grabbed our supplies and hurried back toward the warehouse.

When we arrived, our friends were gathered at the back gate on high alert.

"What happened?" Dustin asked. "We heard gunshots."

We opened the gate and went through, Riley closing it behind as we unloaded all our items.

"Ran into a Mort, but it was on its last legs," I said, out of breath. "Gave us a scare, but not much of a fight."

"Another one? This is getting-" Dustin spotted our newly-acquired artillery. "Wait, *what*?!"

With a smile from ear to ear, he picked up the automatic, studying it like he wanted to memorize it.

"We got gas too, if you were wondering," I said dryly. "And this." I removed the pistol from under my shirt and held it up for Dustin.

Like a child on Christmas, he snatched it from my hand. "These are mega scores. They're police weapons," he said in amazement.

I'd nearly forgotten that Dustin's parents had both been cops. It seemed like a lifetime ago. "You sound like Caleb," I said lightheartedly. "The Mort was wearing a SWAT uniform. Luckiest we've been since getting here, I'd say."

"Well, let's ride this wave of luck. Fill the tank up and get out of here before it runs out," Otto said.

Dustin shouldered the automatic and handed me back the pistol. Riley helped Otto lift the bucket of gasoline into the main room.

Inside, we scrambled to pick up the last few supplies that had survived our stay. Otto poured the bucket's bounty into the fuel neck and, like it was liquid gold, made use of every last drop.

"I'd say we got about forty miles before the gas runs out," he announced, after starting the engine and doing a full scan of the car's condition.

Ava was helping me load the trunk with the last of our inventory when Otto pulled her aside.

"Ava, can I borrow you?" he asked her.

Her eyes were still so full of sadness. She nodded and followed him a few steps away. I listened but kept my eyes on the rations, fiddling with them excessively so as to seem uninterested in their conversation.

"I know you need some space. But I wanted to give you this, as a memory from the old world. Thought maybe you missed it," said Otto kindly.

I couldn't help but glance over my shoulder, and saw Otto holding out Ava's orange dreamcatcher charm that had been hanging from her rearview mirror. I smiled to myself, appreciating Otto's gesture to the extreme. I hadn't even seen him take it, but that small act confirmed everything I already felt about Otto's character, despite Gage's perception of it.

"Otto ... I ... " Ava said, emotion swelling in her eyes, but with warmth this time. She hugged him heartily. "Thanks, Otto. That was really, really nice of you."

He smiled and hugged her back.

"Alright, stop being cute. We're all packed," Dustin said, breaking them apart with a laugh. "The gate's open. New horizons await."

Ava joined Riley and me in the middle row of the SUV, with me between them. She had a renewed softness about her.

Dustin took co-pilot next to Otto at the wheel.

"We're *actually* leaving," said Riley, almost like she was trying to convince herself.

The car pulled out onto the street and Otto stopped it for a moment. We all looked up at the warehouse. It was staggering to think of just how much we had been through within its walls. I hoped the hardest parts were behind us and this decision marked a new start. By no means was I going to miss this place, but for some inconceivable reason, leaving felt strained.

15.

We spent the first half of our drive reveling in the joy of leaving the warehouse that had been home to most of our struggles. The rest of the ride was spent looking out of the cracked window in silence. Since our last excursion, the area had deteriorated even further. In contrast to the additional litter and damage, the only thing that seemed to have lessened was the body count. The haunting truth was that they now roamed the city as Morts.

As expected, it wasn't a straight shot out of the city. Countless times we rerouted, hitting a gridlock of abandoned cars on the road or a military blockade. The state border was several hundred miles away. It seemed impossible to reach in one stretch with so many obstacles, even if we stopped to siphon gas repeatedly. Our plan for now was to drive toward the border, as far as our gas tank would allow. When we hit empty, we'd set up camp, and prepare for the second half of our odyssey another day.

I was trying to keep my anxiety at bay, recharging on the uneventful drive as much as I could. Riley was leaning her head against the door, her eyes closed and her cheeks flushed. I caught myself recalling a similar tableau from the summer we'd started dating. A trip to the beach.

I gently placed my hand on the back of her neck. Her eyes opened slowly and she turned to me.

"You okay?" I asked quietly.

"Yeah...Just thinking."

I could always see through her. Her gaze held so much loss. I kept my tone level, reassuring. "I'm still here."

As if she knew I could read her mind, she said, "I know," and smiled.

A small *ping* broke the moment.

"Shoot, we're near empty," said Otto.

"No way," I blurted in disbelief.

"Feels like we just left. Damn," said Dustin.

I looked out the window at where we would most likely have to anchor. It was an area I recognized. My dad used to take me to the marina there when I was younger. A mix of nostalgia and sadness bubbled in my core.

Luckily, when the car eventually gave out we'd reached Oceana Point, a strip of classic high-rise buildings near the water. The area had once been a sought-after tourist hub. Office buildings and hotels there dated back to the 1940s, but the charm they once radiated had been stripped. They were ghostly and faded now. Still, despite the unwelcoming vibe, it didn't come close to the discomfort the warehouse had offered.

After making sure the coast was clear, we got out of the car and stood in the middle of the street to evaluate our surroundings.

"Buildings, buildings everywhere, and not a home in sight," I chanted.

We'd left in search of a better situation, a better shelter, but now the choices were overwhelming.

"Well, most of them look like corporate buildings. I think the hotels are probably closer to the water," Dustin said, popping the trunk open.

We gathered our meager belongings and headed towards the pier nearby.

As we moved vigilantly, we passed shattered storefronts. They'd been wiped clean of any obviously useful items.

We arrived at the front of a large historic building on the marina. The sign on the façade read *Don Lux Hotel,* a name that went well with its timeless architecture. It was painted coral pink, with a long valet driveway leading up to grand oak doors.

"It ain't a warehouse, that's for sure," Dustin joked. "Stay alert, though."

Riley pushed the front door open. With a dramatic creak, it swung ajar to reveal an enormous grand foyer. Though it was gloomy, light spilled through the giant glass windows to reveal the chic, ornate furniture, vintage carpet, and marble front desk.

Otto's mouth dropped open. "Holy hell."

I patted him on the back. "Welcome home," I said.

We set our stuff down near the check-in desk, but in contrast to the old world, no receptionist would greet us and offer to have our belongings taken to our assigned rooms. The silence was our only welcome party.

Riley peeled her eyes away from the chandeliers above us. Her mood instantly brightened. "Let's explore! There's probably so much in here!" she said.

"Wait, wait, wait," Dustin warned. "We can't assume this place is empty. Let's make sure it's clear. Stay guarded and have your guns out."

We brought our weapons up, realizing our mistake in momentarily forgetting the world we now lived in. I was suddenly conscious of how little ammo there was between us all. There were many floors and hallways that could potentially house a fiend.

As the group dispersed, searching behind the desk and in some of the back rooms, I stood under the grand chandelier and absorbed my surroundings. It felt euphoric to be able to inhale something other than the smell of sawdust, to stand on soft carpet, and to realize that luxury, in some form, still existed.

Though this was a complete upgrade from the drab warehouse, there was still a bizarre energy about seeing a once bustling place like this, abandoned. I pictured the posh guests walking around and chatting about their plans for the day, checking in at the counter, and running after their giggling kids.

My trance was broken by a maid service cart speeding past me. Otto was riding on one end while Dustin pushed it, both of them laughing. It was clear they thought the area was secure after all. Dustin let go and Otto jumped off seconds before the cart smashed into a wall, toppling over and spilling little metallic-looking green squares all over the floor. Otto ran over and picked one up.

"What is it?" I called.

He unwrapped it and put it in his mouth. His face lit up. "They're chocolates! Mint chocolates!" he exclaimed.

As if he had said "first one to reach me gets their parents back," we all sprinted over to him and dived into the trove. No one said anything for a long moment as we stuffed our mouths with the most delicious welcome treat we could have hoped for.

"Wow, that tastes like heaven," said Riley, eyes closed as she took in the rich flavor.

"Hey, come look at this," Ava called from behind the front desk, mouth full of sweets.

We gathered around to look at the sheet of paper she held up.

"Let me see that," said Otto, taking it from her.

I looked over his shoulder. It was a list of the hotel's floor plans. My eye was caught by *Floor 9: Pool.*

"Anyone care for a swim?" I asked excitedly.

Dustin butted in again. "Let's finish securing the place. We should barricade those doors if we're going to stay here."

He made his way over to one of the large couches in the lobby area. "Help me out," he said, reaching under it.

We teamed up, both grabbing an end of the hefty Chesterfield and lifting it with some difficulty. We dropped it against the oak entrance doors. Riley and Ava pushed over two heavy armchairs, while Dustin and I fetched a bulky entryway table and added it on top for good measure. We stepped back to assess the pileup.

"Probably wouldn't hold them long, but at least it'd buy us time," said Otto.

"Pool now?" I persisted.

Dustin rolled his eyes. "Let's check it out, but eyes open-"

"-guns up. We know. Let's take the stairs," I finished with a laugh.

We followed him to the stairwell door past the elevator hall. The prospect of a pool suddenly fell by the wayside as my heart picked up speed.

The thought of how big this place was, and not knowing what could be around any corner, made me grip my gun tighter as we warily climbed the stairs.

The beat of our footsteps was the only sound until a loud bang stopped us dead in our tracks. We had just passed the fourth floor. Frozen, we listened to the pounding growing more frantic. It was close.

Dustin grabbed the handle of the door leading to the fifth floor's hallway. He pulled it open and quickly aimed his gun past the threshold. Nothing.

We cautiously followed him into the hall, finally spotting a violently shaking door, three rooms down. The sheer aggression told us it was most likely a Mort behind it.

The banging stopped when the floorboards beneath us creaked.

We had fallen behind Dustin now. He stood before the front door. "556. Room 556," he said in a whisper.

I instantly understood what that number meant. *Never go in room 556.*

"Do we just leave it there?" I breathed, barely audibly.

Dustin contemplated this as he removed the magazine from his gun to check his ammo, each bullet more precious than the one before it.

"Not worth the fight. Guess it's been in there a while so it can't have much life left...and fat chance it can break down this door," he said softly, and led us back toward the stairs.

Our pace quickened as we ran up each flight, eventually reaching the pool deck.

We exited the stairwell into a beautifully tiled hallway leading to foggy glass doors. The blue water of the pool beyond welcomed us. With weapons still held in defensive positions, we pushed open the door. Salty air kissed my face, momentarily tricking me into believing life was good.

But the alluring scent did not match the scenery at all. The pool was somewhat murky; swimmable, but not the crystal-clear water I'd had in mind. The maintenance neglect had built up.

The hot tub near the bar area was still occupied. We stepped back, seeing the fully-clothed body a millisecond before the foul smell reached us. It was grotesquely bloated from soaking in the water, a clue that it was not a Mort and had been sitting there a long time. Dustin reached into a towel bin nearby, holding his breath as he ran up to the corpse and threw a white towel over it.

A splash in the pool made us jump and we quickly turned our guns on it. It was Riley. She had jumped in, down to her bra and underwear.

She splashed at us. "Let's try and enjoy this a little, yeah?"

I smiled down at her. "Does the water smell?"

"We've swum in lakes before. I think we'll be fine," she said.

All of us except Dustin stripped down to our underwear, set our guns along the edge of the pool, and dived in. He kept scouring the area with his eyes, seemingly too uncomfortable to let his guard down.

"Dust," I called to him after surfacing from my dive, "there's only one door leading out of here and we're nine stories up. The guns are right here. Relax for a second. You need this."

With one final scan of the deck, he laid his gun down, threw off his clothes and joined us with a cannonball.

The pool was clearly a contemporary addition to the historic building. In modern contrast to the limestone flooring and classic bar counter, the edge of the pool lined up perfectly with the horizon of the ocean below, creating an illusion of a never-ending body of water.

"Reminds you how big our world is, huh?" Otto asked as we swam up to the ocean side of the pool.

A contemplative minute passed before Ava asked, "Do you think it's just as bad all over the world by now?"

That thought sobered us, but her tone was thoughtful, not negative.

"Depends on how much we were able to contain it. I can't imagine it's not happening outside the U.S.," said Otto. Perhaps realizing what that meant, he added, "More people working to find a cure quickly, if that's the case."

Dustin, now apparently loosened up, flicked some water at us. "Why don't we keep things light? We're in a pool at a ten-star hotel, for Christ's sake."

"It only goes up to five, bro," teased Riley. "Alright, Never Have I Ever? Truth or Dare?"

"Dare you to lose the top," I suggested, laughing at her instant scowl.

"Why don't you set the bar?" she asked, then dived under and grabbed at my boxers.

I burst out laughing as she tried to pull them off underwater. Otto and Ava grinned at my discomfort while Dustin dived down to help her. They reappeared holding my underwear and threw it across the pool deck.

"Are you kidding?!" I laughed. "That's not how Truth or Dare works!"

They both howled. Riley unclipped her bra and tossed it to the side.

"Fair?" she asked cheekily.

I shook my head, shrouding myself with both hands despite the cloudy water providing some cover.

"Do you remember that summer we were all skinny dipping in Adam's pool when his parents were away?" asked Riley. "His parents came home early and kicked us out but you couldn't find your shorts-" She started laughing, unable to finish the story.

I finished for her. "Yes...and I had to walk home in my underwear and you guys all roasted me for weeks."

"It was cold out, wasn't it?" she jeered, still giggling.

I splashed her. "Watch it," I threatened, but laughed with her.

"I like hearing old memories," said Otto.

Our rowdiness subsided. I looked out at the waves and my thoughts immediately landed on my childhood trips to this area with my dad.

"My dad used to bring me on trips out here. He'd call them 'dad-days,'" I chuckled. "You see those docks out there?" I pointed into the distance. "We'd fish all along there. Rain or sun, we'd never cancel dad-days."

I was surprised by how lovely that memory was, despite the last images I had of my dad. It made me happy that it was separated from the more recent horrors in my head.

I noticed Dustin getting a little misty-eyed, probably thinking of his own parents. I changed the subject. "Anyway, can someone get my boxers?"

We laughed again. Otto lifted himself out of the water and threw both Riley and me our undergarments.

"What about you, Ava?" he asked. "Any fun memories come to mind?"

She turned a little red. "Hmm." She thought for a long while.

"C'mon, I can think of a hundred with you," I said to her, trying to keep her in this light headspace. "The tarot card lady? The play we got kicked out of? When your boyfriend tried to fight me?"

"Okay, that one I need to hear," Dustin cut in with a laugh.

Ava turned even redder but started giggling. I was so happy to see her smiling.

"Wow, that was a mess...Okay, so, everyone always thinks Tye and I are a thing when they first meet us, we've dealt with it our entire friendship," she started.

"Guilty," Riley said, raising her hand.

"Same," Dustin added.

"See!" Ava exclaimed. "Anyway, I've always been a hopeless romantic, since I was little, but when I started dating toward the end of middle school, I was always choosing the wrong boys that were a disaster from start to finish."

Riley and Otto both shot me a look, probably thinking of Gage, her last prospect. I ignored them.

"The *one* time I found a boy my parents liked, he showed up to my house early for our first real date, while Tye was still there helping me not dress like a loser. Tye was the only boy allowed in my room with the door closed...Needless to say, the boy thought Tye was another guy I was seeing, that he'd caught me in the act. Drama ensued."

We all burst out laughing.

"He tried to fight Tye and even my dad stepped in to explain. Long story short, that boy proved he too was a flop, and Tye and I spent the night eating ice cream with my dad."

"But aren't you glad we did?" I asked, putting my arm around her.

"Yes. And the moral of the story is, I never found a boy who *wasn't* a flop," she laughed. Suddenly, her smile dropped and her voice softened. "Well, until ..."

It was clear that memories of Gage had flooded in. I hugged her, catching Otto's eye over her shoulder.

"I'm fine. Sorry," she said, wiping her face. "'Waterworks,' remember?"

She tried to smile through it, but I knew her heart was broken.

"Hey!" Otto piped up, seemingly trying to lift the mood. He crouched at the edge of the pool, tapping Dustin on the shoulder and running off. "Not it!"

Dustin bolted from the pool, chasing Otto around the bar.

I shouted after them, lifeguard-style: "No running!"

Dustin jumped over the bar and slapped Otto's shoulder. "You're it," he declared.

We all caught on and leapt out of the water, grabbing our guns and running away from Otto into the hallway of floor nine in our wet underwear. We scattered as he ran after us, dripping water all along the halls.

We zigzagged, laughing and taking random turns. I turned a corner and Otto appeared out of nowhere, grabbing my arm.

"Tye's it!" he yelled.

Ava ran by laughing and I sprinted after her.

She quickly went through a nearby door to seek cover. The door slammed shut but I pushed it back open, intent on tagging her.

She didn't react. She was frozen in place with a smile, in shock, as she stood in front of five huge jugs of water and a vending machine. We appeared to have found a staff break room.

"Holy crap, Ava," I said in awe, kneeling down beside the water stash.

Each jug held six gallons of clean water; they were the kind used to refill water dispensers. I looked around and, sure enough, in the corner was an empty water cooler unit.

"Ava? Tye?" I heard Otto calling from the hallway.

"In here!" Ava responded, propping the door open with a chair.

The others filed in. Immediately, their faces lit up.

Dustin ran for the vending machine. "Am I dreaming? Water? Snacks?" he asked, pressing his palms against the glass of the machine.

There wasn't much left but a few bags of chips, pretzels, and cereal bars. A major win nonetheless.

"Stand back," said Dustin.

He used the butt of his gun to hammer at the glass. With a shatter, glass shards sprinkled onto the floor. He tossed each of us a snack.

"Help me lift this," said Otto, clutching one of the jugs.

I grabbed the other side and helped him lift it onto the water dispenser. With the barrel resting on top, I pressed down on the button and a stream of water poured out.

"We have water," I announced.

Riley opened some cabinets and handed out glasses. We filled them generously, clinked them together and drank. I'd almost forgotten what clean, non-boiled water tasted like.

16.

After grabbing our clothes, we headed back downstairs to the lobby, sitting in the lounge area to eat our snacks. Otto walked over to the toppled maid's cart and picked up a few more mint chocolate squares.

"Dessert, anyone?" he asked, tossing his empty chip bag in a trash can near the front desk.

As he bent down to grab the last chocolate, he dug into the pocket of what looked like an apron hanging over the side of the cart. He pulled out a white keycard with the hotel's insignia on it.

"Guys..." he called.

We joined him and Dustin took the card in hand.

"If this belongs to housekeeping, it'll work on all the room doors. A master key," he said.

Were we really going to score back-to-back wins like this? Leaving the warehouse might have been the greatest decision we had made in our young lives.

"Floor plans say the top floor's the executive and presidential suites," said Ava. "Just a light suggestion." She smiled.

We climbed to the eleventh floor.

Out of breath, we opened the stairwell door into the hall on the top floor. There were significantly fewer doors here than in the other hallways.

"Try this room," said Riley, pointing to a silver plaque that read *Presidential Suite.*

With discernible pleasure, Dustin swiped the keycard. Knowing that the power was out, I held my breath, but amazingly the battery powered card reader instantly clicked and beeped. We pushed open the bulky door.

As if we had passed through heaven's gates, the grand room before us was decorated in various shades of white and cream. A round dining table sat under a vintage wagon wheel chandelier. Nearby was a spacious seating area with a hefty couch and plush armchairs, and a small wooden desk with a presidential-looking seat stood under a large window. On either side of the main room were doors to the adjoining rooms.

We filed into one of the bedrooms to find two king-sized beds and a marble bathroom.

"No more holes in the ground," I joked, petting the porcelain toilet.

Otto walked over to the sink and turned the faucet. Only a few meager droplets dripped out. "Don't think the water supply is running…"

"Well, with the master key, we can use a different toilet every day of the week," said Dustin.

Riley flopped onto the downy bed. A fine cloud of dust kicked up into the air. She coughed. "Okay, should've thought of that," she said, waving her hand in front of her face to clear the air. "Still feels like heaven, though."

We all collapsed onto the pillows, the wonderful cushioning pulling us down.

"I'll be here until help comes," Ava said, her face in the pillow.

We lay there silently for a while until, finally, Otto broke out of the spell and got up to check the other room.

He came back a moment later. "So, who's rooming with who? The other room's identical. Two of us will have to share a bed," he said, looking at everyone but Ava.

I sent him a playful look, but didn't comment. "Ava and I'll share a bed," I said instead.

She gave me a high five. Otto turned a little red, and hurried over to the glass doors at the other end of the room.

"Looks like we have a wraparound balcony, too," he said distractedly. We followed him outside to take a look.

The eleventh floor was a great vantage point. We could see most of the street below as well as our Expedition in the distance. This area felt even more empty than around the warehouse.

"Are we doing night watch?" I asked, thinking the balcony would make the best lookout point.

"I think if we're all staying in this suite there's no need for it, for now," Dustin said. "We didn't see any Morts here other than 556, who's locked up. We'll latch and bolt the front door and the doors to our rooms. Hard to sneak up on us all the way up here, even if they figure out what room we're in."

"Well, it'll be nice to sleep through a full night, that's for sure," Riley said.

We gathered in the main living area. Dustin picked up the master keycard.

"I'm gonna search some nearby rooms, see if anything good was left behind. Anyone want to come?" he asked.

Otto picked up his gun. "I got you."

"I'll go too," said Ava, and Otto smiled.

"I've got a splitting headache, I'm gonna stay back," said Riley.

"I'll stay with you," I said. "We should probably keep to most of the rules, at least to always have a buddy with us."

Dustin walked out into the hall with the others. "Alright. We'll be back in thirty. Won't go far," he called back to us. They closed the door behind them.

Riley immediately plopped into an armchair. "I swear I've been getting the worst headaches," she said, rubbing her temples.

I started sorting through the last of our rations and organizing it in the closets to get it out of the way. "You'll rest good tonight. We have beds and no wakeup call," I said.

I glanced over at Riley, who was looking out of the window behind the desk. Anyone else would've interpreted her expression as blank, but I knew her implicitly. It was sad.

I closed the closet door and sat in the armchair across from her. "What's up, Ry?" I asked quietly.

She turned to me. Her eyes had welled up, but she couldn't bring herself to speak. I got up and sat on the arm of her chair, realizing this was more serious than I'd thought. I put my hand on her back, and as if I'd hit a button, she burst into tears.

"It's Hunter. I think it happened so suddenly that I was in shock, but it's catching up to me now," she said through gasping breaths.

Hunter had met Riley before I did. Although she went to a different middle school, they dipped in and out of the same circle and spent a lot of the summer before high school together. Within that time, the seeds that would later both grow and destroy our future friendship were planted.

I met Riley independently, so when I realized Hunter was a mutual friend, the three of us naturally spent a lot of time together. We managed to make a great trio until Riley and I took the next step. I never knew the extent of their pre-high-school history, but it was clear Hunter's hate for me was a direct result of whatever had happened then.

"He just had so much anger toward us. Toward our relationship," Riley continued. "And I feel like it was all because of me-"

"Don't do that. You know you're not responsible for how he reacted to our connection. I didn't even meet you because of him, he was just a mutual."

"I led him on," she said. "I *did*. He told me how he felt and I wasn't honest with him. Even when I was with you, I just liked having someone who looked at me the way he did. It was that needy part of me. I strung him along...I think that's why he had so much resentment toward us. He thought he and I were going to be together in the end, and with you as his friend, it was a hard pill to swallow when he had to watch us have what he wanted. I just wish we could've talked it all out before he was gone. I kept avoiding it, selfishly. I should've apologized for playing with his feelings like that."

She was sobbing heavily now. I was quiet, absorbing this entirely new perspective. I felt like I'd been oblivious all this time, but I was caught in the crossfire. I had always thought Riley was just being herself, unaware of Hunter's one-sided feelings, but she'd engaged in it. It made more sense now.

When I didn't say anything, she kept on.

"I just hate how derailed the three of us got. And I really feel I played a huge part in that. I just wish we got back to what it used to be. What he did with the grenade...He wouldn't have done that if the two of us weren't in that warehouse. He did that for *us*. I feel awful. Under all that anger, he really was a good person."

I hugged her tight. "What's done is done. He can feel us now. He knows in our hearts we care about him. More than words would've ever been able to sort out." I wiped a tear from her cheek. "How about this?" I asked, standing up and making my way over to the desk where a pad and pen lay. "I saw it in a movie once. They had balloons, but we can do our own version. We both write a message to Hunter on this paper. Something we wish we got to say in person. We'll take it out to the balcony and let the wind carry it to him."

She smiled, wiping her nose on her sleeve, then laughed. "He would totally make fun of us if he were here."

"Alright, then we'll make him laugh wherever he is," I said, grinning.

She got up and met me at the desk. I tore a piece of paper from the notepad and handed it to her along with a pen. She went back to her seat, looking pensive.

I sat in the presidential chair, picked up another pen and thought for a moment. Words felt overwhelming; I had so many I'd never got to say. A supercut of all our good times played in my head. When my pen touched the paper, instead of words, I began to draw: a simpler version of the very first drawing Hunter had complimented me on in our sixth-grade art class. The beginning of our friendship.

I got a little teary-eyed as I finished the final details on the sailboat. It symbolized a time when he and I had a pure, unbroken connection. I liked that memory. I knew he would too.

I folded my paper a few minutes after Riley did hers.

"Shall we?" she asked, heading to the balcony doors.

Perhaps serendipitously, the ocean breeze was strong, especially from this height. We held our papers tight, folded in mutual understanding that we were going to keep our last messages to Hunter private. We held them over the balcony's waist-high wall.

"To Hunter. One ..." I prompted.

"Two..."

"Three!" we said together, and let the papers fly.

The two notes soared up and out over the street below, carried by a brisk current. We watched as they were swept around a corner and out of sight.

We stayed watching the sunset for a little longer until we heard the front door click and beep, and the others returned.

I could tell by their energy they had scored something. Riley and I sat on the couch as they wheeled in a suitcase. They were all wearing clean clothes, albeit ill-fitting. It was almost jarring seeing what clothes looked like without grime, blood and dirt on them.

"We found some stuff you guys can change into!" Dustin said, unzipping the suitcase on the floor.

I shot up eagerly, taking a shirt and sweats from Dustin. He tossed an oversized shirt, and jeans to Riley.

She checked the label on the inside of the jeans. "It's actually my size."

"Thank Ava for that," said Dustin.

Riley nodded her way. Ava smiled back.

Otto dumped the contents of a plastic bag onto the table. "Toothpaste and toothbrushes! We found eye masks and earplugs too, but we shouldn't get *too* comfortable. Don't want to let our guard down overnight."

Unpleasantly enough, we had so far been forced to use rags with a little bit of baking soda and water as the extent of our dental hygiene. I'd been over the moon to discover it in the warehouse closet, but toothpaste and toothbrushes were a luxury that had me feeling like Christmas had come early.

"I don't know if I even remember how to use one of these," I joked, picking up the light-blue toothbrush.

"Even though we have the water jugs, we still have to ration for the long run. Let's be smart about it," said Dustin.

Before we knew it, the sun had gone down. All dressed in clean clothes, we drew the curtains and split off into our rooms. Dustin decided to take the couch in the living room, insisting he felt safer there in case anything happened, so Ava and I shared a room with beds of our own, while Otto and Riley slept across the way.

I had to admit, it was comforting to know Dustin was our first line of defense. He was the only one of us who rarely dropped his guard.

I expected to black out the second my head hit the pillow—Ava had—but the smell of detergent on the sheets stirred up so much nostalgia. Not of a specific memory, just a different time. It reminded me of many simple things I had completely forgotten were ever part of daily life.

My mind replayed memories until the thread count of the silky sheets finally sent me into the deepest sleep I'd ever had.

When I woke the next morning, I found Dustin and Ava still asleep. For Dustin that was unusual, but for Ava, I expected nothing less. I grabbed my gun and and headed down to the lobby after reading the note Otto and Riley had left on the dining table.

PAST THE CHECK-IN DESK, DOWN THE HALL, SECOND RIGHT

Following the vague directions, I turned the corner to find them in what looked like a billiard lounge. In the center of the room, surrounded by small cocktail tables and stools, stood a pool table. Colorful solid and striped balls were scattered around the black felt tabletop. Riley didn't notice me, and appeared to be concentrating on purple number four, her cue stick lined up.

"How'd you guys find this?" I asked.

Riley's cue nicked the ball and it barely rolled two inches. "Tye! Oh my god, I *had* that," she grumbled.

They leaned their cues against the table, and Otto unfolded a piece of paper from his back pocket. "Floor plan. Decided to check it out again after we ran into that break room with all the water. Thought there could be more treasures, and lo and behold…" He gestured around the lounge like a showman.

"Between this and the swimming pool, maybe we don't need saving after all," I said with a laugh.

"We found out there's a storage freezer too, on the ninth floor by the pool deck. We scoped it out but it needs an actual key, not a keycard. We searched for a while but couldn't find it," said Otto.

Riley was chalking the tip of her cue. "Where's Dustin?"

I guessed she very much knew where Ava was. "He's still sleeping. I think he hasn't rested properly since he got to the warehouse. He takes on a lot of responsibility. Worn himself out," I said.

I watched Otto take a shot and get two stripes into the pocket.

"Ava loves pool. I'm gonna wake her up and check on Dustin," I said, grabbing the keycard off one of the small tables.

I ran through the lobby and up the stairs two at a time. I knew it was a bad idea to be walking around alone, but this place was so vast, it would be hard to stay together at all times. I excused the oversight since it was the first day, but I always got that *feeling*, like someone was right behind me.

Especially when I reached the fifth-floor landing and heard the bangs coming from room 556 again. I'd expected the demon to drop dead by now. Chills prickled my neck and I quickened my climb.

I made it to the eleventh floor and keycarded the suite door, opening it quietly. Dustin was curled up in a ball, his head buried under some decorative pillows.

"Dustin," I said, shoving him gently. He didn't flinch. I shoved harder, then shook him.

He jumped up, and I found myself staring down the barrel of his gun.

"I would've eaten you by now," I said, twisting my face into an impression of a Mort.

His stare was intense, but then softened. He cracked a smile, lowering his gun. "What time is it?" he asked, looking disoriented.

I pulled open the curtains. "Clock in the lobby says just past ten. We found a billiard room downstairs if you want to join."

I knocked on the bedroom door, then walked in to get Ava. "Rise and shine," I said loudly.

Even after I pulled the shades open and daylight hit her face, she didn't budge. I adopted my Mort impression again and jumped on her bed, pretending to gnaw on her arm.

"You're so annoying," she said, muffled by the pillow.

I burst out laughing. She finally opened her eyes. "I'm up ..."

While Ava got dressed, I went back out to Dustin, only to find him still lying on the couch. His forehead was shiny with sweat.

"You okay?" I asked.

"No, actually. Don't feel so good. Think it's all the junk we ate yesterday," he said, screwing his eyes up.

"Shoot. Want me to get you anything? Water?" I offered.

"What's wrong?" asked Ava, joining me in the living area with her weapon.

"Dustin doesn't feel great. Probably the trash we ate," I repeated.

"Can you open that door, let some air in?" Dustin asked.

Ava propped the balcony door open. "You rest up. We have nowhere to be but here."

"Thanks, guys. I'm just gonna catch a few more Zs," he said, turning over and putting the pillow back over his head.

On the way back down, Ava and I gushed over our new sleeping quarters. It was amazing how a good night's rest could revitalize you.

"Morning," Otto said to Ava as we walked in.

She gave him a hug. "Oh, I love billiards," she said.

Riley put her cue stick down. "Sleep well?" she asked, sounding sincere.

It was probably another effect of being well rested, but I liked that Riley and Ava were being better to each other.

Indeed, Ava actually hugged Riley too. "Breakfast?" she asked, offering Riley a mint chocolate square from her pocket.

"Absolutely," said Riley.

She unwrapped it and tossed it into her mouth, then made a face and spat it back into the wrapper.

"What the ... ? I think it went bad in your pocket," she laughed. "Tastes like metal."

Ava took another one out and eyed it. "I just had like three of these. They taste fine! Here, try another one."

Riley was tonguing her cheek. "Think I lost my appetite, but thank you. All yours."

Otto and I exchanged a smile, noticing their renewed energy for one another.

"What happened to Dust?" Otto asked.

"He's not feeling well. Going to sleep it off," I said, picking up the triangle rack to reset the balls. "Riley and me versus you and Ava?"

Otto smiled. "You're on."

17.

Over the next few days, we fell into a new routine. The Don Lux was a far cry from the brutality of warehouse living. We were sleeping well, staying hydrated, and finding moments to relax over billiards or a swim. Having new clothes and access to basic hygiene changed our energy entirely. At the end of each day, we would sit on the pool deck and watch the sun go down over the glassy ocean. If we weren't careful, we'd almost forget this was only meant to be a pit stop on our way to the border.

The main reason for our delay was Dustin's health. He had gone through a Rolodex of cold symptoms in recent days and even he thought being in a closed car together wasn't a smart idea. After nearly a week of living in ideal circumstances but still no improvement, worry was creeping in. He moved to the executive suite next door as a safety measure.

We'd been periodically taking turns checking in on him. After my latest visit, I sat on the floor of the large ballroom off the lobby corridor with the others, sifting through magazines we'd found around the hotel. Seeing all the ads and editorials that had once seemed glamorous and relevant was bizarre. They were relics of the past now. None of this was important anymore.

Riley held up a page of *À La Mode* magazine to show Ava. "She looks like you."

The ad featured a brunette model sporting a tailored khaki trench coat, posing theatrically.

"Oh, come on. She's stunning," said Ava.

I gave her a look, like she had just insulted my best friend.

"Exactly," Riley and I said together.

"I mean, she's photoshopped and wearing tons of makeup and you *still* look like her," Riley went on.

Otto stood up and took a closer look. "I see it," he said. "You are beautiful, you know."

Ava stood up and imitated the dramatic pose. We all laughed.

"I'll take it," she said sweetly.

Riley and Ava had really warmed up to each other in the past couple days. For the most part, we were all in good spirits, but the change in how they addressed one another was significant, considering they had subtly been avoiding each other during our time at the warehouse.

Both had always been two very important girls in my life, but they were so wildly different. Other than a few special occasions, I'd never hung out with them at the same time. Our warehouse stay had proven to be an even less likely opportunity for bonding, between Gage's games and the environment itself. But now, things were calmer.

Ava gathered a few magazines together. "Maybe we should take one of these to Dustin's room. He must be bored out of his mind."

"He's been sleeping mostly. Doesn't seem like he's getting any better," I said grimly.

I instantly regretted saying that out loud. Ava had been growing more and more sensitive to Dustin's situation. Having watched Gage slowly deteriorate still haunted her.

I tried to cover. "I still think it's just a bad flu. We've been telling him he was going to wear himself out eventually. I think it all caught up to him."

Ava wasn't buying my shift in tone. "It's just hard to see him like that. If we hadn't all been around Gage, I'd think Dustin may have caught it from him...but we all feel fine. It's just giving me flashbacks," she said, emotion heavy in her voice.

Otto put an arm around her. "We should definitely do everything we can to get him well. He's been telling us in detail everything he feels, and so far it doesn't sound anything like what Gage went through. If he caught it airborne I imagine it'll be far milder than having a bite. He can beat this. Flu or not."

Ava started tearing up. She quickly hid her face.

"Ava ... " I said gently. "It's going to be okay."

I hugged her. The others joined in around us.

"I'm sorry this keeps happening. I just miss him...I feel like I made peace with it, but it's the feelings I miss. Just felt good having someone in that way," she said.

Riley stepped back a little, but covered her discomfort with sympathy. "We get it. But we all support you. We got you," she said.

I smiled at her over Ava's shoulder.

"It just feels awkward that I keep breaking down, when you guys lost close friends too-"

"Hey," Otto said, grabbing her by the shoulders and looking her in the eye. "We all mourn differently. It's okay."

"Let's take these to his room," I said, scooping up a couple more magazines.

Ava appeared to appreciate the change of subject. "Maybe we should bring some food and one of those water jugs to his room so he doesn't have to wait on us," she suggested.

"Hope he's happy with pretzels again because that's really all we have left," I said.

"I'm still working on a contraption to get that freezer open on floor nine. Tried picking the lock but it won't budge," said Otto.

We parted ways in the stairwell. Riley and I headed to the break room on floor nine, while Ava and Otto made their way up to Dustin's suite to drop off the magazines.

"Are we going to have to carry the thing all the way upstairs?" Riley asked begrudgingly.

I grabbed a housekeeping cart parked against the wall in the hallway. "We'll use this to get it to the stairwell, but yes. Two flights, we got this," I said, wheeling it down the corridor toward the break room.

After a few seconds of listening to the squeaky wheels, I said, "I like that you and Ava seem to be getting along. What changed?"

"Change of location, change of heart," Riley answered simply.

I knew there was more to it than that. "Do you feel like it's helping you move on from the stuff with Gage? I know you were upset at how it all unfolded..."

We reached the staff room and grabbed a six-gallon jug, then heaved it on top of the cart and started back for the stairs.

"It's been easier to think here, getting away from all of it, and I realized Ava had nothing to do with Gage pulling a shit move like that. Girls always go for each other's throats over the asshole actions of dumb boys...and honestly, hearing how she just liked being loved like that, I see a lot of myself in her. I want her to have closure."

I thought about the milestone this marked. "Well, you're both important to me, so it makes me happy to see it," I said.

We lifted the bulky jug off the cart and placed it at the stairwell door.

"Two flights. You ready-"

I was cut short when Riley grabbed a laundry bag from the cart and puked in it. It happened so out of the blue that I reared back in shock.

"Ry?! What was that?"

She took a seat on the ground and leaned back against the wall.

"Are you okay?" I asked.

She was glistening with sweat. "I'm fine. Just got really nauseous."

My heart jolted. "Now I'm getting worried...You *and* Dust?" I asked, taking an involuntary step away from her. "Dust started off with mild-"

"Tye, I'm not sick," she insisted. "You said you'd always have my back, right?"

My concern ramped up at her tone. "Yeah, of course," I said, bracing myself.

She stood up again, grabbing me by the shoulders. "You love me?"

"Yes! Spit it out, Ry!" I said, almost laughing from the unease.

"I think...I'm pregnant. I'm almost sure."

It was the last thing I'd ever expected to hear. The news hit me like a freight train. I hadn't even thought of problems like this considering the state of things. An accidental pregnancy seemed so out of left field, and almost trivial in comparison to the issues we faced now. I started piecing together the situation. My heart sank lower.

"Gage?" I asked in a whisper, trying not to sound harsh.

"Who else? I hadn't taken my birth control since we left your house, and I wasn't thinking straight...with everything going on."

I remained silent as I processed.

"I really never thought this would happen. I've been getting morning sickness. I puked this morning and a few times this week...I'm a month late, too," she went on.

"What are we going to do?" I asked, more to myself.

"I'm sorry for hiding it, but we need to focus on Dustin right now. And I'm not ready to break the news to Ava. We just got on track and this'll open a whole new can of worms I just can't handle right now," Riley said. "I think it's better we don't say anything until we have to. Who knows where we'll be a few weeks from now?"

A whirlwind of conflicting thoughts spiraled in my head. I was already keeping Gage's treachery hidden from Ava, but now this? I would be the world's worst friend to keep this big a secret from her, but at the same time, Riley was asking for my loyalty too. The issue of Gage's messiness always had me stuck between a rock and a hard place.

My lack of response was evidently starting to worry Riley. "Tye? Promise you won't say anything? At least for now. I need you to promise me."

I wanted nothing more than to delay an inevitable blowout. The choice felt like it wasn't mine to make, anyway. "Yes," I said, swallowing hard. "Promise."

She hugged me.

I used the walk upstairs to gather myself. We plopped the bulky water jug at Dustin's open door and rolled it in, staying at the threshold to keep our distance.

"How you doing, buddy?" I called.

Dustin was sitting up in bed reading one of the magazines, a small bag of pretzels by his side. "Head still pounding and feeling weak, but no worse than yesterday at least."

"We brought you some water to keep in here," Riley said.

"Thank you, guys. Probably a good idea not to visit too often," he said, sadness evident in his tone.

"We miss you, but you're gonna beat this," I said, trying to sound confident.

Though isolation had been his idea, it didn't make it any easier on him. If he was infected, we couldn't risk catching it airborne.

"We're one door down if you need us, just holler," Riley said tenderly.

He nodded limply.

Inside our suite, Otto and Ava were sitting at the round table with the building's floor plan laid out. They were mid-conversation when we walked in.

"There you are. What took so long? Everything okay with Dustin?" Otto asked.

I looked at Riley, who answered quickly.

"Yeah, Tye's string bean arms had trouble carrying that water jug up the stairs. All good. What are you two up to?"

I shot her a death stare as the others laughed.

Ava slid the floor plan across the table as we took a seat. "We're still trying to find the key to that freezer room on floor nine. We thought our best bet was the basement floor where they keep all the supplies and the office rooms, but without power or windows, it's pitch black down there. It's like a labyrinth. We didn't have much luck."

"We're low on food, so getting that freezer open could save us from having to venture out again...*if* there's anything unspoiled in there," said Otto.

"So, how can we help?" I asked.

"Well, the more eyes searching the better," said Ava. "Otto and I think the basement floor's worth another shot. With all of us this time."

A dark basement floor in an abandoned hotel sounded as good to me as chewing glass.

"Gotta do what we gotta do," said Riley, catching my expression.

"There's a maintenance room off the lobby we searched yesterday. We can grab some flashlights and get going," said Otto.

Back when we'd acquired the two SWAT weapons, we shuffled who had which gun. The arrangement we had now left us all with half-full magazine cartridges, but ammo was not in surplus. Every bullet counted.

We arrived at the maintenance room. Otto and Ava already knew where the flashlights were stored. They handed us one each.

"Did we already check for the key in here?" I asked, hoping we wouldn't have to make the basement trip after all.

"First place we checked," said Ava.

I opened a drawer just for my own peace of mind. It was empty. Riley copied me with another.

"It's not here, we looked," repeated Otto.

"What about these?" asked Riley with a smile.

She held up a white envelope with the hotel's insignia on it. Inside were a few keycards.

"Keycards?" Otto mused. "It's a solid key we-"

Riley took one out and showed him the insignia on the front. It was a master keycard, like the one we used to open the suites. Finding more of them was a welcome stroke of luck.

"Oh, nice," said Otto with a grin.

Riley handed one to me and another to Ava. "We should give one to Dustin," she said, pocketing the last one.

With flashlights lit, we climbed down to floor zero, stopping at the stairwell door. Like the dark depths of the ocean, no sunlight from above penetrated the area. As an added bonus, it was freezing cold.

"Ready?" asked Otto.

Despite him and Ava saying they neither saw nor heard anything on their last visit, I couldn't help but tense up as he pushed open the door to the hallway.

We could only see what our beams of light touched. A strange stench hung in the air. Most of this hallway was lined with abandoned office rooms, a ghostly contrast to the frantic workplace this floor must have once been.

"Let's hit different rooms, but don't split up too far," Otto said, making his way to an office that was labeled *Head of Housekeeping.*

I turned the opposite way and passed Riley as she entered an office belonging to the *Front Office Manager.*

A chill climbed up my spine as I fell away from the group. They were only a few doors down, but the darkness was stifling.

I shined my light on the door in front of me. It was slightly open and the odd smell was stronger here than in the hallway. The label read *Hotel Manager.* That seemed like a promising prospect. I readied my weapon and pushed the door open, quickly stepping back and pointing my beam inside to make sure I was alone. I saw nothing but an overturned chair and a messy desk.

I moved inside and started to rummage around the office, opening the drawers and going through the contents carefully. When the drawers came up empty, I shuffled through the papers on the desk, hoping the tiny prize would be buried under the mess.

I stopped on a picture of a woman that caught my eye. There was a handwritten note on the back.

See you soon, Mary. God forgive me.

The words made the hairs on the back of my neck stand up. I turned abruptly, shining my lamp across the room. Nothing. I started to calm myself, but the overturned chair on the floor grabbed my attention again. I slowly raised my flashlight to the ceiling.

I turned away in horror. Hanging by braided bedsheets from the ceiling was a man's body, white as snow.

I bolted from the room. I was about to alert the others, when I reminded myself how vital this key was to our survival. Sounding the alarm over a harmless body would deter us from searching thoroughly.

"You okay?" asked Riley, coming out of a nearby room.

"Yeah," I gulped. "Just hate the dark."

"Then let's make this quick," she said, her eyes mocking.

We spent nearly forty-five minutes looking in every nook and cranny the basement floor had to offer, and still no luck. We reconvened in the lobby.

"Maybe whoever had it left with it?" Riley suggested, looking defeated.

"If we search every possibility like we did that basement, I'll accept that," said Ava. "Last places I can think of that'd make sense would be the ninth floor again, where the freezer room lives, and the small kitchen off the breakfast area. Otto and I saw it was already ransacked for food, but we weren't looking for the key at that point. You guys try the ninth floor again and we'll take the kitchenette."

And with that, we split up again.

Riley and I decided the bar area near the pool would be the best starting point. A bar manager seemed like a logical candidate to carry the freezer room key. I hoped he'd left it somewhere we could find it.

I found myself daydreaming about what my spring break would've been like when I finally turned twenty-one. I'd never pictured a wild and messy kind of adventure, but I did fantasize about drinking all day by a resort pool like this one, getting some sun and meeting some interesting girl visiting town.

My pointless reverie was broken by a new smell assaulting my nose. I covered my face, spotting the bloated dead guy still in the hot tub. Thankfully, Dustin had covered most of him with a towel.

"I swear, if we go through all of this and come up empty-handed..." I said, irritated.

Riley had just finished going through the last drawer behind the bar. "Wonder what happened to him?" she asked, glancing over at the body with disgust.

"Must've worked-"

Riley and I both turned to each other. The realization seemed to hit us simultaneously. The man was wearing a hotel staff uniform. We raised our weapons and approached.

"I'm gonna take the towel off. Fat chance it's a Mort, but cover me anyway," I told Riley.

She aimed her gun at the man's face, standing as far back as she could. I inched closer, visions of all the Morts we'd encountered thus far flashing through my head. I grabbed the furthest edge of the soggy towel and swiftly pulled it off.

BAM!

I fell back, startled by the sudden gunshot.

"What the hell?!" I yelled at Riley.

She stood there, gun smoking. "Oh my god, sorry. I thought it moved," she said, shaking.

My panic shifted to elation when Riley said "Tye!" and pointed at a lanyard hanging from the employee's leathery neck. There at the end of it, next to the newly-made bullet hole, was a single silver key.

I kept my gun up with one hand, and pulled the lanyard off with the other. We both ran for the freezer room. My hand was trembling with excitement; it took me a few tries to fit the key inside the keyhole.

There was a click. We paused for a second, smiling. Riley pecked me on the lips, and we pulled open the heavy metal door.

Inside was colder than the outside, but with no power, the freezer room was more like a storage room. A smell that rivaled even the body outside wafted from the bins along the shelves. Boxes were stacked all over the place. Smaller mini freezers were pushed up against the walls. We began our raid, opening everything.

Some of the bins held rotted produce, but others had bags of white rice and beans.

"Big W," I said, happily taking some of the bags and placing them outside the door.

Riley found a few bottles of alcohol, a jar of martini olives and three cartons of coconut milk.

After sifting through tons of expired foods we added a couple cans of fruit, a jar of escargot and the holy grail of all finds, an entire box of cured meats.

"This was worth the scavenger hunt, one hundred times over!" I exclaimed, adding the box to the sizable pile.

Riley suddenly ran out of the freezer room and plopped down on a sun chair. "Sorry, got really nauseous from the smell," she said, trying to breathe through it.

I walked over and sat next to her. "You want me to get you some water?"

"No, even that sounds terrible right now," she said, closing her eyes.

"What else have you been feeling? Are you one hundred percent sure you're-"

"Tye. Yes. I don't know how to explain it but I just *feel* different. Besides the symptoms, I can just feel that something's changed in me..." She put her head on my shoulder. "I'm so scared." Tears pooled in her eyes.

"Why are you scared?" I asked. "I'm going to take care of you, and we're going to get through this before the baby's even close to coming. Even when you start to show, we'll handle it, one step at a time."

"It's not even all that I'm scared of. I've always had my mind made up that I'd never have a kid...even when I was older and married. And I definitely didn't imagine it happening like this."

I felt the pain behind her words. I recalled a brief talk we'd had about future kids when we were dating, in the way teens did when they fantasized that their high-school fling would be who they spent the rest of their lives with. Riley's maternal instincts appeared to be non-existent after the loss of her sister. She had even gone as far as saying she'd get an abortion if it ever happened, but I suspected that was her way of remaining detached from all things family.

"I just can't imagine loving anyone like I did my sister. This world we live in now? If something ever happened to my kid, if I ever have to go through what my parents went through when they lost her... I couldn't survive that. I'd rather never have a kid."

"Riley...you've already gone through what your parents went through, and you survived it. You're stronger because of it. Losing a sister is as close as it gets. This baby's going to come into your life and you'll see its cute little face and you'll forget all this dark stuff. She's going to be strong like you, funny, beautiful, witty...*stubborn,*" I laughed.

Riley wiped her face, laughing too. "She? You already know?"

"I just assume. You're powerful," I said, trying to hype her up.

We hugged, but quickly broke apart when we heard the hall doors opening. Riley wiped her face hurriedly.

Otto and Ava joined us.

"Sorry we took so-" Ava stopped short, spotting the open freezer door. "You found it?! Where?!"

I pointed at the dead body now sinking to the bottom of the hot tub.

"No way!" said Otto, and started to look through our new groceries.

"That's everything that didn't go bad. Did you see the dried meats? We're finally getting some protein," I said.

They examined each new item in awe, and Ava rubbed her stomach. "Can we eat dinner? I'm starving, and searching through an empty kitchen didn't help at all."

Riley and I helped them bring our stash over to the bar. We sat on the stools and unwrapped a huge cylinder of smoked salami. Otto took out our combat knife from his boot and sliced off the tip, then cut a few generous slivers for each of us. We held them up, touching them together like champagne flutes, and bit down, making sure to chew as slowly as we possibly could.

The salty protein immediately reset our mental stamina. We savored and enjoyed as the sun began to set over the ocean, a pink light reflecting off the pool.

"I'm sorry, but this moment really deserves a toast," I said, hopping down from my chair and going around the bar to grab a shot glass from under the bar top.

I poured out a bit of brown liquid from a bottle we'd found in the freezer room, and held the glass high. Dustin had made us agree that, despite all the alcohol around the hotel, it was probably best to avoid it considering it had no health benefits, but this would be the tiniest celebration. My harmless taste of the spring break that would probably never come. I gulped it down. It burned more than I'd expected.

"I'm going to bring a piece of this to Dustin and update him, but I'll leave that part out," Otto said, mock-disapprovingly. He cut a sizable chunk from the cured meat and put it on a cocktail napkin, then picked up his gun, said "I'll be back," *Terminator*-style, and headed into the hall.

"I can't believe you found the key," said Ava after a moment. "And *there*? Thank god it wasn't me up here. Let me guess, Riley was the brave one?"

"Hey!" I protested. "We were *both* brave. I took the key from around his neck."

Ava and Riley laughed.

"I'm shocked," Ava teased. She cut herself a slice of prosciutto. "Anyway, good work, both of you...but mostly Ry."

She laughed again through tight lips, trying not to spit her food out. They high-fived and I found myself loving the moment. We were all in a good place, and had food on the table, the sound of the waves rolling onto the shoreline below, and a gorgeous sunset dimming around us.

The moment was shattered as Riley abruptly threw up onto the bar stool beside her. Ava jumped up at once, grabbing some napkins. She put her hand gingerly on Riley's back as she spat weakly on the ground.

"You're okay," Ava assured her, and turned to me. "Go get her some water from the break room."

My feet were momentarily glued down. I tried to act natural. "The meat must've not sat right with you," I said, working to sound convincing. "I'll go get you some water, but maybe don't eat any more of that-"

Riley burst into tears.

Ava looked between us both, confused. "Riley, are you okay?" she asked, sounding very worried now.

Riley retreated to the sun chair nearby, her face buried in her hands. Ava watched her cry, clearly perplexed by this sudden turn of events.

"What's going on?" she asked me, in a tone that made me feel like she was accusing me of being the reason Riley was upset.

I shrugged. "Nothing. She's just stressed. I think the food-"

"Tye," Riley cut in. She looked up at me, distress plain on her face. "I can't do this ... "

I held my breath, the pressure suddenly on me.

"Guys, what's going on?" Ava asked again, more sternly.

I took Ava's hand and walked her to the sun chair next to Riley's. We sat down together.

“Ava,” I said, leveling my tone to not sound dramatic, but I had no clue how to deliver my next words without gravitas.

“Ava, I’m pregnant,” Riley divulged, beating me to it.

Ava immediately turned to me, blatantly misunderstanding.

“Gage and I … ” Riley added in a whisper.

She couldn’t look at Ava. I didn’t make eye contact either, expecting Ava to wail in grief, but no sound came. When I eventually looked up at her she was staring down at her hands, her face blank.

When she didn’t speak for an uncomfortable length of time, Riley did. “I know you’re angry, but just hear me out. You don’t have to respond right now, I just need to tell you...I swear on my sister, it was one time and there were no emotions behind it. The anger I had was never toward you, it was from feeling used by him, how he was trying to erase that moment and carry on with you after betraying us. None of it was right. I’ve really gotten to know you properly this last week, without my resentment toward Gage getting in the way. I feel so terrible keeping everything bottled up. I swear, it was a mistake I made at the beginning of all of this and it meant nothing. When you and him got so close, I didn’t want to cause drama...but this...I can’t hide this from you. You don’t deserve that.”

I hadn’t blinked for the entirety of Riley’s confession. My eyes stung from the salty air.

Ava finally looked up from her hands, her face wet. “I’m not mad,” she said. “He told me already...that you guys hooked up early on. And I *was* angry. But it was before I really knew him the way I grew to … ” She began to cry more heavily, and moved closer to Riley. “I know Gage had some demons, and it wasn’t right how he played with your emotions like that, but that doesn’t matter now. This is bigger than that.”

Riley pulled Ava close. I stood up and gave them some space as they cried into each other’s shoulders. Part of me was in complete awe that the reveal I’d dreaded had turned out so differently. The other part of me felt a massive weight lift from my shoulders, a weight I didn’t even realize I had come to bear so intensely. It had troubled me having to keep Gage's secret from my best friend, but it was always to shield her from sadness.

Now, the way my two friends had come together—in a moment I'd always imagined would be dark—had me welling up with happiness.

18.

A couple days had gone by since Riley shared her secret with Ava, and the two of them seemed to have started over anew. I felt a lightness now, knowing that I was no longer caught between being a good friend to one and disloyal to the other.

Although the new energy between them was refreshing, we had yet to share the news with Otto or Dustin. For the time being, it seemed to have fallen by the wayside as Dustin's health had plummeted severely. We rallied to keep him afloat. Throughout the night, we took turns checking on him, giving our night watch an entirely new purpose.

It was during my check-in that I found Dustin drenched in sweat and shivering. It was difficult to watch him from the threshold of his room and not be able to go near him. In some ways, I was thankful it was Dustin of all people, because I didn't believe any of the rest of us could stay as tough as he did. With a little encouragement, he could still pull himself out of bed to get water and food.

Ava and I arrived at the door of a random room on floor six. The door beeped and clicked as she swiped the master keycard over the reader. Inside, the room smelled stale but looked as though no one had stayed in it since it had last been cleaned. The bed was still made and the bathroom was stocked with small soaps and clean towels.

Ava pulled the quilt off the king bed and we both began removing the clean sheets for Dustin; we wanted to take him fresh bedding since he had been bedridden for a week now.

I knew Ava was dealing with a lot: Riley's secret, and being sensitive to Dustin's illness, which was clearly giving her flashbacks to Gage's demise. I wanted to give her some breathing room, but now seemed like a good time to check in with her, being away from the others.

"How are you feeling?" I asked, trying not to sound too parental.

She feigned confusion. "About what?"

I busied myself with another pillowcase as she tried to fold the fitted sheet. "Everything? Just asking what best friends are supposed to ask," I said.

She nodded. "I'm actually doing okay. I'm worried about Dustin, but I feel like this place has given me time to process everything else. And I'm glad Riley told me. A big part of my trauma with Gage was how abruptly he was taken away, and knowing part of him's still around...I don't know, it's strangely comforting."

"I gotta say, I'm really proud of you for handling everything coming at you in the middle of all this."

"Well, it's easier with you here. Thank you," she said with a smile. "And Otto's been really sweet, too. He calms me."

I threw a pillow at her.

"Hey!" she said, throwing one back. "What?"

"*I'm* your only friend!" I teased.

"Maybe he's more than that," she teased back.

I made a dramatic gagging sound and we both laughed.

After gathering the fresh sheets and some clean towels, we headed up to Dustin's room. We approached quietly in case he was sleeping.

Caught off guard, we turned to each other when we heard Dustin's voice coming from behind the door.

"Ava, Otto, Tye, Riley...Ava, Otto, Tye, Riley...Don Lux Hotel..."

He repeated the names several times until Ava knocked lightly.

"Dustin? It's us," she said warily.

"Come in," he called.

Ava scanned the keycard and we pushed open the door.

I half-expected to see someone with him, but it was clear he had been talking to himself.

"Everything okay?" I asked, trying not to look alarmed.

His voice was soft. "Yeah...Were you waiting long?"

"No, we just got here ... but we heard you saying our names," Ava said.

He sat up in bed, still looking weak and sweaty. "I'm just making sure my memory's still there...We know that's one of the symptoms, so it makes me feel better if I'm still sharp."

We knew Dustin wasn't doing well, but his own level of concern was far more intense than we'd realized.

I changed the subject. "Well, we brought you clean sheets. Sorry we can't help you change the bed. Just toss those out the window, I guess."

He gave the most feeble of laughs, and nodded. Ava and I made a neat pile of linens by the doorway.

"Need anything else?" she asked.

"I'm good for now. Thank you, guys," he said faintly, his lips trembling from the chills.

We closed the door gently and headed back to our suite.

"I didn't realize he was that scared," said Ava, fear audible in her tone.

We entered the presidential suite to find Riley and Otto outside on the balcony. The curtains were swaying wildly from a strong draft coming in through the open doors.

"What's up?" I asked, but before they answered, I followed their gaze up to the sky.

Ominous clouds churned over the city. They were the darkest shade of gray, rumbling with thunder.

"It was raining all last night. Thought it'd pass, but looks like a bad storm's coming in," said Otto grimly. "Glad we're not at the warehouse for this one."

We watched for a few moments longer until a heavy veil of rain in the distance finally caught up to our building. We ran inside for shelter. The rain pattered against the glass as we sat around the dining table.

"Group meeting? We need to talk about Dustin," I prompted.

Riley and Otto looked concerned, as if something grave had happened.

"He's fine for now," I continued, "but he's not getting any better and he's starting to get worried...which is worrying us."

"I thought he was convinced it was just a normal flu," said Riley. "Are his symptoms changing?"

"Not yet, but he's had a fever for two nights now and he's starting to get worried that losing his memory comes next...like with Gage," Ava said, uneasy.

Otto ran his hands through his curly hair, looking distressed. "So, we can pretty much assume he has the virus, however mild?"

"We can't know for sure, but it seems likely. I mean, this whole epidemic started with a flu, right? Regardless, we should keep treating it like he does. Help him all we can, but be as safe as possible until he's better...Can you heal after getting infected?" I wondered out loud, swallowing hard.

"Well, he wasn't bit, so if it's like any other virus he should develop antibodies to fight against it. We just have to keep him strong," said Otto.

"I don't think I should be checking on him during the night anymore," said Riley, looking at me to underscore what she meant. "I shouldn't be anywhere near him."

Ava and I traded looks. Riley turned to Otto.

"Otto, I'm going to tell you something Ava and Tye already know. This isn't easy for me to share, but we need to all be on the same page."

Otto looked to me as if to brace himself.

"I'm pregnant...It's Gage's," she said.

Otto seemed to experience whiplash from how abruptly the news was dropped on him. His eyes darted to Ava first, but her face was calm. He looked dazed as he processed all that this news encompassed.

"We talked it out. Everything's okay, but we do need to take care of Riley just as much as Dustin. Her body's going to go through a lot of changes," said Ava with care.

The words seemed to be landing with Otto now. "I'm really sorry if my reaction's hard to read, I just don't know what to say," he confessed.

"Well, I prefer it not being a dramatic response, so thank you," Riley said. "Needed to get that out of the way."

"I was thinking maybe you and Tye can room together now, so I can help Riley out," Ava suggested to Otto kindly.

Riley gave her a surprised but appreciative look.

"Whatever she needs," I said.

"It would be nice having another girl nearby. There's things you two just wouldn't relate to," Riley said with a laugh.

A flash from outside lit up our room, followed by a rolling boom.

"Is this a storm we need to be worried about? We're pretty close to the coast," I said, thinking about the hurricanes we would often get during the summers.

With no access to a weather channel, the usual heads-up couldn't be delivered.

"Let's go to the pool deck and see what we're dealing with," Otto suggested.

We had a much better view from the ninth-floor deck without the skyscrapers in our way. The dark ocean was turbulent, crashing against the shoreline in huge swells. The rain was so heavy now and the sun was completely blocked out by swirling black clouds.

In the short time it took us to get there, the wind had picked up significantly. Another lightning strike ended our storm watch. We quickly ran back into the hallway, soaked, despite staying underneath the pergola.

"That's definitely not just a tropical storm," said Otto, wiping the rain from his temple with his forearm.

I took a step back from the glass doors as they started to shake from the wind. "Well, it is hurricane season-"

CRACK. We jumped back as a sun chair was blown against the glass entryway, leaving a large fracture down the middle.

"Okay, let's not stand near any windows," I said, heading back to the stairwell.

We headed back up the stairs toward the suite.

"Our room has all those glass doors. Maybe we should move for tonight. 'Til the storm passes," Riley said.

"The ballroom doesn't have windows. We could move some mattresses in there for the night," Ava suggested.

"Let's tell Dustin," I said, turning down the hallway toward his room.

"Dustin," I called through the door. "We checked outside. Hurricane's coming in strong. We're going to move some mattresses into the ballroom downstairs to stay away from windows. Meet us down there and we'll find a spot for you somewhere safe."

Faintly, he answered, "Good call. I'll need a minute to gather the energy."

"Sorry, buddy. If we don't see you down there in a little while, we'll come check on you. We'll make you a bed down there," Otto added.

Back in our suite, we rushed to grab our belongings, praying the rattling balcony doors wouldn't give out and destroy our new home. We hurried down to the first floor.

I swiped the master keycard on a few rooms and we dragged a couple queen-sized mattresses down the stairs, across the lobby and into the large ballroom. There was a sense of mischief and fun among us, like kids prepping for an epic sleepover.

We put our mattresses in a circle at one end of the room, and Otto and I moved another to a corner just for Dustin. The room was spacious enough to keep our distance but still have eyes on him.

I'd just returned from a second trip up to the room to fill our canteen when a loud banging sound startled me. The others heard it too, freezing in place as it continued its rhythm.

"Is that 556?" Riley whispered.

"No way. All the way from here? It's way too loud," I answered.

The banging continued consistently. Otto and I raised our guns and cautiously headed toward the lobby. We peered out of the foyer windows, trying to make out the source of the noise through the heavy water streaming down the glass.

Hanging from the third floor of the building across the street, a window washer platform slammed against the façade as the wind tossed it left and right. One of the cables suspending it had snapped and it flailed in the wind like a wild ribbon.

"Not good. That noise is going to attract every Mort in the area," said Otto, visibly stressed.

"We should cover these windows in case any come snooping around here," I said, pulling the cascading drapes over the glass, just in time to block a bright lightning flash from outside. A boom shook the oak front doors.

We met the girls back in the ballroom. They were already sitting in the beds they'd claimed with the comforters pulled up to their laps.

"We're probably gonna have to get used to that banging," I said. "It's a platform strapped to the next building. It's going haywire."

The girls looked relieved.

"Wow, that's a lot better than the things I was imagining," said Riley.

Dustin, dragging his gun and pillow behind him, entered the room. He was out of breath, clearly having exhausted all his energy to get down to us.

"You okay?" Ava called to him.

He nodded weakly, spotting the bed in the corner and plopping down onto it. He pulled the covers over himself.

Otto and I chose our mattresses. Him beside Ava, and me beside Riley. We spoke in a hushed tone to let Dustin rest.

"I swear, if our room gets trashed from this hurricane, I'm giving up. That was our first source of comfort since leaving home," said Riley.

"I was actually going to talk to you guys about that," said Otto. "I don't think we should get too comfortable here. Our goal has to be to make it to the border. That radio message we heard definitely mentioned something about the border. It's the best hope we have right now. I don't want to get complacent."

"We're on the same page," I said. "Once Dustin's better, we can move on."

An eerie howling noise sounded around us. The wind outside rose in intensity. Ava cuddled up against Otto. It was only then that I spotted her holding something in her hand: the dreamcatcher from her car. The way she held it reminded me of a kid and their teddy bear. It was a comfort to her. I smiled, and she noticed.

"Let's say there *is* salvation at the border. What do you think that even looks like?" she pondered.

The question stumped us for a second. I hadn't exactly contemplated that.

"Well, I doubt it'll be very welcoming. Definitely some crazy measures to make sure we're clear of the virus," Otto said.

"And then what? We just get released to a neighboring state? Shipped to another country?" I asked.

"What if they run some weird government tests on us? Keep us in some underground secret lab-"

"Riley ..." I said, lightly touching her arm.

She laughed. "What? Is that really hard to believe after everything our world's become?"

"No, that's why it's giving me the creeps," I said.

Riley pushed back her comforter and started fanning herself with her hand.

"You okay?" Ava asked gingerly.

"Yeah, just got a little hot and queasy all of a sudden," she said. Her forehead was glistening.

"Do you want water?" asked Ava, handing her the canteen.

Riley poured some into her mouth.

"Maybe take a walk, get a little hallway air?" I said, half-joking.

"Actually, yeah. It's a little claustrophobic in here," she said, standing up.

Ava stood up too. "I'll go with her, we won't go far."

They grabbed their guns and the two of them strolled out into the hall. I saw Otto's expression of concern as his eyes followed Ava out of the door.

"You're really in love, huh?" I teased.

He turned red, but didn't answer. Instead, he reached for the canteen and took a swig of water to avoid the subject.

"Well, I'm all for it. We'll be like brothers-in-law one day," I said, messing up his hair.

A loud clap of thunder answered for him.

"What's wrong?" I asked, noticing that his smile had faded.

"I do love her, you know that. I just get a little nervous that she's moving so fast. I don't want her to project her feelings for Gage onto me without realizing. Just hope I'm not just a source of comfort, and she really feels what I feel."

"Hey, I get it, but I don't think that's what it is. You said it yourself, when you guys had night watch together, your connection was undeniable. You felt it. We all see it, and I know she does too."

He smiled, but it faded again. "You know, my mom told my dad that she wasn't meant to be a mother...before she left. She had a lot of stuff from her past she never worked out and she put it all on my dad. I think I get anxious when things start going well with a girl."

Otto's vulnerability caught me by surprise. Although he was sensitive, he always led with his intellectual side. "You're afraid to get too attached?" I asked, trying to handle his openness with care.

"Yeah, pretty much," he said. "I was lucky I got close with my stepmom, but I always think about my mom. Been coming up a lot lately. Wonder if she's out there somewhere."

"When's the last time you saw her?" I asked.

"Other than in photos? When I was four...but I spotted her once, randomly, two years ago at a shopping center ..." he said, his eyes far away.

"You didn't talk?" I asked curiously.

"No, I froze. She didn't recognize me. I was actually with Xander at the time. Bawled my eyes out for an hour straight. Hit me out of nowhere. That's kinda when I realized I had all this stuff built up that I never dealt with."

"Well, Otto, whether your parents are still out there or not, you have a family in us now."

He smiled from ear to ear. "Thanks, Tye. Lucky I got stuck with you through all this," he said, throwing an arm around me.

"Can you two stop being adorable? I'm trying to sleep," Dustin called from across the room.

"You're awake?" said Otto.

"Barely," he answered, sitting up in bed. "Where's the girls?"

"Riley wasn't feelin' so hot. They took a lap," I said.

"Oh no, is she getting sick?" he asked worriedly.

Otto and I exchanged a look, realizing we'd slipped up.

"No, she just got a little claustrophobic," said Otto quickly.

"In this giant-ass room?" Dustin called back through a cough.

"Want some water?" I asked.

"Yes, please," he replied, just before plopping back down onto his pillow.

I was keen to avoid the subject of Riley's pregnancy when Dustin was in this state. Any added stress could break him. "I'm gonna grab a glass for you," I said, standing up.

Riley and Ava passed me on my way out of the ballroom.

"You good?" I asked.

"Yeah, much better," Riley said.

"I'm getting a glass of water for Dustin," I said, heading for the stairwell.

"Hey," Ava called to me. "No going anywhere alone."

"I'll be two seconds. I'm just going up to the first floor and grabbing a cup from the first room I see," I said.

She gave me a stern look. "Hurry back," she said.

In the stairwell, I got the usual surge of adrenaline, feeling like something was right behind me. Being alone in the dark hotel, especially to the soundtrack of a storm, was terrifying at best.

I reached the first floor, ran into the very first room I saw, snatched up a glass from the bar tray, then ran back down to the ballroom. I nearly missed the last step when I heard the distinct banging of the door to room 556, several flights above me.

Back in the ballroom, Ava was pressed up against Otto again, and Riley was playing Tic-Tac-Toe with him on a pad of paper.

"Who's winning?" I asked, trying to cover my racing heart.

"Too soon to say," Riley answered. "But probably Otto. I mean, with that brain? So not fair."

He laughed as he filled in one of the spaces with a circle. I grabbed the canteen and poured Dustin a glass. With my shirt lifted over my nose, I jogged across the room and placed the glass next to his bed.

"Leaving your water here, dude," I said softly.

With difficulty, he turned over and grabbed the glass to take a sip.

After another hour of chitchat over a shared can of fruit, we laid our heads down for the night. The howling wind accompanied the banging from outside, but I was eventually able to zone out. The last thing I heard was Dustin, mumbling in his sleep.

"Ava, Otto, Tye, Riley...Don Lux Hotel."

The first thing I noticed when I started to wake was the morning silence that greeted me. No wind, no banging, no rain drumming against the walls. I turned over in bed and noticed Dustin was the only one there, still asleep across the room. The others were gone. I jumped out of bed and walked out into the lobby.

The three of them were sitting on the Chesterfield pushed up against the entrance door. The curtains on the towering windows were drawn, but it was still hard to see outside. Several fallen tree branches now blocked the view.

"Morning," Otto greeted me.

"Everyone make it through the night okay?" I asked.

"With all that banging, I only fell asleep a few hours ago when the storm passed," Riley said groggily.

"Are we sure it passed? This could be the eye. Very good chance a second wave could come in," said Ava.

"Let's get Dustin up to his room, then we can check the pool deck and get a better idea of what we're dealing with," I suggested.

We gently called out to Dustin from the threshold of the ballroom. After several minutes of tossing and turning, he stirred sluggishly.

"We're going up to the pool deck to assess the damage. Do you wanna head to your room? We'll walk up with you and stay a few paces behind," I said.

Too weak to vocalize his answer, he nodded, grabbed his gun and headed up the stairs ahead of us.

It took us nearly ten minutes to get to floor nine. We made sure to stay one flight below Dustin as he used all his strength to climb back to his room.

"We'll be up in a sec," I said to him as we reached floor nine, and he continued upward.

As soon as we pushed the stairwell door open, we entered a war zone. The glass doors leading to the pool were shattered. Shards were scattered over the corridor floor. We put our stuff down near the elevator, dodged a couple branches and sun chairs and walked out to the deck.

The pool was completely filled with debris and stools from the bar area. The body that was once in the hot tub was now grotesquely hanging off the side of the pergola. Leaves, trash, and soaked towels were strewn over everything.

The gray sky only drizzled now. The ocean was choppy, but in the distance, no darker clouds could be seen coming in. It seemed the worst of the storm had, in fact, moved on.

We looked around at what was an area of luxury only a day before. Now, it was another tableau of what this decaying world had to offer. Even the beach below was covered in all sorts of junk and wreckage.

A softer rumble of thunder echoed in the sky. I listened as the sound seemed to roll in the pit of my stomach.

After a few moments, I realized the sound was lasting unusually long. Otto and I suddenly connected the dots, his widened eyes meeting mine.

It wasn't thunder. It was a plane.

19.

In a blink, Otto dug into his pocket for the makeshift flare and the lighter he always kept on him. The rest of us shouted at the top of our lungs, waving frantically at the plane flying parallel to the coast.

"Over here!!!" I howled, but I knew this scene well.

There was no way they could see us from this far. The flare was our only hope.

With seconds to go before it was too late, Otto lit one end of the cardboard tube and the gunpowder inside blasted out of the top like a firework. A stream of smoke trailed behind the projectile. He wasted no time, grabbing a second flare and igniting it a split second later. Another stream of smoke snaked up to the clouds with a bang that reverberated around the neighboring buildings.

The plane was too far away now to waste a third flare. My throat felt raw from screaming so loud. We watched in silence as the plane disappeared out of sight.

BAM. A gunshot had gone off somewhere far away, leaving an intense echo. We turned to each other, as if to make sure we'd all heard the same thing.

"Someone else letting a flare off?" Riley asked.

Otto and I ran to the edge of the pool deck, scanning the coastline for any sign of another smoke signal. Nothing.

Otto's words were ominous. "That was definitely a gun. Guess we're not alone out here."

"Do you think the plane saw us?" Ava asked, shifting to the more pressing matter.

"Hard to tell," I said.

These aircraft flying over, but never actually helping, really left a bad taste in my mouth. The possibility that these planes could be the source of the virus was even more disturbing. I had to refrain from letting my mind run too wild with conspiracy theories.

"Quick thinking with the flares, Otto. Good job," Riley praised him.

Otto was still looking forlornly up at the sky. Rain fell a little harder now, the residuals of the storm. We ducked back inside the messy hallway.

We headed up to our room, fearing the wind had done away with our balcony doors, but when we entered I was elated to find the room mostly like we left it. Other than a few cracks in the glass, it had survived the hurricane.

Out on the balcony, we pushed aside the overturned patio furniture and peeked over the banister to the city below. The streets were flooded and disheveled. The sight of our banged-up Expedition, still where we had left it, came as a small relief. We would need him again.

I scanned the streets for any movement, half-expecting to see the source of the gunshot, but was relieved to see nobody. No Morts, either.

"I really hope Dustin pulls through soon. We can't stay here much longer. If the streets flood too much it'll be impossible to get the SUV out," said Otto, looking worried.

"We have to give him a few more days. Is there any prep we can get a head start on?" I asked.

"I think we need to get a better idea of the area so I know how far the border is, and what kind of drive we can expect to make. Then we'll know how to prep accordingly," he said.

"There's maps in the brochures behind the check-in counter. Saw some when I grabbed the floor plans," said Ava.

We quickly checked on Dustin first, relieved to find his room had made it through the storm as well. Down at the reception desk, we rummaged through the pamphlets by the concierge station.

We took some back to the suite, where Ava spread out a map on the marble countertop. Otto traced his finger down some red-lined roads until he found the Don Lux Hotel.

"Damn," he said.

"What?" Riley asked.

"We're way further from the border than I thought, but not impossibly far," he said.

"What's that mean?" I asked, glancing at the map and understanding very little.

It looked like a mess of lines and squiggly markings to me. What I would've given for a working smartphone.

Otto took a beat longer, running his finger up the markings, counting to himself. "We're about five hundred miles away from the border," he said, swallowing hard. "But the good news is that it's little more than a seven-hour drive. If we fill the SUV to the top and do the trip in two parts, refilling halfway, we can make good time."

The logistics and anxiety of a trip that grand, and what it would entail, filled my stomach with lead. "So we need to do some major siphoning on the cars out there," I said.

"Yes, but we should definitely wait 'til the flooding goes down. It's hard enough to get away from Morts without it. We need to work smart, not hard," Otto said.

"I think it's good we stay put for a few days regardless. In case the plane did see us and sends help," Ava said, with hope in her eyes.

I had already let the plane prospect go, but I didn't want to negate her optimism.

Riley opened the closet and grabbed the small radio we'd brought from the warehouse. She put it on the table and flicked it on.

… … … … chttt… … … … … … … … … … … … …… … … … … …..chhhhsss hh… … … … … … … … … … … … … … … … … … …… … … … … … … … tsch hh… … … … … … … … … … … … skkkt… t chht… … … … … … … … … … … … … … … … … …… … … … … … … … shh h… … … … … … … … … … … … … … … … … …

After a few minutes of static and fumbling with the dial, she turned it off again. "Worth a shot. We should keep-"

The sound of a car alarm cut Riley off.

We ran back out to the balcony to look at the street below. Down the block, a Mort had just pulled a dead body from an abandoned car and torn a chunk from the cadaver's neck. Even from up here, we feared the Mort would spot us. We ducked behind the banister and spoke quietly.

"That's the first one we've seen around here. I knew that banging would be bad news," said Otto, looking distressed. "The car alarm doesn't help either."

"There's about to be two when that body comes to life." I grimaced. "We need to fortify the lobby. It's the only way in here. As long as we keep this place a fortress, we'll be safe."

We bolted back down to the lobby and began our reinforcements. We closed the curtains and took our mattresses from inside the ballroom to lean against the windows for a sturdy second layer.

It was all hands on deck as we dragged, lifted, slid, and piled up every piece of furniture from the billiard room, the lounge and the breakfast area. Our final touch was the pool table. It took all four of us to drag it down the hallway, flip it on its side and press it snugly against the pileup we'd created.

Exhausted, we plopped onto the lobby floor, reveling in the new fortifications. It felt like a war bunker now. We listened to the rain against the windows and sat in the dark, now that no sunlight could come through.

Riley was pressing her palm into her abdomen.

"What's wrong?" Ava asked.

"I'm good, just cramping. Probably shouldn't have helped with that last one," she said, stretching. "When do we think I should tell Dustin?"

She'd directed her question at me.

"That's your call. My only concern is, I know he'll go into caretaker mode and stress himself out since he can't help right now," I said.

"It just feels so weird that we all know and he doesn't," she said wistfully.

"Out of all of us, I feel like he'd take it the best," Ava said. "I wouldn't be worried."

"Tye, I'd prefer if you told him, whenever it feels comfortable. You're the closest to him," Riley said.

"Whatever you want, I got you," I said.

"You have a name for it yet?" Otto asked.

Ava laughed. "It?"

"What? We don't know," he said with an innocent smile.

"I know, just sounded funny," she teased.

"I think it's a little early to be thinking of names, no?" I asked.

"Every girl has a list of names they've pre-picked for their future babies," Ava stated.

Riley looked uncomfortable. "No names, honestly," she said, and the rest of us could read the room.

Otto considerately changed gears and started telling us about his first invention as a kid, a soda can he rigged with some wires and a lightbulb to conduct enough static that the bulb could light up.

Maybe it was our brief talk of babies, but my dreams were tumultuous throughout the night. All of them centered around Riley's pregnancy going awry. Images of a malnourished baby being born on the sidewalk of some chaotic street as gunshots and alarms blared in the distance; Riley crying over the lifeless body of a stillborn baby; a little girl being swarmed by ravenous Morts.

I felt a hand on my shoulder and bolted upright in bed.

Otto was shaking me from my night terror. The sound of rain brought me back to the moment, reminding me I was truly awake. It was the middle of the night.

"You were tossing and turning. You okay?" he asked gently.

"Yeah. I may need that dreamcatcher for myself though...Nightmares. Sorry I woke you."

"It's okay, I should probably go check on Dustin," he said groggily.

"I'll do it. It'll give me a chance to shake the dreams off," I said, getting up and pulling my pants on.

With a flashlight in hand, I walked quietly down the hall to the executive suite. I scanned my keycard and gently pushed the door open. In the glow of my flashlight beam, I could see Dustin's eyes slowly open.

"I'm good," he answered automatically. "Can't sleep though."

"That makes two of us," I said.

"What's wrong with *you*?"

I hesitated to reveal what was really on my mind, but then recalled Riley's wish to tell Dustin when the time was right. It didn't feel good to keep dodging the subject, and I had Riley's blessing now.

"Had some nightmares...about Riley," I said, trying to word the news with care.

Dustin sat up now, fluffing a pillow behind his neck. "You guys good?" he asked.

"Yeah. She wanted me to tell you some news. We all know and we're staying positive, so I don't want you to stress."

His brows pulled together.

I kept my tone light. "She's pregnant from her thing with Gage. Having all the early symptoms, and she's really anxious about it...but it's all good."

Dustin stared at me with his jaw nearly to the floor. "She's one hundred percent pregnant?"

"Ninety-nine," I said.

Dustin coughed and I backed up to a few steps from the doorway.

"I know you're thinking of every way you can alpha-up and help, but get through this and that'll be the greatest thing you could ever do for us," I assured him.

He laughed weakly.

The next morning, the rain had doubled and as a result, the streets continued to flood. Periodically, we would take to the balcony to make sure our battle-Expedition was holding up. Apart from obvious wear and tear, the only major damage to it was coming from the rain drenching the interior through the broken windows. As long as the cars on the street remained above water, we had hope, but for the time being we were still stuck inside.

When Otto and Ava came back to the suite from room-raiding the third floor, they joined Riley and me in the bathroom where we were brushing our teeth over the sinks. Ava threw a small bag onto the counter.

"She's in rare form," Otto warned.

"They're mushrooms," she boasted. "The hippie kind."

"What the hell?" I sputtered, laughing through a mouthful of toothpaste. I spat into the sink. "Where'd you get those?"

This was so out of character for Ava, and definitely not in my wheelhouse.

"Look, I know we never got into this kind of thing, but can we please, *please* have just one day where we let loose, no drama, no setbacks. Just be messy and normal for *one* day?" Ava implored.

I laughed at how seriously she was pleading even though she was smiling. "Riley can't do these," I said, studying the little brown mushrooms.

"She can still have fun! We need this. Blow off some steam," she pressed.

I looked at Otto, gauging his reaction to this new side of Ava, but surprisingly he seemed to find it charming.

Riley took a swig of water from the glass nearby, spat, then burst out laughing too. "Honestly, even sober, I could use some de-stressing. This'll be so entertaining," she said.

"Break room. Now," Ava said with a smirk.

Cut to, Otto lining up three caps and stems on the break room counter.

"How many times have you done this, Otto?" asked Riley, eyeing the fungi.

"A fair share," he laughed. "It's natural. Prefer this over alcohol any day." He handed one to Ava and one to me. "Maybe you guys should take half since it's your first time. I'm warning you, it tastes terrible."

"Oh god," I said, sniffing it and regretting it.

"How long does it last?" Ava asked.

"Probably a half hour to kick in, then it lasts a few hours."

"We really doing this? Dustin would not approve," I bantered.

Ava popped one in her mouth and immediately made a face while she chewed. Otto and I mirrored her. It tasted like I'd just swallowed a mouthful of dirt.

"That is awful, *wow*," I said, recoiling.

"And now, we wait," Otto laughed.

Just when I thought my mushroom may have been a dud, the effects started kicking in. We'd been sitting on the break room floor chatting for the last twenty minutes, when the three of us exchanged a look of comradery, the psychedelics kicking in simultaneously. We giggled more and more until every ounce of rigidity we had built up over the last few months melted away.

I'd never been one to experiment with drugs, so these sensations were foreign to me, but surprisingly they were mild enough to be pleasant.

The tiled floor beneath us seemed to be moving with a ripple effect. Riley laughed at my face as I stared at it in awe. After a few more minutes, I knew I was way past the threshold of full coherence.

"Should we go swimming?" Ava asked, giggling.

Otto hugged her. "Did you see the pool? That's like swimming in a dumpster."

"Hide-n-seek?" I suggested.

"Yes! Why are we five years old?" Ava wondered.

"I'm obviously going to win since you're all tripping," Riley teased. "This place is huge, though, so how about one of us hides, but three of us search?"

I felt too euphoric to object.

"Not it," the three of them said almost simultaneously.

"What the ... ?!" I yelled.

"Tye, you go hide," Riley prompted. "But no going into rooms or outside to the pool deck. Hallways or lobby only."

I picked up my gun and ran out into the hall as they started counting. "Am I even allowed to have a weapon when I'm inebriated?" I called back to them.

I heard them cackling, then continuing their count.

I pushed open the stairwell door and ran down a few flights. Through my haze, I tripped over several steps, landing on my gun awkwardly as I hit the sixth-floor landing. A sharp pain flared in my ribs. I was sober enough to note how lucky I was that my safety lock was on.

Laughing at my clumsiness, I pushed open the door to the sixth-floor hallway. I stopped for a moment to admire how pretty the burgundy carpet looked before I turned the corner, searching for an alcove in the walls to tuck myself inside. I noticed an open door ahead of me, but remembered Riley said no hiding in rooms, so I turned back from what would've been the perfect hiding place. I passed a few rooms in the opposite direction. Room 553, 552, 551...

I froze. My eyes landed on the number five and a numbing sensation overtook me. I strained my eyes to make sure it was not a mushroom illusion, but I felt sober in an instant. I had mistakenly gotten off on the wrong floor, not properly looking at the number on the stairwell landing. Even in the dim hallway, there was no mistaking that the open door behind me led to room 556.

I turned, slowly, holding my breath for fear that even my breathing would be too loud. My shaking finger clicked the safety off on my gun. As I took a single step back toward the stairwell, the floor creaked. I froze again. I felt a warm sensation trickle down my leg, and realized I had just urinated in my panic. I counted to three in my head. My only chance was to make a run for it. *One. Two. Three-*

I darted toward the stairwell and in the same instant, a Mort turned the corner and grabbed me by the neck, slamming me hard to the floor. The wind was knocked out of me; the drugs in my system turned the room upside down. I stared into the horrifying obsidian eyes of a decaying Mort, pushing my forearm against its body with all my strength. My gun was pinned to the ground under its weight. The creature's mouth got so close to my face, one of its teeth kissed my forehead. My heart pounded with such force it felt like it was pushing against the Mort harder than I was.

I thought momentarily of my friends, several floors above, laughing as they searched for me. If they found me soon, I'd be a bloody carcass. If they found me later, I'd be a Mort.

A tear ran down the side of my face. I was losing my grip. The Mort snarled, its screech piercing my ears. Then, an even louder sound came.

BAM!

Blood sprayed over me and for a moment, I thought it was my own, but then the crazed body on top of me fell limp. I pushed it aside and jumped up, almost losing my balance from the blood rushing to my head.

When my vision came into focus again, I looked up to see not one of my friends, but a stranger. A girl with ebony skin, holding a smoking pistol.

I thought maybe this was another illusion, but she approached me. In the time it took my brain to fully recognize what was going on, I took every bit of her in.

She wore a tattered graphic t-shirt that fit more like an oversized dress. Around her neck was a black choker she must have made herself. Her dreaded hair was fastened in two messy buns on either side of her head. A dirty backpack hung from her shoulder. The septum ring in her nose was the final detail I caught as she walked past me and into room 556.

I heard another gunshot go off and remembered I had a weapon too. I raised it in a defensive position but only the girl came out of the room, still in one piece.

She seemed calm. "There was a body in there. They must've been feeding on each other," she said simply.

I finally found words. "How'd you get in here?"

"Tried the front door but it wouldn't budge. Found a door in the basement and picked the lock."

My mouth fell open.

She spoke again when I didn't say anything. "Are you here alone?"

"No...There's five of us. They're probably looking for me," I said, eyeing the dead Mort on the ground.

"Were you bit?" she asked calmly. She got closer, scanning my neck, face, and arms. Her gaze was unreadable, the hazel eyes in stark contrast to her dark skin.

"No," I said, eventually. I felt the last of the mushroom's effects fall away. "I'm Tye."

She looked into each of my eyes, as if trying to see something deeper than just my name. "Willa," she said.

20.

I thought it would be best to wait in the lobby for the others to find us rather than wander around the maze of hallways searching for them. Willa was drying her locs with a towel as I dabbed at the wet spot on my pants, trying very hard not to draw attention to the result of my panic. She spared me the embarrassment by redoing her two buns, looking into a hanging mirror on the wall.

Maybe it was the fact that we had not met anyone who wasn't hostile since Otto and company, or that she'd just saved my life, but there was a familiarity about her that comforted me. I was mesmerized by her quiet power. Her energy seemed at home in this way of life.

She turned from the mirror suddenly, and I pretended I wasn't staring.

"I'm still stunned you got to me when you did. Where did you come from?" I asked, covering.

She sat on the floor next to me. "I saw the flare when the plane went by. I let off a gunshot so you'd know someone was out here. Haven't seen anyone in weeks, so I went looking for you guys. When I tried to push open the door, it moved a little, but I could feel it was barricaded on the other side so I figured people were staying here. Picked that lock down in the basement and made my way to the stairwell. That's when I heard the Jumbee attacking you."

"The Jum-?"

"Jumbee, sorry," she said, clocking my reaction to the foreign word. "It means demon. It's a nickname my friend and I gave them..." Her expression grew sad. "I met a girl when I left home. She and I stuck together after that, but... she didn't make it."

"I'm sorry. We lost friends too," I said gently. "You can stay here with us if you'd like."

The stairwell door opened and Ava ran across the lobby toward me. I could hear the others sighing with relief behind her.

"Tye! We were looking-"

They stopped in their tracks at the sight of Willa and my bloodied shirt, half-raising their weapons, but seeing that she was calm and sitting close to me, they let their guard down.

"This is Willa," I said.

She waved up at them as they stood around her, looking from her to me and back again.

Riley broke the tense silence. "I'm Riley. This is Ava and Otto...Sorry, can you guys fill us in?"

"She just saved me from 556. The Mort got out," I said. I turned to Willa to clarify. "We call them Morts."

She nodded in understanding. The others looked pale.

"Are you okay?" Ava asked, scanning me for wounds.

"I'm fine. Willa was just telling me how she saw our flare, came looking for us and got here through the basement," I said.

The group had missed so much in such a short time. They sat to join us, looking perplexed, yet fully sobered up.

"Sorry to burst in like this. I've been on my own for some time now," Willa said.

"Don't apologize, we're just surprised. We haven't seen anyone in weeks," Riley said.

"Do you want any water, or food?" Otto asked.

"I'm okay. I have some stuff in here," she said, patting the backpack next to her.

It was only now that I noticed her unique weapon. The pistol had a very long magazine cartridge that protruded from the bottom of the grip.

"What's that?" I asked.

She removed the magazine to show us. "It's a magazine extension. Holds thirty-three rounds instead of the normal fifteen," she explained.

"Wow, how'd you land that?" Otto asked, clearly intrigued by the mechanism.

"Early on, a group of looters were ransacking a gun store. I took advantage. I have two more of these things in my bag," she said proudly. "And already been through a couple."

I was impressed.

"Can you tell us more about you?" Ava asked. "From the beginning, if you don't mind. We've all been with each other since the start so I'm dying to hear someone else's story. Like, what you've been through and seen out there."

She seemed to be picking up the same vibe that I had: Willa was different. She almost seemed like she'd been raised in this chaos, not thrown into it like we had been.

Juxtaposed with her hard exterior, she was softly spoken when she talked. "We've got nothing but time," she said with a hint of a smile, but it quickly faded. "My parents went out of state to visit my brother at college. I stayed behind. Few days later, I wake up to my neighborhood evacuating. I knew if I left home I'd be lost in all the chaos, so I stayed put. Even when my area was filled with undead, I waited. I tried to call my parents but the lines were down. I lasted about two weeks barricaded inside my house before I ran out of supplies and started to accept that there was no way they were going to get back home. One morning, I noticed the undead had moved on. It was my only chance to get out of there. I had no plan, I just packed a bag, got my dad's gun from the attic, and got as far away from there as I could. It wasn't long 'til I met a friend along the way, Imani."

Just like before, her face completely shifted at the mention of her friend.

"We went through a lot. She was by my side for most of my travels, but she didn't make it...After that, there were groups I'd bump into, but none were helpful. Some were hostile, some predatory, some just useless.

Honestly, I was doing better on my own, so I kept it moving. I just bounced from place to place.

"Did you ever find out if your family is okay?" I asked her thoughtfully.

"Not officially, but there's never been a doubt in my mind that my brother and parents are still out there. I've been making my way to the state border to find them. A few weeks back, I had the idea to find a place with a backup generator. I know hospitals have them for when the power goes out. I figured I could maybe catch a news update, something, *anything*, to point me in the right direction-"

"Did you find one?" I asked, unable to contain my excitement at her genius.

"Yes, but it was swarmed with Jumbees—Morts, as you call them. *But*, I did get into City Hall. It had a working generator, and I got a TV working."

Otto looked like he was struggling to keep still. "What did you hear?" he asked, wide-eyed.

"I watched it for hours, but it was just one emergency broadcast on repeat. Basically, the border's set up a checkpoint where they test civilians before allowing them to cross into the safe states. They've isolated a large area from the infection. Refugees can go there to get a vaccine-"

"Holy *shit*!" I blurted, jumping to my feet.

The others stood up too, as in the dark as I was about why Willa wasn't freaking out at the news.

"We heard a broken message over the radio saying something about the border. We've been trying to prepare for a drive there," Otto said.

"You have a car?" Willa asked.

"Kind of. It's out on the street, but it'll need some work before we make the trip. Do you?" Riley asked.

"No, I don't know how to drive," said Willa.

"You can ride with us when we're ready if you want to come to the border with us. We're just waiting for our friend to get better," I said.

"From what?" she asked warily, no doubt concerned she had joined the wrong group.

"We think he may have the virus, but he wasn't bit. We've kept him isolated in another room. We think he can pull through," Otto explained.

"What symptoms does he have?" Willa asked.

"Right now, mainly a bad fever. Small cough. It could just be a normal flu, but we're being safe," I said.

"I passed a pharmacy a few streets over when I was tracking your flare," said Willa. "It's beat up, but not empty. We can make a run to grab some essentials that could help him."

Willa was evidently a lot braver than any of us. We weren't even considering a step outside until the day we decided to leave. Yet the prospect of medicine that could aid Dustin's recovery was highly appealing.

I looked to my friends for their reactions. Ava was looking at Otto. Riley was looking at me.

"How far of a walk?" I asked. "Did you see any Morts on the way here?"

"I'd say about fifteen minutes. And no, not today. The rain actually masks the sound of our footsteps. It'd be best to go before it stops. We're less likely to attract any undead."

"We need Dustin on his feet so we can get the Expedition and get going. It's our biggest priority right now...I think it's worth the risk. I'll go," I said.

"I'll lead the way," said Willa confidently.

"We can't ask you to risk yourself for our friend," Riley said. "You just got here. Rest."

"You guys have a car. If helping your friend means we're one step closer to making it to the border, I'll do whatever we need to do. I'm grateful you guys are letting me tag along," Willa said. "Tye and I can do it. Smaller group would be more stealth."

Adrenaline immediately began pumping inside me. The addition to our team and this impromptu mission had come out of left field.

"We can go out the basement door you came in from," I said, ready to begin.

The rest of the group walked with us down the stairwell. Willa took a flashlight out of her backpack, clicked it on and shined it into the dark halls beyond. A shiver ran through me as the familiar stench met my nose.

"Please be quick, and be safe," Ava said, hugging me.

Riley and Otto joined in, squeezing me. I embraced the warmth of their bodies, savoring it, knowing there was a very real possibility I wouldn't make it back.

I pushed the thought away. I needed to be focused.

"If you see any vitamins, grab them too. Will be good for all of us, but especially Riley," said Otto.

"I'll grab as much as I can," I said.

After a few more hugs, I followed Willa into the dark.

Even in soft daylight, I squinted when we emerged out of the pitch-black basement. Willa tossed the flashlight back into her bag, then raised her pistol in a defensive position. We exited the side door into a sloping alleyway, where a stream of water poured down from the street above. We went against the current, climbing up the ramp until we made it to the sidewalk out front.

We kept our eyes peeled, weapons raised in opposite directions to make sure our surroundings were clear. The storm had thrown debris over every corner of the city but we saw no movement, so we cautiously crossed the street and ducked between two buildings. The rain continued to pelt down and we sloshed through the ankle-deep water, sticking to narrow alleyways rather than the open streets.

"It's a straight shot past the next two blocks. Once we hit the main street I'll have a better idea if it's to the right or left," Willa said, leading the way.

As we trudged on, we stayed close to the buildings to avoid as much of the rain as we could, but it wasn't much use.

Willa spoke quietly. "You and your friends seem very close. What's your story?" she asked. Maybe she was just making conversation, but she sounded genuinely interested.

"Dustin went to school with me," I said. "I dated Riley for a bit, and Otto we met along the way. Ava's like my sister, I grew up with her."

"Must be nice having familiar faces around. I miss my brother a lot."

"I can imagine. You guys were close?" I asked.

"Very. Only person on earth that truly saw me, and understood me. This is his shirt, actually," she said, turning to show me the collegiate graphic on the front of her baggy tee. "I'm not close with my parents. They're in their late fifties. I just feel like they don't get me at all. All we did was fight. My brother's the brains of the family and makes them proud. Me, on the other hand... I hang out with people they like to call 'delinquents.' I'm into art and music, that's my scene."

"Nice. I draw and paint. My mom was an artist," I said enthusiastically.

"Sick. Wish my parents respected me for it. Even though my brother and I were so different, we'd always say we were 'from the same planet.' We just had a crazy connection."

"What was his name?" I asked.

There was pain in her eyes. "Malik."

We arrived at a crossroads. We scanned the area vigilantly before running across to the adjacent alleyway. We were making good progress, still keeping close to the walls.

Willa stopped suddenly and I bumped into her. We had reached the back door of a building and she was staring at an insignia on the metal—a sheriff's star.

"Is this-"

"A police station," she said, dropping her backpack and rummaging through it.

"What are you doing?"

"Jimmying the lock," she said simply, removing a pointed metal pick. "There could be weapons in there. It's worth the detour."

My heart started to race as she stuck the pick into the lock, fidgeting with it aggressively. I wasn't entirely sure this diversion was necessary, but Willa had the presence of a leader, so I followed.

The lock clicked and she pulled the door open.

Inside was dark. Willa took her flashlight out again, crossing her wrists while holding it in one hand and her pistol in the other. The glass on the floor drew my attention to the broken front windows. This place had definitely been paid a prior visit.

Slowly, but with purpose, Willa led me to the back of the station. We passed a *General Office* and *Detectives' Unit,* and wandered until we found a door near the *Interrogation Room* that said *No Unauthorized Personnel Beyond This Point.*

"Looks promising," Willa said, pushing it open.

With the power out, all the electromagnetic doors were unlocked. We found ourselves in a hallway leading to a barred room. At first I thought it was a cell, but as we approached I saw the entryway was labeled *Armory.* The gate was already open. Willa raised her pistol an inch higher and I mirrored her.

We entered the large room to find a collection of boxes and weapon lockers. All of them were open and empty, except for a padlocked closet in the corner, apparently not worth the time of the ransackers who had been here before us.

"Cover your ears," said Willa, aiming her gun at the lock.

I covered them a second before she blasted it to pieces. She shook her head, recoiling from the loud bang, then swung the doors open to reveal a gun rack, with several automatic weapons and pistols resting in their placeholders.

"Willa ..." I said in awe.

She grabbed a duffel bag from under the nearby table, smiling from ear to ear. "Told you it was worth the stop. Hurry up," she said, throwing a few of the bigger guns into the bag.

I grabbed a few of the handguns and boxes of ammo from the bottom shelf. There was enough firepower in this closet to arm a small platoon.

A *crunch* in the distance made us freeze. It sounded like a boot on glass.

"Hide," Willa said, pushing me into the closet and shutting it.

She pushed the duffel bag under the table and ran to the locker opposite me, shutting herself inside. I heard more footsteps now. Someone, or something, was definitely coming.

I tried to even my breathing to stay quiet, but my heartbeat jumped from fast to racing in an instant. I peered through a thin gap in the door to see a man walking into the armory, a revolver in his hand. It was hard to tell his age; he was bearded and unkempt. He scanned the room, clearly having heard the gunshot moments earlier.

He turned toward the closet Willa was hiding in. His hand lifted for the handle. I grasped my gun by my side, but there was no space to raise it.

He swung the locker door open and pointed his gun at Willa. Like me, she couldn't raise her weapon in time.

"Drop it," he croaked in an accent I couldn't place.

She set the gun on the floor.

"Out," he said.

She calmly stepped out, keeping steady eye contact with him.

"This my territory and these my guns," he said sternly. "Who you here with? I heard voices."

"I'm here alone," she said simply.

He pressed the gun to her forehead. "A lot of people been through here. I ain't getting robbed again...None of them were pretty like you, though."

He laughed as his palm grasped her breast. As if his touch had turned her to stone, her expression became vacant. I felt rage build up inside me. I wanted to jump out and shoot, but the way he was angled in front of her, my bullet would have passed through him and hit her. Plus, his gun was still pointed at her head. Any sudden movements and I could lose her.

"Wait," she said, her voice unexpectedly strong.

She put her hand on his cheek.

"At least let me enjoy this."

They were the last words I ever expected to come out of her mouth, but for the briefest moment, she made eye contact with me through the tiny opening in the closet door. I understood.

The man laughed, no doubt intrigued by the prospect of a willing girl. "You been needin' it too, yeah?"

She grabbed at his belt, but he still didn't let his guard down. The gun stayed pressed to her forehead and he kicked her weapon away. It slid across the floor.

"I can't do a good job like this," she said, looking up at his revolver.

He grunted, but then slid his gun across the room to join hers. "Don't try nothin'. I still have fists," he said with a deep chuckle.

My blood boiled. In one fluid motion, Willa dropped to her knees, positioning herself so that she was no longer in my line of fire. My trigger to act, and I didn't hesitate. I barged out of the closet and, with one shot to his back, sprayed the wall with the man's innards.

Willa stepped back, grabbing her gun from the floor. The man was clearly dead, but for good measure, or maybe just on principle, she fired one more round into his head.

"Let's go," she said, tossing more handguns and ammo into the duffel.

She handed me the bag, threw her own backpack over her shoulder and led us back to the alley with her flashlight.

Willa continued down the stormy street as if we'd never stopped. I was impressed by how seamlessly we were working as a team.

"Are you okay?" I asked, feeling extremely protective over her after what I had just witnessed.

"I'm fine," she said, seeming unfazed. "I think the pharmacy's to the left."

We reached the main street, a hub of brick and mortar, all destroyed and pillaged. We remained watchful of our surroundings. The encounter we'd just escaped proved that Morts weren't the only threat out here. Despite the city looking like a ghost town, it was far from it.

We finally reached the local pharmacy. Like its neighbors, the storefront had been demolished. The once automated glass doors were now just a shattered entryway into a disheveled store. As always, we approached with caution, scanning the inside before stepping out of the rain. Fortunately, the store was small enough that we could sweep and clear the place quickly.

Willa pulled the retail security gate down over the entryway. "So no one sneaks up on us this time. I'm sure our gunshots were heard," she said.

"You're sharp, you know that?" I asked with a smile.

She smiled back. Unlike her usual subtle smiles, this one seemed to have more behind it. She wore her survival journey on her face, so seeing her light up in a moment of levity stirred something in me.

Willa kicked at the piles of items around her feet, scanning what was on the floor and what was left on the shelves. She grabbed two small boxes of pills, checking the labels.

"This is fever reducing," she said, throwing it into her backpack.

I mimicked her, throwing in some Vitamin C packets I'd spotted. Anything that boosted the immune system was a keeper.

We foraged through half the store, gathering an assortment of flu medicines and vitamins. Behind the pharmacy counter, the medications were too complicated to risk taking, so we tried to stick to the named brands with simple descriptions. There was no proof that any of what we were bringing back would cure Dustin, but if it at least relieved his symptoms, we could give him a fighting chance.

The rain outside was finally starting to die down and the sound of us sifting through the last of the shelves became our soundtrack.

I caught Willa fiddling with her septum ring. "Did that hurt?" I asked her.

"Don't remember," she said with a dry laugh. "This dude did it for me."

"You trusted someone to do that?! A boyfriend or something?" I asked, rubbing my own nose as I imagined it.

"No, I don't like boys," she said flatly. "Not in that way at least."

I cringed internally. That light had gone out quickly.

"I don't like anyone. Never really have, and don't think I ever will." She turned to me when I didn't respond. "It's not some trauma or anything. I just genuinely don't need it."

She was looking at me, likely expecting a response, but I had completely tuned out of what she was saying. When my hand reached for my gun, Willa turned and spotted what had caught my attention. Beyond the security gate, three Morts wandered the street out front. The group of undead could clearly sense us nearby, but hadn't spotted us inside. They limped aimlessly, seemingly listening for any sign of life.

Barely audible, Willa whispered, "Let's leave through the back."

"*Shit*... The guns," I swore softly.

The duffel bag, with all our new weapons, was still near the entrance.

She raised her pistol at the Morts. "Slowly. I'll cover you," she said.

I got down on all fours and like a timid animal, crawled toward the bag. At the pace I was going it felt like an eternity, but the Morts had still not clocked us. At last, my shaking hand wrapped around one of the straps. Slowly, as patiently as I could, I dragged the bag back toward Willa who was waiting for me by the counter.

I tensed, then froze. Some ammo inside the duffel had shifted and made a clinking sound. One of the Morts turned to face us and I made direct eye contact with it. It broke into a run toward the gate. I sprung up and ran for Willa, who had leapt behind the counter. I joined her, taking the duffel with me.

The gate clattered loudly as the group of monsters slammed into it and started pulling at it violently. It held long enough for us to run to the back exit. Willa pulled open the door, but immediately shut it again and locked it. Pounding could be heard as she backed away.

"There's a ton out there," she said, wide-eyed.

"A ton? We're surrounded?" I asked, panicked.

Willa took one of the extended magazine cartridges out of her bag and slipped it down her boot, obviously preparing for a fight. She cocked the pistol in her hand.

"If we shoot our way out we're going to attract every Mort in the area," I said.

Willa's brain looked to be churning. "That's not a bad idea. I need you to cover me from behind the counter," she said. "Shoot off as many rounds as you can. Hit as many as you can. The sound will attract the others out back to the front. I have a plan from there."

I was about to ask for more details, but Willa was already heading for the front. I followed, ducking behind the counter and cocking my own weapon. With her eyes, she gave me the signal.

I stood and fired a round into a Mort behind the gate. There were already twice as many of them as before and I knew the gate would not hold for long. I fired one shot after the other as Willa combed through the store, clearly looking for something specific. She had announced the plan with confidence so I trusted she knew what she was doing. I continued to provide cover fire.

After a couple minutes, the corner of the security gate began to tear from its support rod. Luckily, Willa had found what she was looking for: a bottle of rubbing alcohol and what looked like a box of tampons. She also grabbed a glass jar of pens off the countertop and dumped them out.

The gate creaked as two more Morts jumped onto it, flailing wildly, desperate for our flesh.

Willa uncapped the alcohol and poured it into the jar. She tore open the tampon box, removed one, unwrapped it and dipped one end into the jar with the string hanging off the side.

"Tye, my bag!" she called to me.

I ducked behind the counter to grab it and threw it to her. The gate was now hanging on by the skin of its teeth. I fired three more rounds, but for every Mort I hit that fell away, another would take its place and more were arriving every second. "Willa!" I urged.

"One second!" she said, rummaging frantically through her belongings.

The horde was overwhelming now. My thoughts landed on my friends back at the hotel. The last hugs they gave me. There was no way we were going to make it back there. I pictured Ava waiting for days for me to come back, and eventually realizing I hadn't made it. Riley's reaction to losing another person so close to her. Otto, and Dustin. The thought of all their faces flooded my heart with sadness. I wasn't going to see them again. All that, for nothing.

"Found it!" Willa yelled.

She held up a small Zippo lighter.

She ran toward the gate, lit the string hanging from the jar and with immense force, smashed the glass over the gate's metal bars. The jar shattered, spraying the Morts with alcohol. The tiny flame on the end of the string sparked the liquid into a firestorm, spreading across the ground at great speed.

Willa fell back as a fiery explosion torched the Morts. The entire storefront went up in smoke, the flames licking their thrashing bodies.

She jumped over the counter and grabbed me by the arm. Weapons raised, we rushed to the back exit where she unlocked the door and flung it open, immediately firing off a few rounds. Two Morts hit the floor, but no others were in the alleyway now.

"Come on!" she yelled.

We raced down the flooded streets back toward the hotel, a massive cloud of black smoke at our backs.

21.

The moon had replaced the sun while we'd been inside. Willa and I ran three blocks through dark, flooded streets without stopping, before collapsing onto the carpeted floor of the hotel lobby. We caught our breath as we listened to the others' frantic footsteps thunder down the stairs.

"We saw you guys from the balcony!" Ava said, sounding relieved.

"We got worried when we saw the smoke. Are you guys okay?" Otto pressed.

In sync, Willa and I both sat up.

"We're good. We got the meds, but barely made it back," I said, still short of breath.

"Do you guys need anything?" Riley asked, concern in her eyes.

"I'm okay," said Willa. "A towel, maybe."

We were like two soldiers who had just returned to the village from war. Ava ran to the lobby restroom while Riley and Otto sat beside us attentively. Ava rejoined us a moment later, handing us both white towels. Willa let down her locs and wrung them gently with the cloth. I dried myself too, feeling my breathing finally settle.

"Unzip that bag," I said to Otto.

He pulled the duffel between us and opened it halfway. "How the F did you snag this?!" he asked, looking mesmerized by the arsenal.

"Sheriff's station not far off. It'd been raided already, but these were overlooked," Willa said.

Riley and Ava pulled out two large automatic weapons, studying them in awe. "*And* ammo?!" Riley exclaimed, spotting the boxes of rounds inside the bag.

"It was Willa's find. We wouldn't have made it back without her," I said.

She smiled softly. "No, it was a team effort."

"I'm just happy you guys are safe. What's with the smoke? Was that you?" Ava asked.

"The pharmacy was surrounded by Morts. We were cornered, badly. Willa made some crazy fire cocktail with stuff inside the store and gave us a window to run. I'm still kind of in shock that we made it out."

"Shit...So there's definitely more than a couple Morts in the area," Otto noted.

"Who knows how many after our purge, but there were far more than I ever thought were around here," I said. "I think enough time's passed that their numbers have increased drastically. More bodies, more hosts. Way more than we were dealing with in the beginning."

"Another reason we need to set out as soon as possible. What medicines did you find?" Otto asked.

Willa unzipped her backpack and started piling up our stash. "A bunch of random anti-inflammatories, Theraflu, Tylenol—all stuff that'll help his fever and symptoms. And I'm sure we could all use some of this," she said, holding up some multivitamins.

"This may have been the most rewarding mission yet. You guys are heroes," Riley raved.

"We should make sure Dustin gets these flu meds in him as soon as possible," Otto said. "He still seemed like he had a mild fever last time we checked on him. I'll take some to his room."

"And you two should get some dry clothes," Ava said. "Otto and I found a few rooms with suitcases while raiding the tenth floor. Why don't we walk up with you and you can meet us back at the suite. We'll put some food out and have a little dinner. Willa hasn't even had time for a proper welcome."

She and Willa exchanged a warm glance.

"I'd like that," Willa said.

Willa and I tried a few rooms with the keycard before finding one with two open suitcases on the bed. Otto and Ava had been there already, and a few items of clothing hung over the sides of the unzipped bags, the aftermath of their digging.

Willa overturned the suitcase onto the bed, going through the pile.

"You gonna tell me where you learned how to be an arsonist?" I asked, lightheartedly.

She looked at me coyly. "All my friends were 'delinquents,' remember?" she teased.

Having saved my life—twice—Willa was already solidifying herself as an integral member of our clan.

She shook out a wrinkled silk slip dress, held it up and shrugged. "It'll do for now," she said, lifting her oversized tee over her head.

Her casualness took me by surprise. I turned away, grabbing a pair of shorts and a long-sleeved shirt, then headed into the bathroom. I closed the door behind me.

It may have been a little overly cautious, but after seeing Willa objectified by the man inside the sheriff's station, I wanted to show as much respect as I could. Even in the short time I had been around her, the eventful experiences we'd shared had connected us in a way that surpassed typical chemistry. It was a tangible bond.

I threw my sopping shirt and jeans to the floor. My naked reflection caught my eye in the mirror. I'd lost so much weight in the last few months that my face was barely recognizable—partly due to the grueling toil my day-to-day had become, but mostly because I hadn't really looked at myself like this in ages.

Just after I'd pulled up my shorts, a mark on my shoulder caught my attention. I looked closer and realized it was two parallel scratches. My body was no stranger to bruises and injuries, so I wouldn't have noticed them had it not been for the strange, pale blue discoloration around them.

The image of gnashing teeth flashed in my mind. The Mort from 556...its fingers digging into my shoulder as it tried to devour my face. *Did it scratch me?* The discoloration didn't look normal.

There was no evidence that a scratch could pass the virus ... But then I remembered the Mort's blood, seeping through my shirt after Willa shot it. I started to sweat, imagining it's infected blood trickling into my open wounds. I felt nauseous. Not from sudden symptoms, but from pure and profound terror. *Am I going to become a Mort? Are my friends infected from being around me? If I tell them, will they turn on me?* The onslaught of worries flooded in. I turned and threw up into the toilet next to me.

"Tye? You okay?" Willa called from the other room.

It took me a long beat to reply. "Yeah, sorry ... Think I'm a bit dehydrated," I said.

I heard more shuffling in the suitcase and was relieved she wasn't pressing the issue.

There was just no way this small scratch meant I was infected...Was it inevitable? Even so, I felt perfectly normal aside from the anxiety that now boiled inside of me. Surely I was a very low risk to my friends. We had been around Dustin before he'd shown symptoms, and none of us showed any signs of infection. Even being around Gage wasn't detrimental because we were careful. I would be careful too. I could monitor myself, like Dustin, testing my memory and taking note of any changes in my body—

A knock snapped me out of my racing thoughts.

"I'm dressed. You good?" Willa called from behind the door.

"Yeah, just tying my shoes, sorry," I said, hurrying to finish dressing.

I took one last look at the festering scratch before putting my arms through the shirt sleeves. I had to keep this to myself while I had no symptoms. I'd already been around my friends since my run-in with 556, so being around them now would make no difference. After a deep breath to gather my composure, I slid the bathroom door open.

"Ready?" I asked.

Thankfully Willa was fixated on tying up her locs, because my expression would have fully given away that I was not okay.

We reached the presidential suite, now in our new clothes. Willa had brought her brother's shirt along to hang dry.

Ava and Riley had set up a small meal of cured meats, fruit, and water for us on the round dining table.

"Wow, I should've broke into a hotel earlier," Willa bantered, looking around the luxurious room as she hung the shirt on a closet door.

"We put all the extra weapons in there," Otto said, pointing to the stretch of closet space.

"You guys want some food?" asked Ava, sitting at the table.

Their voices seemed muffled. I was still battling the fear swelling inside of me.

The rain had finally stopped and our balcony door was slightly ajar, letting in a gentle breeze that kept me from puking again. If I didn't eat something, I would definitely be questioned. I hadn't eaten all day. I sat at the table and picked up a piece of fruit.

Willa joined me. "Are you sure I can have some of this? I have protein bars in my bag," she said.

"Are you kidding? You more than paid your dues. Eat," Riley insisted.

Willa cracked a smile and took a few pieces of dried meat.

"I love your nose ring," said Ava warmly.

"Thank you," she said, touching it habitually. "Bad decision, good result."

The others joined us at the table, picking at the small selection in the middle.

"So, Willa, you were saying you kept it moving, but where did you stay before getting here?" Otto asked.

"All sorts of places. Mostly empty homes, but more often than not they were still occupied...and I don't mean by survivors," said Willa. "It felt safer to keep moving. The thought of getting surrounded by a horde of Jumbees and being trapped inside somewhere was my biggest worry."

"Other than your friend, you never found anyone you knew?" Riley asked. "I'm impressed you were mostly on your own. I can't imagine it."

"It was tough when I lost Imani. It's been a month on my own ..."

"I'm sorry," said Otto, "but you got us now."

"Thank you," Willa answered softly. "I'm telling you, I know my brother and parents are out there. I just feel it in my gut. If I can make it to anywhere near his campus, I'll find them."

I had kept quiet, still mechanically nibbling at the same piece of fruit. My thoughts had wandered to what Willa had said about testing people before letting them through the border. My innards twisted into a knot. *Will I be denied passage through?*

"Willa," I said, my voice slightly cracking from how dry my throat was, "that emergency broadcast said there's a vaccine, right? Did they say anything about how it's being administered? Is everyone getting it?"

"The message was repetitive without much detail, but from what I gathered, everyone gets tested and if you're cleared you're admitted into the safe zone," Willa said. "But it sounded like all refugees require vaccines. Not sure what happens if someone's infected, though. Let's pray your friend really does just have a bad flu."

I swallowed hard.

"What are your thoughts on the virus? Have you learned anything?" Otto asked.

"There's a lot of confusion out there amongst who I ran into, but I have my own theories," said Willa. "Whether it was our own government or another, or a secret major international coup, I'm fully convinced this virus was a ploy that went haywire. There's an ulterior motive somewhere."

A heavy silence filled the room. Going by the minimal details we'd picked up along the way, her theories sounded all too plausible.

"Well, whatever comes after, there's no chance it's worse than this," Riley said.

“We’re almost at the finish line. Let’s finish strong,” Otto urged. He clasped Ava’s hand and held it lovingly.

Ava steered the subject away from conspiracies. “I made the couch into a bed for you,” she said to Willa.

Willa peeked over Ava’s shoulder at the sheets and pillows that had been set up to accommodate her. “Seriously, thank you so much,” she said, rising from the table and hugging her. “You guys are by far the nicest group I’ve met out here.”

“We should probably all take these, now that we got some food in our systems,” said Otto, dumping a handful of vitamins into his palm.

Riley poured us a few glasses and like alcohol shots, we each tossed back a gulp of water with our pills.

My anxiety had subsided briefly, mostly from the sheer exhaustion of the day catching up with me. I stayed seated as my friends hung up their clothes and headed to their assigned spots to sleep. Willa was tying her hair back, watching me with the same penetrating eyes as when we first met. Like she was seeing through me.

“You sure you’re okay?” she asked calmly.

Solely to derail her intuitiveness, I flipped the conversation. “Was thinking about Dustin. I’m going to check on him. Want to come meet him?” I asked.

She nodded.

I knocked lightly and pushed open the door to Dustin’s room. He turned over and sat up, a lot quicker than usual.

“Hey,” he said, looking happy to see me. “The others told me about today. Major win. Thank you.” He looked at Willa, clearly liking what he saw. “I heard a lot about you. I hope it’s all true.”

“Someone feeling better?” she asked.

“Slightly. Crazy after taking the flu meds how quick my fever went down. Finally feel like I got some of my strength back,” he said.

"Well, don't get too ahead of yourself. Keep taking them, but rest. The rain stopped, so we're going to start planning our trip out of here. Contingent on you recovering," I said. My stomach hollowed for a moment, remembering my scratches again. "Well, we just came to say goodnight. We'll check on you again later."

"Thanks, buddy," said Dustin. He nodded to Willa. "Nice meeting you."

"You too. Rest up," she said, and we headed back to our suite.

I lay awake for most of the night, tossing and turning amid turbulent thoughts. After I had checked on Dustin for a second time in the small hours of the morning, I finally felt my body give in and sleep overtook me.

What felt like minutes later, Ava and Otto's distant voices woke me. I opened my eyes, staring at the ceiling. I could hear them talking to Willa outside. For a sliver of time, I had forgotten about the scratches on my shoulder, but the fear came flooding in again when I realized I had kept my shirt on for bed.

My mind was racing now. I knew I'd never get back to sleep, so I decided to join my friends outside.

"Morning," Willa said. She was standing on the balcony with Otto and Ava, wearing her brother's shirt again.

I stepped out to join them. "Morning. What's going on? Where's Riley?" I asked.

"She's still sleeping," said Ava. "We were checking how many cars are left out on the street that we could potentially siphon for the Expedition."

I peered over the edge to the street below. Unlike the congested streets we had passed on our journey over here, there were very few abandoned cars parked out front. "Doesn't look like many."

"The flooding went down a lot, but the clouds are still gray. We need to act fast," said Otto. "There's four close enough to attempt a gas run. We have two empty six-gallon water jugs we can fill. That should get us halfway, assuming there's enough gas in these cars to fill ours."

"We'll need one of those maid carts for maneuvering them once we're out there. They'll get heavy if we can fill them," Ava said.

"Who's we? Who's going?" I asked, conscious of how drained I was after no sleep. I couldn't imagine another stressful mission this soon.

"Otto and I," she said, obviously trying to sound confident. "Riley shouldn't go, and even though Dustin said he feels way better, it's best he stays put."

"I want to go," said Willa.

"You and Tye did your time yesterday. Let us help," Ava said.

"I'm a good shot, and I really want to repay you guys for bringing me in," Willa insisted. "You're the first group I've met that's treated me like a friend. It would mean a lot to me."

Ava looked to me, then back to Willa. We all knew Willa was a lot more self-assured when it came to survival. "Okay. Tye and I can play watchdog and scope things out from up here. We can give you some cover fire from overhead if anything happens."

I scanned the street. It was eerily empty, but the cars were so spread out that it wasn't going to be a quick task. It'd require speed, efficiency and covertness. I was grateful for Willa and Otto's eagerness; I was running on empty. Keeping a bird's-eye view for my friends would be a much safer contribution in my current state.

Ava and I switched out our weapons for heavier automatics. While we all loaded our weapons from our closet arsenal, Riley joined us. We filled her in as she walked with us down to the lobby, where we righted the overturned housekeeping cart and cleared it of its items.

Together we carried it down the steps to the basement door. Willa and Otto placed the plastic jugs onto the cart, clicked on their flashlights and readied their weapons.

"Remember the market raid? First sign of danger, you do whatever it takes to make it back to the hotel, even if it means leaving the gas behind. We'll cover you," Ava said.

"We'll give you a thumbs-up if the coast's clear. If you hear any gunshots, beeline for the hotel. We'll shoot if anything's coming your way," I said.

They nodded in agreement, looking like the mission nerves were finally taking hold. Otto took Ava's hand. I hugged Willa and from the corner of my eye, saw Ava and Otto exchange a kiss.

"Good luck," Riley said, and Otto and Willa disappeared into the dark basement hall with the cart.

We ran back up the stairs two at a time and rushed onto the balcony. Moments later, we saw the cart turn the corner and roll out front of the Don Lux. Otto and Willa did their own assessment of the area before looking up at us for confirmation. I scanned up and down the street, between buildings and down toward the SUV. The area looked deserted. I gave them a thumbs-up and they quickly made their way through the puddles to the nearest car to the hotel.

The green Hyundai's passenger door was ajar. Dried blood spattered the interior. Only days before, a Mort had fed on a cadaver inside the abandoned vehicle, though the remains were nowhere to be seen now. A chilling absence. I rested the barrel of my automatic weapon on the banister, preparing for any sign of an attack.

We watched Otto park the cart and remove the rubber tube from Willa's backpack. She raised her pistol to cover him as he knelt down and began the siphoning. He put one end into his mouth, sucked the air through, and quickly set the tube to pour gasoline from the tank into the empty jug. Almost a minute later, the tube came up empty. The car was nearly dry.

I watched the two of them quickly reset to make their way to the second car, a little further down the street toward the Expedition. Otto pushed the cart as Willa led. He was forced to move slowly so the wheels wouldn't make too loud of a rattle on the bumpy street.

Ava was standing on top of the small patio table for a better visual on them. She kept her weapon raised. Riley was to my left, her weapon fixated in the opposite direction as she squinted to see any distant movement.

Otto inserted the tube into the gas tank of a dented white sedan. Again, Willa scoured the block with her pistol up. This time, the stream of gas was bountiful.

"Thank god," Riley whispered to my right.

Willa and Otto exchanged a quick smile as the jug filled to the top right before the tube gurgled, signaling the tank was depleted. Together they lifted the heavy container onto the cart, then wheeled it toward the third car, an older, rusted orange model.

Riley, Ava, and I shifted our positions as our friends headed further down the street. I was barely blinking and my eyes stung in the ocean breeze. Otto and Willa repeated the same steps and we watched in anticipation as the amber liquid filled up the second jug. From their body language, I could tell they were disappointed. When they removed the tube, I saw that the car had only provided half a jug of gas.

They hurried to the furthest car, a silver van near our Expedition. I could see Otto was nervous by the way he dropped the tube twice as he fed it into the gas tank. It was the furthest he had been from our shelter. Despite Willa scanning their surroundings like a hawk, he was clearly feeling the pressure.

The three of us jumped as the van's car alarm suddenly went off, its blinking lights illuminating Otto and Willa's terrified faces. Otto ripped the tube out of the tank, liquid spilling onto the ground. We tensed our weapons, checking all corners of the block for movement, and right away I saw a Mort scurrying down an alleyway.

"Cover them," I said as I turned my weapon in its direction.

With one eye squeezed shut, I aimed at the moving target. I pulled the trigger, but missed. The Mort stopped at the sound and I fired again, this time hitting it in the chest. I turned back to see Willa and Otto hurrying back to the hotel, but the heavy cart was slowing them down.

Otto grabbed Willa by the arm. "Leave it!" he yelled over the alarm.

"Tye!" Ava said, tapping me hard on the shoulder.

She pointed to further along the street. Several Morts were running into view, revealing themselves from their hidden corners. The three of us fired as they started in the direction of our friends.

With our shots raining down, Otto and Willa knew the situation was dire. They bolted into the alleyway where the basement door was, never looking back at what may be behind them. We ceased fire before running down to the lobby to meet them.

Willa and Otto collapsed onto the lobby floor, wheezing from how quickly they'd darted back. The car alarm continued to scream in the background.

"You're safe. You made it," I said, my hand on Otto's back.

He thumped the ground in frustration. "We were so close!"

"It's not a lost cause," Willa said through heavy breaths. "The cart's not going anywhere."

Ava hugged Otto tightly.

"Guys ..." Riley said quietly.

I looked up. Through the tiniest opening in the curtains, I could see the shadows of movement outside. The swarm of Morts had found our stronghold.

Instinctively we backed toward the stairwell door, but a bang on the glass froze us in place. Either they could sense us inside or they'd seen Willa and Otto run into the building.

"If we run and hide and they get in, they will overtake the hotel and we'll never make it out of here. We need to stand and fight," said Willa, raising her weapon at the glass.

A forceful shove shook the oak doors. They were definitely adamant about making a meal out of us.

"If this is anything like the pharmacy, we need to be ready. Stay here," I said, rushing into the stairwell.

I climbed up to our room as fast as I could. My lungs burned by the time I reached our suite. In a flash, I grabbed the duffel from the closet and refilled it with the surplus ammo and a few more guns. I raced back down the stairs, feeling lightheaded from pushing my endurance into full throttle.

When I returned to the lobby, the oak door was pushed slightly open and some of the furniture we'd used for our barricade had shifted. My friends had ducked behind the check-in desk like it was a war foxhole. I joined them, dropping the duffel bag at their feet.

We set the barrels of our weapons in a line along the marble countertop: five guns, all ready to shoot if the door gave way. It rattled violently. I could only imagine the number of Morts now congregating out front. The sheer strength it would take to push the thick wooden doors in and move our fortifications was immeasurable, yet they were doing just that. Just as the thought crossed my mind, we heard a crack in the glass.

Willa bolted out from behind the desk.

"Willa!" I called, realizing too late I should keep my voice down.

She turned back, and quietly explained, "All our firepower coming from one direction isn't as effective as us splitting their attention."

Her words confirmed my own fear. She had already accepted the Morts were getting in.

She ran to the doorway of the lobby bathroom and tucked herself behind the wall. Otto and Ava hid behind the corner leading to the billiard room.

I stayed behind the counter with Riley who, for the briefest moment, put a hand to her stomach. Looking into her eyes, I could see the fear that these may really be our last moments. I gave her a look she knew well. I was there with her, and we were in this together.

The wood of the entrance door splintered and we could hear ravenous growling. Another creak came from the straining glass as still more weight pushed on it. Finally, it shattered.

Simultaneously, our barrage of bullets ambushed the wave of Morts now pouring into the lobby. Some dropped the moment they entered and others tripped over their bodies. Blood splattered as our trigger fingers refused to let up. The wooden doors cracked open from their hinges and the tower of heavy furniture toppled over. More and more creatures chaotically trampled over one another to get to us.

Adrenaline pulsed through my veins. I had tunnel vision. Aim, fire, repeat. Even with bodies everywhere, the flow of Morts persisted. We were doing well at keeping enough distance between them and us, until my gun clicked, and across the room I heard someone else's do the same. I reached quickly for the bag; Riley continued to fire to buy me time. I reloaded, sloppily dropping a few bullets to the floor. I grabbed a box and threw them to Otto.

A Mort reached its arm over the counter and grabbed me. Riley shot it in the face, point blank. I resumed my stance and returned to firing. Otto joined in a moment later.

Another Mort made it to the bathroom door a fraction of a second before Willa, with a fresh magazine, buried two bullets in the monster's chin and forehead.

"Shit, I'm empty," a voice said to my left.

I turned and saw a very pretty girl fumbling through a bag of weapons on the ground. She threw her gun to the side and picked up a handgun, then continued firing.

"Tye! What are you doing?!" she yelled.

It was Riley. The pretty girl was Riley. How could I have forgotten *Riley*?

I continued to fire aimlessly. I felt a chill spread throughout my body, realizing I had just suffered a highly concerning malfunction.

Two Morts made it around the desk, forcing Riley and me to jump ship and make a run for the bathroom. We stopped next to Willa, who had just shot down two more.

Otto and Ava had no choice but to retreat behind the overturned pool table that had fallen away from the entrance. It was only a matter of seconds before they too were out of ammo. Making a run for the duffel bag was out of the question with Morts filling every inch of the lobby.

I was still dazed from my memory glitch. I knew that was more than just a blackout...It had to have been my first sign of infection.

"Otto, Ava! Get over here!" Riley called, her words snapping me back to the moment. She must have also realized the others' ammo situation was getting perilous.

The pair shot through a handful of Morts and made it into the bathroom. Willa slammed the door shut and we worked together to move the heavy vanity from under the sink to up against the door, then sat with our backs against it for added support. The door jolted forcefully.

"We're trapped!" Otto said, sounding utterly defeated.

The undead were scratching and hammering at the door. A sharp pain pierced my spine as the vanity convulsed. Impulsively, I looked to Willa. She had saved me twice from near death so far. The blank look on her face was all I needed to know that this time, she was truly at a loss. Like us, she'd felt so close to finally reaching salvation. We'd escaped the brink of death so many times, but it had never felt this hopeless. In all the bedlam we'd endured, I recalled times where I'd felt this level of fear and desperation, but never had I felt all hope was lost...until now.

The door shuddered again.

Ava was crying into Otto's shoulder. "What do we do-"

BAM. BAM. BAM. BAM. BAM.

A hailstorm of shots sounded in the distance and the pressure on the door eased.

BAM. BAM. BAM. BAM. BAM. BAM.

There was more growling, but further away from the bathroom now. Collectively, we jumped to our feet. Willa was the first to squeeze past the vanity and open the door, her gun raised. The rest of us followed.

At the threshold of the stairwell door stood Dustin, a piece of fabric wrapped around his face like an old western cowboy. He held a smoking assault rifle.

He had given us a window to break free from our corner, but there was no time to celebrate. Though the heaviest wave had passed, more undead were trickling in.

We jumped back into our offensive positions, reloading from the ammo supply and spreading out, firing from different corners of the lobby. Little by little, the invasion dwindled. We regained control and eventually only a single Mort waded in, toppling over the blanket of dead bodies. With one final round to the head, Dustin disposed of it. We held our positions, waiting to see if any more would come, and a long beat passed before we finally lowered our weapons.

The battle was over. Even the car alarm had ceased.

The lobby was now the scene of a total bloodbath. Glass, furniture and nearly fifty bodies littered the once luxurious space. We ran toward Dustin who sat with his back against the wall, visibly exhausted.

I wanted to hug him in gratitude but his mask was a sure indication that, although he felt better, he still considered himself a risk.

"Sorry I didn't get here sooner. Took a lot out of me to get down that many steps," he said.

"If perfect timing could be defined, that was it," said Otto.

"How are you feeling?" Riley asked him.

"Still weak, but I don't feel like I have a fever and I haven't coughed since the first pill I took," said Dustin. "The meds really brought me back. Thanks, guys."

"We're glad you're back," Ava said.

I realized I hadn't yet greeted Dustin. My mind was still processing his bounce back and picturing my own decline, sooner or later. "Think you have enough energy to get to the SUV? The hotel isn't secure anymore. We need to go," I said.

"Today? What's with you and impulsive departures?" Dustin joked.

"If we retrieve the gas on the way to the Expedition, I'll only need a few minutes to refill the tank. We'll have to stop on our way to the border to siphon more cars, but we got enough to get us going," said Otto. "Anyone have a reason why we shouldn't get on the road quick?"

No one did.

"With all these bodies around, there's no chance others won't show," Ava said, grimacing in the direction of the nearest corpse. "The sooner we leave the better."

We started gathering the bare necessities, repacking our weapon supply, stashing our last rations of food, and lugging down a jug of water we hadn't opened yet. A half hour later, we reconvened in the lobby.

Ava handed us all a piece of fabric. "I made these for us from pillowcases. Who knows if it's foolproof, but Dustin had the right idea. Better safe than sorry if we're going to be sharing a car," she said.

As my friends each tied a torn cloth around their face, I secured mine with some relief. If Dustin could be around them with face coverings, then my minor scratch would be no different.

But although the masks were a small comfort, I still couldn't fully shake the overwhelming guilt of my secret.

22.

We decided to watch one final sunset from the beachfront as an impromptu parting ceremony. We walked barefooted on the wet sand, absorbing the nostalgic energy of a calm, vast ocean. The water reflected a vivid pink from the sky above as the waves gently rolled up to meet our toes. We didn't know what was in store with our journey to the border; this could be either the first of many peaceful moments to come, or the last one we ever had.

"I haven't felt the sand and sea since last time I went surfing," said Dustin, wistfully.

"Should we go in?" Ava asked with a smile. "We could all use a bath!"

Answering without words, Dustin stripped off all but his mask and boxers and ran into the water. Ava and Otto copied him.

"Shoot, I just stepped on a shell!" Otto said, laughing and holding his foot.

Riley rolled up her pants and trotted into the shallows. It wasn't long before they were all splashing each other and roughhousing. Memories of the warehouse and the first time it had rained came back to me. I thought about how much Xander, Gage and Hunter would have loved to be here, feeling full of hope that salvation could potentially be one final drive away.

"You going in?" I asked Willa next to me.

"In a sec. Just taking it all in," she said, staring out at the horizon. "You know, I think the last family outing I had was to a beach like this, the summer before my brother graduated."

"I hope you find them, Willa. I want that for you."

She gave me her signature subtle smile. "I do too," she said. "I keep thinking, if I'd only gone with them to visit my brother...I didn't go because all me and my parents ever did was fight. I always felt like a disappointment to them in comparison to Malik, but I'd take back so much of what I said to them. I wish they knew how much I regret all those silly arguments."

"You'll tell them yourself soon," I said encouragingly.

With a hopeful nod, she stood up and threw off her clothes, diving into the water and coming up again like a spellbinding siren.

"Tye, come in!" Dustin called to me.

I was about to do so, when I remembered the scratches on my shoulder. I hadn't even looked at them since the previous day. It could be twice as bad as I remembered.

"The water's freezing. I'm gonna keep watching the sunset," I replied.

"Alright stinky!" he called out with a laugh.

As the others swam and splashed around, Riley came out of the water and joined me. "How are you doing?" she asked, taking a seat on the sand. "I feel like you're always making sure we're okay but we forget to ask you."

The whirlpool of anxiety churned within me. She could never imagine what I'd been going through in the last twenty-four hours, battling my intense loyalty to my friends with logical justifications about why my secret should be kept to myself. We were at the homestretch. I had told myself that no symptoms meant low risk, but I had, albeit briefly, experienced loss of memory, which we already knew was a sure sign of turning.

The tremendous guilt was infinitesimal compared to the fear of losing my group after everything we'd endured. I kept feeling this major panic that they would abandon me if they found out I was infected. A life alone in this warzone would be torture.

More justifications pushed back on my worries. *We're all wearing face masks and they're heavily armed. If I start to turn, I'll be no match for them. It'll be over before I know it.*

"I'm good," I said, hoping Riley wouldn't think anything of my slowness in responding. "We should get going before anything else gets in the way."

She stood up and grabbed my wrist, pulling me to my feet. "Alright, naked mole rats, let's get back on track," she called to the others.

They came ashore, drying off with scattered beach towels left on the sand. They quickly dressed and with one last glance at the dim orange glow beyond the horizon, we congregated in the hotel lobby for departure.

Everything we owned was collated outside of the oak lobby doors. We tiptoed over the sea of dead bodies and shuffled along the valet driveway, raising our weapons in different directions to cover all bases.

The maid's cart holding the two containers of gas was still ditched halfway down the street toward our SUV. I couldn't imagine more Morts in the area after the surge we'd witnessed, but anything was possible. Staying on high alert was still crucial.

In formation, we started along the street, moving swiftly but silently. There was no time to look back and get sentimental over the Don Lux. We needed to have tunnel vision on our goal.

The pungent smell of gasoline carried on the ocean breeze. Otto took hold of the cart without missing a beat, wheeling it along as we advanced. My heart fluttered as we approached the Expedition.

Otto spared no time in funneling the tube inside the jug. In reverse this time, he sucked the gas through until it poured into the Expedition's tank.

Like a pride of lions protecting their young, we surrounded Otto with weapons poised. I surveyed the dark alleyways and side streets for any threats. Minutes passed before both of the repurposed containers ran dry and the SUV was fueled and ready to go.

"Done," Otto confirmed, taking out the car keys.

The trunk popped open and we loaded the car in a flash. Putting the empty jugs in last, we closed the trunk and jumped into our seats. Otto was navigating, so he sat in the passenger seat with Dustin driving. Willa and I took the middle row, and Ava and Riley took the back.

Sitting in the Expedition again was like reconnecting with an old friend. It had been with us through all our pivotal moments. Otto's revisions had proven to be worthwhile. The seats were still soaked, and the damage to the outside was significant, but otherwise it provided us a sense of protection.

The engine coughed, then roared to life. Even through my face covering I could smell the gasoline fumes. With a last glance at our surroundings, we pulled away.

As we passed the strip of buildings, I wondered if this part of town would ever recover. Ten, twenty, thirty years from now, would life ever return to how we once knew it? I thought about Riley's kid and if they'd ever have family outings to the beach like Willa, or me with my dad.

Daydreams of my parents and the old world played in my head like a supercut. I thought about some of my friends' families. Riley and Otto's parents could still be out there somewhere, and hopefully Willa's. I remembered my own distant family members, none of them as close to me as my parents, but I wondered if I'd see any of them on the other side of all this.

We drove cautiously, passing parts of town we hadn't yet seen. Main streets that were once bustling with shops and restaurants had been stripped to the bones by desperate vagabonds. Anything still unscathed had been turned to ruin by the hurricane that pummeled through. Some areas were still flooded.

Each time we drove by clusters of abandoned cars, I couldn't help but wonder where those people were now. What were their stories? It gave me the same odd feeling I'd had when I saw the sea of tombstones at the graveyard where my grandfather was buried. Like those stone monuments, each vehicle represented someone's lost life.

I felt queasy thinking about death. Although I had seen many people close to me pass, I myself was feeling very mortal knowing that I was infected. I kept counting to one hundred over and over again in my head to test my memory. I recited the names of artists I'd studied and the titles of their most famous works. I said the names Xander had given to me several times over. *Beckett and Parker Taylor, Beckett and Parker Taylor.* It seemed my head was still clear, but the thought of another random memory failure was grim.

In the second hour of our drive, we passed a dense suburban area and saw numerous Morts wandering the neighborhoods. The presence of damaged military vehicles shed light on more of the early attempts to control the outbreak. Clearly, the forces they'd sent in weren't enough. I was angry to know our country was one of the most powerful in the world and mere scraps had been sent in to help its own people. An initial wave to show initiative, then nothing.

Hour three of our drive presented us with multiple reroutes which took more of our precious gas than we would have liked. Dustin and Otto worked tirelessly to find alternate routes to the border that would incur the least mileage.

Even now, as we drove along open roads in the middle of nowhere, we spotted Morts. One in particular caught my attention. It looked like it was once an older woman. It was wearing a nightdress and walking aimlessly down the barren road. Dustin drove past it quickly, but I felt a sadness within me. It was the first time I had looked at any of the creatures with empathy. Humankind had many different beliefs about what happens when you die, but I don't think anyone could picture such a hellish existence. If memory loss being a symptom was any indication, I was at least comforted by the thought that, when one did turn, they knew nothing of what their life was before. Maybe it was just a void as far as their previous consciousness went. If I turned, I didn't want to be aware of what I was.

Somewhere deep in thought, I drifted to sleep huddled against the car door.

It was Willa who woke me sometime later with a gentle shake of my shoulder. "Hey, we hit empty so Otto pulled into a lot," she said.

It was dark without street lamps, but I could tell we were still in one of those in-between towns that no one ever visited and locals never left. The parking lot was off a boating canal that ran through swamplands and as far as I could see, there was nothing else in any direction for miles. The handful of parked cars abandoned in their spaces meant filling up on gas would be easy pickings. A welcome convenience.

Dustin and Willa took charge and approached the vehicles with their guns up, checking to make sure they were in fact empty.

Ava and Otto decanted some water from the jug to fill up the canteen. They passed it around, everyone understanding to pour the stream into their mouths rather than touch their lips to it. Willa took a small silver bar out of her backpack.

"What's that?" Otto asked.

"It's a magnesium fire starter," she said. "If we find something to burn we can start a little bonfire. Warmth and light."

"I'll check in some of these cars," Dustin said heading for the parking spots along the canal.

"You got everything in that bag, don't you?" I asked Willa.

She laughed. "Just about. You guys want some protein bars?"

"Yes please," Riley said. "Eating for two."

Most of us laughed, but Willa looked confused for a moment. I realized that Willa hadn't been filled in, but judging by the change in her expression she seemed to pick up on the context clues.

Dustin came back carrying some car manuals, newspaper and an old phone book. He plopped it a few feet away from the car. Willa knelt beside the pile and scraped some magnesium flakes over the pages, then turned the small bar over and struck the rough side. It sparked a few times, and the heap set ablaze.

"Let there be light," Willa said.

Dustin sat on the asphalt, coughing slightly behind his face covering.

"How you feeling?" I asked him, taking a seat by the fire.

"Energy's back. Just still feeling a little off. Not sure if it's from the cocktail of pills I'm mixing or my flu," he said with a little laugh.

"You saved our asses today," Riley said, sitting down as Otto and Ava joined too.

"You have no idea how good it felt to be up and running again, and to be able to help you guys. You all saved me. And you didn't give up on me," he said, looking serious. "Being isolated in that room...it really changed me. I went from nonstop chaos and survival to sitting still and having constant quiet. Constant time to hear all my thoughts, and I gotta tell you, it got dark."

Dustin got choked up. Ava reached out as if to put her hand on his back, but refrained.

"It was tough facing all the memories of my parents, my old life, my old friends," he went on after a moment. "And I was so scared I was going to turn on you guys. I really thought about ending it ... so you guys wouldn't have to deal with me if things turned bad, so there was no chance I could hurt you. But you guys never left me alone for long, checking on me and caring for me. That's what gave me the strength to fight on. You guys weren't giving up on me, so neither was I."

For a moment the only sound was the cicadas singing from the marshlands. Unseen by the others, I wiped away a tear that had escaped my eye. I felt Dustin's words in ways the others could never guess.

"We're glad you're back, Dustin. We missed you a lot," Otto said.

He smiled, running a hand through his hair. "Love you guys."

"We love you too, Dust," Ava said.

We took a moment to devour the protein bars Willa had passed out. I looked up at the stars, silently taking in the glittery galaxy. With no light throughout the state and not a cloud in the sky, I had never seen the stars quite like this. Similarly to when I'd looked out at the ocean, the vastness of space was humbling...powerful.

We lay back, and had a quiet hour of reflection.

It was only when Dustin yawned audibly that I realized the others were dozing off too.

"We doing night watch?" I asked. "I napped on the way here so I can go first."

"Yeah, we should," said Dustin. "Let's keep the buddy system, though."

"I'll stay with him," said Ava, sitting up from cuddling with Otto.

"We'll fill up in the morning then?" he suggested.

"First thing," I agreed.

The group shuffled back to the car as Ava moved closer to me.

"Should probably get some more stuff to burn," I said, poking at the smoldering embers. I felt the need to distract myself from what was really on my mind before it came pouring out. Ava had always been the easiest to talk to, but the hardest to lie to.

We strolled over to the grassy area and began picking up anything dry that could serve as tinder. My reticence was quickly noticed.

"You excited to reach the border tomorrow?" she asked, but I could see she was masking her concern.

"I don't know if excited's the right word. More like anxious."

Ava nodded. "I get it. We don't really know what awaits, but any hope's better than none."

We walked back to the pile of embers next to the car and tossed in our haul of sticks and some flammable trash we found littered around. They caught fire and we sat before the flames once again.

"Tye," Ava began.

"Yeah?"

"I'm really happy you're here with me through all this. I don't think I would've made it this far with anyone else," she said.

I smiled a real smile for the first time in days. "We've been through a lot, huh? Even before all this."

"It all feels like a lifetime ago. I guess it is, now," she said, the last part almost to herself. "Thank you for being a good friend."

I scooted closer to her with the intention to hug her, but held back. Instead, I looked her in the eyes and delivered my words with the same energy as an embrace.

"Whatever happens tomorrow and beyond, we're family and I'm here for you," I said.

"Back at you," she said warmly.

It tore at my heartstrings to know deep down that my fate was completely up in the air. I still had no idea what would happen to me if my infection was discovered...either by my friends, or at the border.

We spent an hour poking at the fire and recalling funny memories from middle and high school. We laughed until our stomachs were sore and our eyes burned from fatigue.

When it was time, I walked up to the driver-side window and tapped lightly on the cracked glass. Dustin, whose seat was all the way reclined, sat up, shaking off the sleep.

"I'm up, I'm up," he said, grabbing his gun from beside him and hopping down from the SUV. "Any trouble?"

"Nope, crickets," I said.

"Good."

Otto stepped out of the car, rubbing his eyes. "My turn?" he asked groggily.

"You're up," I said.

He kissed Ava quickly as she passed him.

"Goodnight," she said, and we both got into the car to take our window of sleep.

Willa and Riley appeared to be out for the count. I could faintly hear Otto and Dustin chatting by the fire as I reclined my seat and closed my eyes.

I thought sleep would come rapidly, but the suspense over what was to come crept back in. I tossed and turned for a half hour until I gave up.

"Ava," I whispered, "you awake?"

I could hear her heavy breathing from the backseat.

"I am," Riley replied instead.

I flipped around to see her eyes were open. "Why are you awake?" I asked quietly.

"Just the anticipation. That we might actually make it out of this," she said.

"Sooner we sleep the sooner it'll be tomorrow," I said, trying to make light of it. I noticed her eyes looked glossy. "Ry, were you crying?"

She wiped her eyes automatically. "For a sec. Otto and I had a moment. We were talking about how our parents might still be alive, which led to him sharing some stuff about his birth mom, and...something just clicked. For the first time, I really feel excited about having this baby," she said, and tears came again. "I'm going to be a good mom. I'm going to make sure of it." A tear dropped onto the fabric of her face covering.

"I know you will be. I'm proud of you, Riley," I said.

"Girl or boy, I'm going to name them after my sister. It was my biggest fear to have a kid and for anything to happen to them, but I want her to know how much I still love her and I know she's going to protect them with everything she's got."

"She will...We all will," I said.

Riley and I left it at that. Having each other close came as a comfort, and I was able to finally get some shut-eye.

We awoke to the sun shining through the cracked windows of our car. Riley and Willa were already up having taken the last night shift, during which they'd put out the fire and refilled the canteen. The rest of us hopped out of the Expedition and took a swig of water. Dustin took his meds and the rest of us popped some vitamins in lieu of breakfast.

"I really like her," Riley said quietly to me. I figured she and Willa had hit it off during their watch.

“Otto and I will go get gas from some of these cars. Do you guys want to make sure all the weapons are reloaded and put all the seats up?” Dustin proposed.

“Got you,” I said, and they took off with the container and the rubber tube.

Willa and I opened the trunk and took out the duffel bag. We sat next to it and removed our magazine cartridges, counting how many rounds we had used and replacing them. Willa refilled her extended magazine with a handful of bullets, clicking them in one at a time.

Usually it was Willa who would catch me staring at her, enamored, but on this occasion I looked up from my gun to find her watching me with a thoughtful expression. I was nervous that she was about to call me out for hiding something, but when I looked in her eyes I could see they looked friendly.

“What’s up?” I asked, half-laughing.

She went back to loading a few more bullets. “Just wild to think we’ve known each other forty-eight hours.”

“Hmm, you’re right. Feels like years,” I said.

“I feel like I must’ve known you in a past life,” she said softly.

It made me feel good to know that Willa also felt this potent connection we had, though it wasn’t a romantic one. It was beyond that. Maybe past lives did exist.

“You believe in that?” I asked, genuinely curious.

“I do. I think certain people, we meet for the first time, and others, we’ve met before and find them again,” she said, standing up and clicking the long clip back into the butt of her gun.

“Well, nice to meet you, again,” I said with a smile.

“Big win,” Otto said as he and Dustin jointly placed a full jug of gas next to the car.

I loaded the duffel bag into the trunk while they filled the gas tank back to the top.

Once we were strapped into our assigned seats, this time with Dustin navigating, Otto took the wheel and the engine hummed to life.

We pulled out of the lot and drove along the road parallel to the canal for a while. We passed a few run-down shops and a fishing boat rental place before veering off onto the main road toward the interstate.

It was smooth sailing for a half hour until we hit a dense line of deserted cars. Otto pulled off onto the grass to get around the congestion. The hour thereafter was mostly a straight shot toward the border, with only the occasional detour.

"If we don't hit any major blocks, how long do you think until we reach the border?" Ava called to Otto from the backseat.

"Guessing a little less than four hours," he answered.

"Okay, we need a road trip game, then," said Riley. "I'm gonna think of an animal. You guys each ask a question to narrow it down. You can only guess once, then you're out for this round. Go."

"Is it a narwhal?" I guessed.

"Bro, what?! How'd you get that?" Riley protested.

"You *always* pick narwhal when we play this," I laughed.

"No I don't! When?"

"*Every time* we play this!" I repeated.

"I got something. Not a game, but a prompt," Ava proposed. "What's one simple thing you miss from the old world?"

"Oh shit, just one?" Dustin quipped. "Probably surfing. I really miss waking up and paddling out with my board." He sounded thoughtful. "Being able to conquer something as powerful as the ocean for just a moment...Each wave had its own feeling. I miss that."

Even through his mask, I could hear the smile in his voice.

"Honestly, I miss Wi-Fi," said Otto, jokingly at first. "Not for dumb stuff, though. Just being able to have access to everything with a touch of a button. I took it for granted."

"I miss my bed," Ava announced.

We all laughed.

"I *do*! Even at the Don Lux, the beds don't come close. There's just something about your own bed that hits home, you know?"

"I feel that one," Riley said. "I think what I miss more though is restaurants. Eating good food, good service...Seems like a crazy concept now."

The Expedition stuttered as we off-roaded around a flipped semi-truck.

"I miss the movies," I said. "The whole experience of it. A good movie coming out and everyone talking about it and getting those good seats. The concessions and the moment the title hits the screen, then your problems melt away for those two hours and you get to talk about it after. I loved a good movie night."

"That was concerts for me," Willa chimed in. "Going downtown every weekend to watch live bands play. The energy of the crowd. The total escape from the real world."

We reflected for a while on all the wonderful but simple comforts we may never experience again. We had been so lucky, and we never knew it.

Three hours into the drive, Otto and Dustin switched places while the rest of us were in and out of sleep. We passed a small throng of Morts feeding on cattle in a field. Although the glimpse of it was brief, it stuck with me.

I struggled to find a position for my head where my neck wasn't straining. I eventually gave up and sat upright, lamenting that I couldn't recline the seat much with Ava fast asleep behind me, when I felt something wet drip onto my shorts.

My first instinct was to look up at the car ceiling, but a slight tickle in my nose made me reach under my face cover. I retrieved my hand to see a drop of blood smeared on my fingertip. I quickly wiped it under the seat and pulled my mask away from my face so no more would leak onto the fabric.

My throat tightened and my heart started to pound. I quickly recited all my friends' names, going back as far as Caleb and Elle to make sure my memory was still sharp. I turned to Willa to check whether she'd seen the blood, but she was looking out the window, apparently lost in thought. I reached under my shirt and located the wound on my shoulder. The entire patch of skin was numb to the touch. I pressed harder, and still felt nothing.

As I battled with my thoughts, the faint sound of a helicopter made Dustin slow down.

"Look! Up ahead," he said.

With a start, everyone was awake and alert, seeing not one, but three helicopters circling the sky in the far distance.

"What's the map say? Are we near the border?" Riley asked.

Otto traced his finger across the map. "Yeah, we're about three miles away! This is it, guys!"

A buzzing energy filled the car. We sped forward for another mile before we started to see barricades and cones funneling traffic toward the border. It was in our fourth hour that we finally slowed down and joined a line of cars, but this time they were not abandoned. Brake lights blinked on and off as the other cars inched forward in the stop-start traffic.

"I guess we wait in this line," Otto said.

"Can you see anything up ahead?" Ava asked.

"Just cars for the next mile, it seems. This is gonna take a bit," Dustin answered.

Helicopters circled above and army Humvees drove along the shoulder every ten minutes. It was mind-blowing to see this many cars full of people. The last I'd seen anything like it was the day I left home with Hunter and Riley. There was less chaos in this traffic, though. With the amount of military presence surrounding the sea of cars, it seemed organized, official.

Everyone was waiting anxiously in their cars, hoping for some guidance on what came next. I, on the other hand, was not filled with hope. I suddenly grew hot and felt clammy. I wrote it off as anxiety about my unknown fate. I certainly wasn't feeling enlivened like the rest of the group.

Forty long minutes passed, our car inching forward. I could now see a massive wall dividing our state from the next. Cars were being diverted into separate lines. Hundreds of people on foot were in a line of their own. Armed military personnel wearing hazmat suits walked up and down each lane.

"Can I say something?" asked Willa, delicately. "I just want to thank you guys for welcoming me into this group the way you did. I talked about this moment—the 'end of the tunnel'—with my friend Imani. I always pictured her here with me for this, but I'm so grateful to be with you all. It feels safe. Like I found my pack after being a lone wolf."

"Thanks, Willa. You're one of us now. Now and always," said Otto from up front.

"Bonded for life," Riley said, reaching from the backseat to put a hand on Willa's shoulder.

"Speaking of life, what are we all going to do with ourselves after this?" Ava asked.

"Maybe we can get a big house and all live together. For old times' sake," Dustin said.

"With what money?" Riley bantered. "We're gonna need jobs."

"Bet I can get a job at an auto shop, or helping with military mechanics," said Otto eagerly.

"Maybe I can join the police academy or special forces, follow my parents. Guaranteed, anything they throw at me would be a cakewalk now," said Dustin.

"You'd be great at that," Ava said enthusiastically.

A heavily-armed soldier in a hazmat suit approached the car in front of us. We couldn't hear what their exchange was about, but we'd soon find out for ourselves. My heart began to race again. My mask was catching the beads of sweat rolling down from my forehead.

"Whatever we end up doing with our lives, we're going to always be there for each other. I love you guys so much. Really," I said, trying with immense difficulty to hide the pain in my voice.

"None of us would've made it through all this without you," Dustin said earnestly.

All of my friends reached out and placed an affectionate hand on me.

I jumped as the soldier tapped on the driver-side window. Otto lowered it. Two other hazmat soldiers stood off to the side, on standby. It was the first time we had seen grown adults in a while—a sign the area had been stabilized.

"Anyone in the car currently experiencing any symptoms?" the man asked sternly.

I swallowed sharply.

"No. We're all good," Dustin answered.

"Does anyone have ID on them?" he asked.

We answered together; "No."

"Any weapons in the vehicle?" the soldier went on.

"Yes, we're all armed and there's some in the trunk," Otto replied calmly.

The soldier removed a stack of papers from inside his backpack and clicked a pen, handing everything to Otto.

"You will all need to fill this information out individually, and also note the weapons in Section C. They'll be confiscated up ahead, logged and returned to you once you leave the containment zone if they're registered to your name. I'm going to take everyone's temperature now. Please lower the remaining windows," he said, taking out an infrared thermometer gun.

My entire body went numb. This was it. The exact moment I had been dreading since finding the scratch. Everyone else was worried about Dustin's potential reading, but little did they know there was a wolf in sheep's clothing amongst them. The garments I wore came with the heaviest of burdens.

After pointing the laser at Dustin, the soldier said "Cleared" to the man beside him, who tapped something on a tablet. The tension inside the car noticeably lifted.

The soldier next cleared Otto and Willa, then walked around the car to my broken window. I was sweating more than ever now. He raised the thermometer gun to my forehead and clicked the laser on.

He glanced at the tiny screen on the reader, looked up at me and said, "Step out of the vehicle. *Now.*"

23.

I froze, stunned that my worst nightmare was coming true.

"Step out of the vehicle!" another soldier yelled, more aggressively this time.

"Why?! What's going on?" Ava screamed from the back as I was pulled from the car.

"101 fever," said the man. "Rest of you will be escorted to the priority line. You've potentially been exposed."

He spraypainted a red X onto the side of the Expedition, as three other soldiers beckoned Otto to follow them into a separate lane further along. At the same moment, an armored medical vehicle pulled up next to me. The soldier lifted me inside the back of the carriage. I heard my friends screaming my name as the door locked behind me, leaving me in darkness.

I was alone now. I felt around and found a low bench, which I sat on for a silent minute until the truck lurched and drove away. My hands trembled.

Was that really the last time I'd ever see my friends—my family?

I spent ten minutes in the dark before I felt the truck come to a stop. The doors opened with a blinding flood of sunlight and two hazmat soldiers pulled me out.

As my vision cleared, I saw before me an expansive tent city constructed near the curve of the mammoth border wall. The military presence here was even more extreme; there were soldiers in hazmat suits stationed everywhere. One of them escorted me to a white plastic tent where I was sprayed down with some strange-smelling fog. He then walked me through a long hallway that looked like a giant plastic tube connecting several tents together.

We only stopped when we reached a mechanical door where he had to enter a security code. In the few seconds that we stood there, I peered beyond the translucent wall into a tent across the way. A soldier stood over a young girl who was strapped to a gurney, her eyes black as tar. The next moment, she was shot dead. My hands went from trembling to convulsing.

The doorway slid open into a larger tent. It was cold and sterile with nothing but a doctor's examination table at the center. A man wearing a thicker-looking hazmat suit approached me. Through the window in his face covering I could see his eyes were kind, which relaxed me for a second, until I realized my armed escort wasn't leaving. Instead, he stood by the door as the doctor invited me to take a seat.

"I'm Doctor Chiron," he said calmly. "Look here."

He raised his tablet and took a photo of my face.

"Tye. How are you, Tye?" he asked, reading from the screen.

"I'm...I'm ... "

"Were you bitten?" he asked.

"No...A scratch."

"Did you come in contact with any bodily fluids from the infected?"

I calculated my next words.

"...I don't know."

"I see ... May I take a look?" he prompted.

Warily, I lifted my shirt. I was scared to look down at the wound, but from the doctor's expression, I knew it had gotten worse.

"Are you experiencing any symptoms?" he inquired kindly. "Memory loss, nosebleeds, increased temper?"

I was not about to hand them a pass to shoot me on the spot.

"No," I said, weakly. "Can you please, *please* tell me what's going on...and what's going to happen to me and my friends?"

The doctor looked at me, sympathetic. "I am being fully honest with you. I was drafted into service to treat patients and run tests. I probably know very little more than you do.

"The president addressed the nation a few days ago. She said the virus has been significantly contained. Crossover zones like this one have been set up outside all of the contained states. People are flocking to them by the thousands, so things are still a work in progress. According to protocol, your friends will be examined at the border. If they're cleared, they'll be vaccinated and moved to a halfway camp where they'll be housed until they're released to the adjoining state.

"As for you, we're going to test you to see how serious your infection is and administer a post-exposure injection. The best results usually show when it's given before someone's symptomatic. It's not a cure, but it helps to subdue the virus and keep patients from turning. We've seen a handful of cases become undetectable if we administer it early enough."

I stared blankly at some needles on the side table.

"Can you count backward from one hundred, please?" he asked.

It took me a beat to realize this was one of his tests.

"One hundred, ninety-nine, ninety-eight, ninety-seven, ninety-six..." I recited.

I reached number one with ease. The doctor entered some data into his tablet, then placed five differently-colored cards next to me on the examination table.

"Ten seconds, memorize the order," he said.

I spent the first three seconds confused, then quickly snapped an image of the cards in my head. The doctor picked them up, shuffled them, then set them down again in a different pattern.

"Rearrange them into the original order," he said.

I racked my brain for the image I'd mentally recorded. I moved them to match what was in my head: yellow, blue, green, red, orange.

"Am I right?" I asked flatly.

The doctor took a photo of the cards. "Yes. Correct."

After the doctor had spread some foul-smelling ointment onto my discolored scratch and checked my pupils and vitals, he tightly wrapped a band around my bicep and clicked the cap off a needle. After a quick sterilizing wipe of the skin, he stuck it in my vein and administered the serum. He then took a small blood sample and stored the vial in a nearby container.

"There's no record of scratches transferring the virus, but it's possible you were exposed through your open wound. You definitely show signs of a significant infection, but your cognitive tests and vitals don't seem to match the severity of your exposure. That's not common, but it's a good sign. I'm hopeful we can stop the virus from developing to any serious level."

The doctor tapped on his tablet for a few seconds.

"You'll be taken to a lodging tent for the night and we'll check to see if the treatment shows significant results in the morning. If it takes, you should be back with your friends in a few days," said Dr. Chiron gently.

The thought was comforting. "Thank you," I said.

The soldier stepped forward and motioned for me to walk ahead of him down a second tube-tunnel. We entered a tiny pavilion that only fit an electronic monitor and a cot. He had me change into what looked like medical scrubs.

"Stick those on your chest," he said, gesturing at two sticky pads at the end of wires connected to the machine. "They'll track your vitals overnight."

I did as I was told and lay back on the stiff cot. The soldier exited, but his shadow remained at the opening of my tent. I was under lock and key.

A faint smell filled my room; a misty vapor was wafting in through the vents. Almost instantly, I felt sleepy. Although it was clearly chemically-induced, I welcomed any form of rest. I allowed the euphoric sensation to drag me into black.

Beep. Beep. Beep.

My eyes opened at the sound of the alarm. My rest had been short-lived.

I could hear urgent whispering outside my tent. An unfamiliar woman walked in and scanned the barcode near the entrance with her tablet. She scrolled through something on her screen, then nodded to the soldier next to her.

"Up," said the soldier sternly.

"Where am I going?" I asked, growing impatient with the constant vagueness.

The woman answered. "We're transferring you to a monitoring center for further observation."

"What? No!" I protested as the soldier grabbed me.

The demeanor of my handlers had gotten more aggressive overnight. I was tossed, once again, into the back of a military vehicle. It drove for a few minutes before I was pulled out by two more hazmat soldiers. I felt like a baton being passed along in a relay race.

We were inside a building lit by unpleasantly bright white lights. Where it was, I couldn't tell. I was escorted down a few halls where we passed through several key-coded doors until we came to a final doorway that slid open. The larger space beyond housed a single cell that looked like a glass box at one end of the room. I quickly noted the cameras in each corner. The soldier entered a code and the door to the holding tank slid aside. He pushed me in, closed up, then left without a word.

"I want to speak to whoever's in charge!" I shouted after him, but I was ignored.

Looking around the chamber, I saw a small restroom off to the side, a water fountain and four cots. Sitting on two of them were a teen boy and girl, both staring blankly at me. She had wild hair and caramel skin. He was freckled and had a buzzcut.

"Do you guys know what's going on? No one's telling me anything," I said.

"I've been here eight days and I still don't know," the boy said dully.

"Eight days?!" I asked, my anxiety spiking again.

"I've been here four," said the girl. "They won't give us answers. They just pop in and keep checking our vitals, give us shitty food and pills ... Not even sure what we're taking."

My knees weakened and I crumbled onto the cot next to me with my head in my hands. I couldn't believe that after everything I'd been through, I ended up here. I tried to calm myself, reasoning that maybe the shot just needed a little more time to take effect and I'd be off to join my friends again...It had been less than a day, after all.

"I'm Ivy," said the girl, like she was trying to sound friendly.

I looked up from the floor. "Tye."

"You'll be okay. It's not too bad if you keep yourself busy. I've got an extra book if you want," she offered, holding up a thick novel with a green cover.

"I'm alright. Thanks, though." I turned to my other companion. "How about you? What's your name?"

"Parker," said the boy.

I froze. My head suddenly spinning. "Parker ... Not Parker *Taylor*, by any chance?"

His eyes widened. "Yeah...Have we met?"

"No, but—one of my friends, he knows your brother! Beckett, right? Beckett Taylor?"

He shook his head, looking baffled. "I don't have a brother, dude. You feeling okay?"

It felt like someone had slapped me across the face. He had to be messing with me. "Wait, your name's Parker Taylor, right? You don't have a brother named Beckett?" I repeated.

"That's my name, yeah, but no, I don't."

Ivy was staring at us like we were both mad.

There's no way I've just met a different person with the exact name Xander gave me.

My train of thought was interrupted by two men in hazmat suits entering the room, one heavily armed, the other holding a tablet. It all seemed never ending.

"Tye?" asked the doctor.

I raised my hand reluctantly.

"We're going to need to take another blood sample," he said.

"Again? Why?" I challenged.

"Let's make this easy," he said, sliding open the chamber door.

I made eye contact with the stoic-looking soldier through his face mask and decided to present my vein willingly. The doctor wiped my forearm and drew my blood into a vial. It took several minutes to fill.

"Thank you," said the doctor, capping the vial. In no time, he was out the door.

"Why do they need so much of our blood?" I asked the others. "I just gave a sample last night."

I noticed Parker had dozed off, and Ivy answered. "They do that sometimes. Not sure what they're doing with it."

Something felt off, but everything had been so chaotic up until that point that I didn't fight her on it. "So, what's your story?" I asked, realizing I was going to be here a while.

"Made it to the checkpoint with my mom. Somehow she was cleared, but I tested positive. I guess the shot didn't work, so they sent me here."

"Your mom made it?" I asked, feeling slightly hopeful that my friends' parents had survived after all.

"Yeah...My dad didn't. He was older," she said, sadly. "How about you? Any family?"

The question was a punch to my gut. "Only friends. We were separated at the border too."

I eyed a bloodied rag at the foot of her bed. Ivy caught me wincing.

"Nosebleeds," she said simply. She looked over at Parker, then back to me. "By the way, he does have a brother. I think his memory's going," she whispered.

I sat up straighter.

"When I got here he was with another boy. I didn't get his name, but they acted like brothers and they looked alike. A few hours after I arrived, his brother collapsed and was unresponsive. I have no clue if he was alive but they took him out of here. He never came back."

"Took him? Where?" I asked.

"I have no idea. A nurse came in with a gurney and hauled him out. Parker cried for a few hours and then never mentioned it again. I stopped asking about it when I realized he doesn't remember him," she said.

I looked at the sleeping Parker. Maybe losing his memory after the loss of his brother was a blessing in disguise. Although I was heartbroken not to be able to pass along Xander's words, Willa's view on past lives came to mind; I felt a wave of optimism imagining Xander and Beckett reunited in the next one, at peace in whatever realm they now lived in. They would finally be able to reconnect, without judgment. I felt better, knowing that possibility was more powerful than any words I could have delivered myself. I dabbed at my eyes with my sleeve.

My blurred gaze landed on the water fountain across the cell, and I got up and took a long, refreshing drink from it. I realized I hadn't been taking care of myself at all. The scratch had become such a burden, it had erased all my attention to self-care.

"I'm going to wash up," I told Ivy.

She nodded, then went back to a book that was under her pillow.

I slid the bathroom door closed behind me. Even here there was a camera, which made things highly uncomfortable. I held my middle finger up to it, defiantly, then removed my clothing.

I caught my reflection in the cloudy mirror above the faucet. My entire right side from torso to shoulder was bruised and withered. It showed no signs of healing from any treatment, but it hadn't worsened. I tried not to react, knowing I was on camera.

I stepped into the tiny square shower and turned on the showerhead. I couldn't even feel the water's pressure on the decaying parts of my body.

As the weak stream of water dribbled over me, I got lost in a flood of thoughts. If the post-exposure treatment didn't work at all, I would inevitably turn and they'd kill me, without a doubt. The chances of seeing my friends again looked bleak. This chamber would probably be where I'd live out the last of my days—unless I figured out a way to get out of here.

Thinking back on the number of armed guards I'd seen within the maze of hallways outside made that fantasy seem hopeless. I just didn't want to be another number in their system. I was a human being. The way they'd shot that girl when she turned replayed in my head, over and over. Once someone turned, they weren't a person anymore. I couldn't let that be my fate.

The water suddenly shut off. I pulled at the lever, but of course, it was on a timer. This place was feeling more and more like a prison. I didn't even have time to revel in the fact that I'd had my first real shower in months. I grabbed the rag hanging on the hook, dried off quickly, and redressed in my scrubs.

Back in the main cell, I claimed one of the available cots in the corner across from Ivy. Parker was still sleeping while she read.

She looked up from her book. "What luxury, huh?" she asked sarcastically, nodding toward the shower.

"Yeah. You'd think we were prisoners, not patients."

The main door opened and a woman in a hazmat suit wheeled in a cart carrying three trays of food. An armed guard followed her.

"Just wait 'til you try the food," said Ivy under her breath.

The cell door opened halfway and the lady slid the trays inside. "Leave these by the door again when you're done," she said dryly, then trotted out with the guard.

I tapped Parker awake, and we all picked silently at our food. The pills Ivy had mentioned were in a small cup beside the off-color potatoes and rubbery turkey. I eyed them suspiciously.

"Just take them. Symptoms get worse if you don't," said Parker, tossing back his own meds.

At this point, nothing fazed me. I took them with a swig of chlorine-flavored water.

To my surprise, the main door opened again and this time a whole group of hazmats walked in. I recognized one of them as Dr. Chiron. They congregated along the glass wall of our tank, like we were exotic animals on display at a zoo.

"That's him there," said one quietly, pointing at me.

Both Ivy and Parker looked at me as if I had gotten us all into trouble.

The observing group retreated and talked in whispers for a moment before a man approached the glass again. I could see that under his hazmat he was wearing a suit and tie.

"Tye. How are you feeling?" he asked in a faux-friendly tone.

"Annoyed... but fine."

They continued to whisper as Dr. Chiron stepped forward.

"We're going to need to check your vitals and take another blood test," he said with care.

"Again?! What the hell's going on?" I demanded, now thoroughly frustrated.

"We just need to run a few more tests," said the suit.

"No! Why aren't you taking this much of *their* blood?"

"Once we have a little more data we'll give you a full diagnosis," Dr. Chiron insisted.

Two armed guards stepped through the cell door. By their body language, I knew that if I didn't cooperate, things were going to get bad. One vial of blood was better than a puddle of it. I reluctantly presented my arm to Dr. Chiron as he entered.

I relinquished myself to his needle and checkup, my mind racing. Something wasn't right here. The superfluous testing was making me paranoid that I was going to be subjected to something worse than a cell...maybe worse than death. *Did they find something wrong with me?*

"All set," said Dr. Chiron, entering some data into his tablet.

"Let's expedite this," said the suit. "Let us know if you need anything else, doctor."

"Thank you, sir. I'm going to hang back and ask my patient some follow-up questions," said Dr. Chiron.

With a nod from the main suit, he and the other men filed out of the room while Dr. Chiron packed up. Two guards remained.

"I'd like my patient to be comfortable. Can you wait outside the cell, please?" the doctor asked of them.

They stepped just beyond the threshold of the glass.

"Can you tell me why you need all this?" I asked. "Am I going to turn soon?"

"Everyone taken to this part of the facility has been flagged because their blood shows a unique reaction to the virus..."

"I feel perfectly fine."

"That's exactly it. The post-exposure injection didn't take, but despite that, your blood shows an almost untraceable amount of the virus... It's significantly decreasing by the hour."

I stared at him blankly, not fully grasping what that meant. Something was said over the guard's radio outside the cell.

"We need to go," one of the guards called to Chiron.

"We will probably be seeing a lot of each other," said the doctor gently, but somehow the words were ominous.

The visitors left the room. Ivy and Parker were staring at me in wonder.

"What was that about?" Parker asked.

My head was spinning. "Shot didn't work," I replied flatly.

They looked concerned, but didn't pry.

When the lights in the cell finally dimmed, indicating it was time for bed, I lay on my cot wishing the chemical fog would fill my room again, but it never came. I stayed awake, processing Chiron's words.

If my blood was somehow special, there was no chance in hell I'd be let free, even if I fully recovered. I may even become a lifelong prisoner of the government if it meant they could study and utilize me. Ivy and Parker would probably suffer the same fate.

At first I tried to write the imaginary scenarios off as anxiety, but when I remembered they had already collected three vials of my blood in about twenty-four hours, my chest felt empty. Any hope of a life beyond the hell I'd endured in the many months thus far, evaporated. Immunity to a fatal virus sounded like a godsend...but was it actually a blessing if I was to be made a science experiment?

I mulled over every possible outcome, but all lines of thought seemed to lead back to the same fear. They needed me now. If the additional tests confirmed their theory, then I was a rare and valuable commodity...and if history was any indication, rare commodities were exploited and fought over.

I have to escape. The idea returned in full force. I tried to mentally retrace my steps in the halls of the facility, but I'd barely seen any of it. I didn't even know where exactly we were—not even which side of the border wall this prison was built on. Even if I managed to get out of this cell, which seemed unlikely in itself, I would be shot in a blink. Then, like Beckett, I'd be another body hauled out on a gurney and donated to science.

Beckett! Ivy had told me that a nurse came to retrieve his body when he was unresponsive. That was my way out! I would stay unresponsive until they wheeled my body out of this chamber. If my blood was unique, I would probably be transported somewhere less occupied for testing. Before they ran their tests, I could make a run for it ... How and when, I wasn't sure, but waiting around to be made a specimen looked like the worse option.

As impossible as my plan seemed, I was fully committed to making the attempt.

I lay somewhere between asleep and awake for hours before the white lights brightened again. I refrained from opening my eyes. I made my body as limp as it would go, like liquid. The numbness in my right side helped. I heard Ivy and Parker shuffle awake. One of them went to shower.

After a half hour, Ivy shook me gently. "Tye," she said softly.

I remained motionless, letting my hand flop off the bed.

"Tye? Wake up," she said, a little louder.

It took every fiber of my being not to move and to keep my breathing even.

She stopped, probably figuring I was beat from my first day.

I listened to my two cellmates go about their business for another hour, until-

"How is he *still* sleeping?" whispered Parker.

"We should check on him," said Ivy.

I felt her hover over me. "Tye, wake up," she said. She nudged me harder. "Tye ..."

"Is he ... ?" came Parker's voice from across the room.

"I don't know," whispered Ivy. "Hey! Something's wrong!" she called out, most likely waving at the cameras. "Can someone help?"

Five minutes later, the front door slid open and I heard footsteps. It sounded like two people. Probably the nurse and a guard.

"I think he's dead," said Ivy, her tone sad.

"Another one," came a second voice.

It was getting progressively more difficult to stay still. One of my legs was tingling sharply. I heard the cell door hiss open.

A hand touched my neck, checking my pulse. The nurse shook me again. I remained still.

"Possible coma. We'll need to transfer him to the ICU," said the nurse.

Suddenly I was being lifted and I felt something envelop me. A zipper closed up and the light penetrating my eyelids dimmed. They were putting me in some sort of sanitation body bag.

I felt myself glide across the room on wheels. This was it. I was out of the cell.

I paid close attention to every detail I could gather as we moved. A door opened. I was out of the chamber now and probably in the hall. Minutes passed where all I heard were the wheels of my gurney. Then, the low hum of a running engine; I was being loaded into a transport vehicle. The doors closed and everything went even blacker. It was all happening faster than I'd imagined—they were moving me with urgency. I swayed as the truck took off.

Surely the drop-off point for unresponsive bodies was not going to be heavily monitored, but wherever they took me thereafter most likely would be. When those doors opened again, it would be my one and only chance to make a run for it.

I reached up and felt around for the zipper. *Found it.* I unzipped myself from the bag and slowly stood up. My legs and arms prickled from the ache of being still for so long.

We passed over a few bumps and the truck slowed down. With a deep breath of anticipation, I gripped the gurney next to me. It was my only weapon.

I heard voices and to my relief, it didn't sound like many. The driver's door slammed and I heard the latch on the outside being lifted. *Three, two, one—*

The carriage doors opened and I shoved the gurney with all my strength. The man in front of me yelled in agony as it slammed into him. He fell to the ground with a thump. I jumped out, immediately ducking as two hazmat soldiers shot off a handful of warning rounds. I ran around the truck. Bullets ricocheted off the metal façade. I barely had a plan so, impulsively, I ran for the driver's seat.

Leaping inside, I ducked as the glass shattered from a near-lethal shot. I hit reverse and slammed on the gas. The tires screeched and I heard two loud thuds as the soldiers' bodies rolled underneath the truck. Then, silence.

Did I really just do that?

For a few beats, I waited for more military personnel to surround me, but none came. I shook myself and slowly jumped down from the vehicle. Peeking around the hood, I saw no one but the bloodied soldiers lying limp on the ground. They were the first non-infected I'd killed. I had no time for regret. I snatched up one of their guns.

I was in some sort of docking bay. At one end there was a single doorway; it seemed like it would be suicide to go through and confront more people. At the other end was the wide tunnel the truck had come through, but it looked endless. More trucks were bound to turn up and I'd be spotted with nowhere to run. I'd hit a dead end.

I looked down at my gun in defeat. Maybe this was the end of the road...but better to be in control of my fate than to suffer a lifetime of examinations as a prisoner.

I raised the barrel to my temple, but only for a second. I thought of my friends. Through everything, they had become my family. I recalled every moment I'd shared with them, and more powerful than the hardships were all the profound moments along the way. We had grown together. We were kin, for life.

As I daydreamed of our journey, I slowly realized what I was staring at. A large metal grate at the bottom of the wall.

I ran over to it and pulled with the last ounce of my strength. It moved. I slid it aside and, without any clue to where it led, jumped down through the gap. To buy more time, I replaced the grate before heading off.

I'd found myself in a catacomb of tunnels. The only light came from sporadic grates above my head. Every so often a stream of rancid liquid would run past my ankles. I removed my scrub tunic and tied it around my face like a mask.

I walked and walked around bends and corners, for so long that I lost track of time. I deludedly imagined my friends awaiting me at the end of wherever this led. They'd jump into my arms and we'd celebrate. Maybe we could start planning that shared house Dustin mentioned, so we could all readjust to a new life together.

It could have been delirium, but random memories swam through my mind with intense lucidity. The time Ava and I were thrown out of a theater because we couldn't stop laughing at the overly dramatic performance. And another, when Riley planned a romantic picnic by the ocean and a rogue wave washed our stuff away. Dustin changing our grades on the teacher's computer when she stepped out of class for a moment—a skill that had helped me pass. I saw Elle's eyes. Heard Caleb's and Hunter's voice. Xander, Otto and Gage's smiles. The look Willa would give me when she was reading my soul. My mother's easel. My father's laugh lines.

I reached a brighter section of the tunnel. At the far end was radiant, golden sunlight. I picked up the pace, my legs feeling like jelly from the trek.

I came to a stop at the bars of a large exit gate, beyond which was an expansive stretch of barren land. It was padlocked shut. Remembering Willa's move at the sheriff's station, I tightened the shirt-mask over my ears and aimed my gun at the lock. *BAM.* It popped off with a spark.

I pushed at the metal door and with a clang, it swung open. I stepped out onto the soft dirt and let the sun's rays kiss my face. It was the first non-artificial light I'd seen in two days.

I looked back at where I had exited from and saw, towering above me, the behemoth border wall. Very far in the distance I could see the line of cars funneling into the checkpoint lanes. I'd escaped, but I was on the wrong side.

I fell to the ground, exhausted and defeated. Rolling onto my back, I stared up at the sky. I looked to my right, then to my left, and saw nothing but land. This was an unmonitored area, but it was only a matter of time until someone realized what I'd done.

I forced myself to my feet. I had to get far away from here, and fast. I jogged toward oblivion, the orange orb of the sun slowly setting beyond the horizon. I knew my friends were probably watching the same sunset.

EPILOGUE.

"Look here, please," said the large woman behind the counter.

She held a tablet up to my face and something clicked. After reading the screen, she looked up at me and asked, "Willa?"

"Yes," I said, distracted as I took in my surroundings.

After passing the checkpoint of the priority line, we'd been funneled into a huge atrium. All of us here were cleared and administered with a vaccine. Every corner of the space was filled with refugees. What few belongings we had were taken to be registered and supposedly returned to us later, but for now, we were given a mask and one bottle of water each while we waited for our numbers to be called in no particular order.

"You're assigned to zone three, dormitory eleven. Go through security and show this ID card. Follow the street signs," the woman said flatly.

"My friend was taken somewhere at the border. He had a fever. Where will he be?" I asked.

She gave me a look that suggested she'd been dealing with similar inquiries all day. She spoke mechanically. "He's most likely at the medical facility. They'll run some tests and treat him. He should be checked into the halfway camp in a few days if he's cleared."

Irritated, I took the ID card from her. It read '311.4Willa.' *I guess we're reduced to numbers now.*

I looked back at my friends sitting along the wall, waiting to be called up. We were all shaken by Tye's blunt departure. I waved to them, trying to look reassuring as I headed for the security gate beside the counter.

I presented my ID card. The armed guard scanned the barcode, patted me down courteously, then let me pass to walk through a metal detector.

I was now in a second atrium with fewer people. The crowd here were all gathered in front of a massive LED screen showing endless rows of text, organized in columns. A closer look revealed they were all people's names, with tiny symbols next to each one. Every minute the names would shift and be replaced with new ones in a continuous loop.

A man across the atrium let out a desperate scream, dropping to his knees. I looked around and saw several people in tears, while some, by contrast, were smiling.

I looked back at the electronic screen and saw at the bottom right was a legend, explaining what each symbol meant. The screen seemed to be displaying all the names and statuses of civilians who were accounted for.

I quickly spotted my own name and next to it, a white square. According to the legend, it meant *Halfway Camp*, clearly having just been updated. I scanned the charts hurriedly, stopping when I saw my parents' names. Next to them both was a blue circle. My heart raced as I checked its meaning. *Alive*! They were alive!

Where they were it didn't say, but for a blink my heart exploded with relief. Then, urgently, I searched for my brother's name. The names on the screen shifted to a set of new ones and I stood there for what felt like a year, waiting for the previous names in the loop to reappear. They changed again, and I immediately looked under *M*.

Malik...Malik...Malik...

Finally, I found his name. Beside it was a symbol I hadn't seen anywhere else on the board: a red circle. It apparently meant *Reevaluating*. The vague title made me feel even more confused than before.

"Any trouble?" came a voice from behind me.

It was Otto, with Ava next to him.

"What is this?" she asked.

"It lists the status of every civilian in the system. My parents are alive, but I don't know what the symbol next to my brother's name means."

Both wore multiple expressions at once on their faces, taking everything in and probably wondering what the fates of their own loved ones were. They hesitantly approached the board.

I spotted a kiosk against the wall. Stationed at it was a calm, official-looking man. I ran over to him.

"Excuse me. What does 'reevaluating' mean?" I begged. "It's next to my brother's name. Malik."

He looked up from his tablet, calming my frustration with his patient energy.

"It means it's being updated from a previous status, so it could mean a number of things. Either he was retested recently and something changed, or maybe he was admitted into one of the in-state facilities. I wouldn't be too concerned, though, if there isn't a deceased symbol."

I stared at him skeptically. These days it seemed there were far worse things than being deceased.

"We'll register you as family and update you if any new information becomes available. Sound good?" he asked, like he was trying to be comforting.

"Yes...please."

"Look here," he said, raising the tablet and taking my photo. "Alright, Willa. All set." He entered some data.

"You okay?" asked Dustin, having appeared to my right.

"For now...Parents are alive, but can't tell about my brother," I said as we walked over to rejoin the others.

"Just looked mine up. Says 'missing,'" he said dismally.

"I'm sorry, Dustin...How about yours?" I asked Ava and Otto, who were embracing.

"'Missing,'" said Ava, wiping her eyes.

"Mine aren't even on the board, but my birth mom's alive," Otto said, a small laugh escaping through his tears.

We all hugged, heads together. The closure of receiving any update at all was still healing in a small way.

"Where's Riley?" I asked Dustin, realizing the group hug felt light on people.

"They took her to a med tent nearby to run some extra tests since she's pregnant. She was assigned housing though, so we'll probably see her there," he said.

"Is Tye on here?" Ava asked, quickly scanning the board.

We all joined in the search.

"Found it!" Otto said a second later.

"...'Pending,'" Ava read aloud, sounding defeated.

"He's a fighter. He's gonna be back with us in no time," said Dustin, rubbing her back. "He wasn't bit so if it's anything like what I had, he'll pull through."

"What dorms are you in?" I asked them, eager to alleviate the heavy mood.

They all checked their assigned ID cards.

"We're together in zone three, dorm twenty-two," said Otto, pulling Ava close.

"Same zone," said Dustin. "Dorm nineteen."

"Good, we're all close. I'm in eleven," I said, and we headed for the atrium's exit.

Military personnel were on every corner. Among them were staff helping civilians find their assigned housing. The whole place was utopian. It clearly used to be a manicured suburban area, now converted into a halfway camp to hold us until we were released into the state beyond.

My steps felt lighter. I didn't have to worry about a Jumbee jumping out from behind every corner. Even though I felt naked without my gun, the sense of safety I felt now was unfamiliar, nearly uncomfortable.

Clashing with the homely streets of cookie-cutter houses and buildings was a distant, towering fence. This was a camp indeed. It still wasn't clear how long we'd be here, but we had nothing to our name. I imagined our temporary boarding wasn't going to be very temporary.

The street signs had been taken down at each corner and replaced with arrows and directions to zones one through forty. We walked as a group, following the signs that pointed to *Zone 3*.

We arrived at a side street lined with houses. It seemed every single one had a soldier stationed out front. A gun in one hand, a tablet in the other. The houses were marked with big red numbers. We arrived at number eleven.

I turned to my friends. "See you in a bit?"

"Hope so," Dustin teased.

"Love you, Willa," Ava said, looking emotional.

I smiled back. "Love you. All of you, you hear me?"

They laughed and continued on. I approached the soldier with my ID card. He scanned it with his tablet.

"You'll be in room four," he said.

I nodded and approached the house.

The door was open, and inside there was no furniture like a lived-in home would have. I heard voices coming from a nearby room. The door was labeled with a number two. Figuring room four was on the second floor, I climbed the stairs and turned the corner to a bedroom off the hallway.

Inside was a tiny desk, a dresser with a phone on top, and a single bed beside a small window. On the bed was a plastic bag and a towel. I sat on the stiff mattress to check inside the bag and pulled out a document that listed guidelines and house rules for my stay. I tossed it aside, rolling my eyes, and continued rummaging through the bag.

There was a change of clothes—basically a prison jumpsuit—and some miniature toiletries, a credit card with *$100* written on it, and a map showing where the cafeteria and medical tents were.

I pushed the bag off the bed and lay back, staring up at the popcorn ceiling and listening to the constant hum of distant choppers.

I was exhausted, but my mind was still racing, thinking of Malik. I tried piecing together how my parents could be alive, yet my brother was being 'reevaluated.' Did they ever even reach his campus? I knew he wasn't dead because I could still feel him. I was confident that if anything had happened to him, I'd know deep down...and I *knew* Malik was still out there, with the same certainty I'd had this whole time that my parents were alive.

And I had the same feeling about Tye. I could still feel his presence somewhere in the area. He was one of the most powerful energies to have come into my life, despite being one of the briefest.

I really hoped he was going to be okay. I really hoped I'd see him again.

As the sun went down outside my window, I finally unglued myself from the mattress and, mostly out of sheer boredom, gathered my toiletries and bath towel and headed out into the hallway.

A door labeled *Bathroom* was in between my room and room number three. I knocked lightly.

"Just a minute," came a female voice.

A beat later a girl opened the door, her hair still dripping and a towel wrapped around her. "Wash your hair first," she advised. "There's a timer for the water."

"Great ... " I said as she walked past me and back to her room.

I visited the cafeteria after my brief shower. It was crowded, but organized. Everyone was now in the same light-blue jumpsuit we'd been given with our care packages. I scanned for any familiar faces, but saw none, until-

"I spotted your hair before I spotted you," said Riley, looking up at my locs.

I laughed, happy to see a friend. We hugged.

"Keep it moving, girls," said a guard, motioning for us to step forward in the line.

"Everything okay with you?" I asked Riley.

"I guess. They said the baby's healthy, but gave me some vitamins to take daily. I have to check in every other day. How about you?"

"I'm fine. Did you see the status board? My parents are alive but my brother's status is still updating… "

"Shit, Willa! I know how close you two are...but at least it doesn't say he's gone. My mom is...Dad survived though. And I found one of my favorite aunts here. Feel pretty lucky, all things considered."

She wiped her glossy eyes as we were handed trays of premade food. We found a seat at a long table.

"Any word on Tye?" I asked, hoping Riley had found out more than I had.

"No. The board said 'pending.' I'm sick to my stomach thinking about how scared he must be. He must've got whatever Dustin had."

"Hopefully it's just that."

Riley picked at her food thoughtfully. "He's special, huh?" she asked.

"He is," I agreed simply.

I tried to down as much of the food as I could, but even after all the shitty things I'd eaten on my journey, it was just about comparable.

"Ry, can I ask you something?" I ventured cautiously.

"What's up?" she asked, not looking up from her food.

"The day your sister passed...Did you *feel* it, before you found out?"

She seemed to become overly invested in a single pea on her plate that she was trying to fork. I knew her sister was a sensitive subject, but since we'd opened up to each other about our siblings during our night watch together, I hoped she could feel my intentions.

"I've thought about that before. I'm not sure if I remember it differently in retrospect...but that day felt so *off*, even before I heard anything about the crash," she said, her gaze faraway. She finally looked up at me. "Willa, I know where your head's at, but don't start mourning him before you need to. I wish I could buy a single day where I don't feel that for my sister. You'll see him again. Trust that."

I allowed myself a smile. It felt good to be reassured out loud, especially by Riley.

Back in my dormitory, I tied my hair up and prepared for bed. My body was achy from our long drive and being up and about all day. I melted into my mattress.

RING...RING...RING...

I jumped up from the bed. *The phone!* It scared the shit out of me.

I picked up, waiting a beat before saying, "Hello?"

"Is this Willa, zone three, dorm eleven, room four?" came an official-sounding voice.

"Yes ... Who's this?"

"We have an update on the status of your brother, Malik."

My legs buckled. I sat on the edge of the dresser. "Is he alive?"

"His profile says he's reentered the contamination zone, voluntarily."

"...*Excuse* me?! What does that mean?" I asked, my voice coming out weak.

"I'm only reading you the update. I don't have any further information. You can visit the Civilian Relations office tomorrow after nine a.m.," said the voice.

The line went dead.

"Hello?"

I slammed the phone down hard.

Reentered the contamination zone? Voluntarily?

I fell to the floor, covering my face with my hands. Tears dripped through my fingers. The realization hit me like an oncoming train, because I knew. I knew deep down that once the news had reached him about what was happening in our hometown, and that I'd stayed behind, he would've wanted to come get me. Malik was like that. Calm and collected until it came to his family.

Did he have any idea what he was willingly putting himself through? I didn't know going back in was even an option—who would want to? I was sure he'd seen the Jumbees on the news, but nothing came close to facing one in person. *Malik! Why?!*

I cried and cried, wrestling with any other logical possibilities, but I couldn't shake what I felt in my core. At last, my body gave in to a shallow and restless sleep.

The only two nights I'd slept that bad were the first night after I left home, and when Imani died.

After an hour and a half of waiting outside the small construct marked *Civilian Relations*, my name was finally called.

"ID?" asked the clerk.

I handed it over and she scanned it, then looked up at me questioningly from behind her mask.

"I got an update that my brother Malik apparently 'voluntarily reentered the contamination zone.' Can you please tell me, in more than a sentence, what happened to him?" I asked sternly, but trying to maintain a polite tone.

She typed something quickly on her keyboard. "I see here you're listed as family. It looks like your brother signed all the documents and paperwork releasing him beyond the wall a week ago."

"What documents? Why would he do that?" I asked, distraught. I had missed him by a whisker.

"The documents sign away our liability and some of his rights if he decides to reenter. Most cases of people voluntarily going beyond the wall are to find family members that never turned up at any of the border facilities. We highly advise against it, but there've been a handful who decide to start their own search party. We don't have the resources right now for individual investigations out there."

I ran my hands through my locs. It was exactly what I'd imagined. He went to look for me. My brother was strong, stronger than me even, but no one should be out there alone. Just as I knew Malik inside and out, he knew me in the same way, and because we had that mutual power between us, he would expect me to stay put until he came to get me. And I would have—

I'd wanted to—but it would've been impossible to survive inside our house any longer than I did. After two weeks of no one showing up, I didn't think anyone getting to me was a possibility anymore, so I left.

I decided here and now, without a second thought, that I would go after him. If I left soon I'd be able to arrive home at nearly the same time, maybe even before him, since I knew how to function in that world now.

"How do I sign the same papers? I want to be released back," I said, with such conviction that the clerk didn't even attempt to advise against it.

"I can give you the documents now. Just know, if you come back through any border, the process will be much more difficult-"

"I'll take it."

She adjusted her glasses, clicked a few things on her computer, then got up to go fetch what was being printed behind her. She returned a few minutes later, handing me a stack of papers and a pen.

"Before you fill that out, I'm required to ask..." she began, in a noticeably quieter voice than before. "Since voluntary reentries are rare, we'd like to offer you the chance to be part of our FORESIGHT program. In exchange for collecting data and noting observations while you're in the contamination zone, we'll provide partnership and significant survival aid."

I was hearing a lot of words, but understanding very little. "What does 'survival aid' mean?" I asked.

"Weapons, survival gear, direct contact with us and even an expedited reentry if you return," she said. I didn't miss the fact that she'd said 'if.' "It'd mean an additional set of paperwork, an evaluation and basic training before you're allowed beyond the wall."

I wanted to leave as soon as possible, but the offer was undeniably appealing. The world out there was brutal. I had very little interest in helping the government in any form, but if it gave me an advantage in finding and retrieving my brother, then...

"Where do I sign?"

www.ingramcontent.com/pod-product-compliance
Lightning Source LLC
Chambersburg PA
CBHW060807310726
48980CB00002B/267

* 9 7 9 8 9 9 3 3 3 1 5 2 2 *